THE LOOK OF LOVE

Book of Love, Book One

Meara Platt

ARE YOU SIGNED UP FOR DRAGONBLADE'S BLOG?

You'll get the latest news and information on exclusive giveaways, exclusive excerpts, coming releases, sales, free books, cover reveals and more.

Check out our complete list of authors, too!

No spam, no junk. That's a promise!

Sign Up Here

www.dragonbladepublishing.com

Dearest Reader;

Thank you for your support of a small press. At Dragonblade Publishing, we strive to bring you the highest quality Historical Romance from the some of the best authors in the business. Without your support, there is no 'us', so we sincerely hope you adore these stories and find some new favorite authors along the way.

Happy Reading!

CEO, Dragonblade Publishing

Additional Dragonblade books by Author Meara Platt

The Moonstone Landing Series
Moonstone Landing (novella)
Moonstone Angel (novella)
The Moonstone Duke
The Moonstone Marquess
The Moonstone Major

The Book of Love Series
The Look of Love
The Touch of Love
The Taste of Love
The Song of Love
The Scent of Love
The Kiss of Love
The Chance of Love
The Gift of Love
The Heart of Love
The Hope of Love (novella)
The Promise of Love
The Wonder of Love
The Journey of Love
The Dream of Love (novella)
The Treasure of Love
The Dance of Love
The Miracle of Love
The Remembrance of Love (novella)

Dark Gardens Series
Garden of Shadows
Garden of Light
Garden of Dragons

Garden of Destiny
Garden of Angels

The Farthingale Series
If You Wished For Me (A Novella)

The Lyon's Den Series
Kiss of the Lyon
The Lyon's Surprise
Lyon in the Rough

Pirates of Britannia Series
Pearls of Fire

De Wolfe Pack: The Series
Nobody's Angel
Kiss an Angel
Bhrodi's Angel

Also from Meara Platt
Aislin
All I Want for Christmas

To all who are kind at heart

CHAPTER ONE

London, England
July 1815

L ADY OLIVIA GOSLING was minding her own business, browsing along the musty shelves of Gresham's Antiquarian Books, when one of those books suddenly fell off the top shelf and landed on her head. "Ouch!"

She peered around the corner, certain that someone had carelessly knocked over the tome bound in faded red leather. But she was alone amid the narrow stacks bulging with old texts and piles of dust.

"*The Book of Love*," she muttered, reading the title after picking it up and dusting it off. She placed it back on the shelf and sighed, for love is what she sorely needed to rescue her from her desperate situation.

The book promptly fell back atop her head. "Oh, for pity's sake. Do that again and I shall toss you into the ash bin."

She rubbed her head where a small lump was beginning to form. "Love, indeed." The way her life had been going lately, she would never find happiness. She was doomed to have an unsuccessful debut Season. Doomed to be a wallflower. Doomed to be a spinster. Or worse, cast off in marriage by her guardian to one of his unsavory friends. "You are most certainly getting tossed into the ash bin."

"Talking to books now, are we? Good afternoon, Goose."

Olivia glanced up, startled. No one ever called her that except... oh, *him*. She did not need Alexander Beastling, the proud and mighty Duke of Hartford, adding to her dismal day. He'd thought himself quite witty when giving her that silly name all those years ago. *Goose*. Because her family name was Gosling. And that's what he'd called her when she was a girl, Little Goose. His Little Goose.

She tipped her chin up and meant to frown at him, but he looked so big and wonderful, just as she remembered him before he'd gone off to fight Napoleon. And now he'd come back a war hero.

Well, he'd always been her hero ever since rescuing her from drowning when she was six years old. That was the day they'd first met. That was the day he'd christened her Little Goose. That was what he'd called her every summer afterward. *How's my Little Goose?* he would always ask, and await her answer as though he truly cared.

He'd saved her life, so she found herself smiling at him. "What are you doing here, Beast?"

"Picking up a book on ancient Roman military tactics. The Punic Wars." He glanced at the one clutched in her hands and grinned. "*The Book of Love?*"

"Stop smirking. I did not choose it." She cleared her throat when it suddenly turned dry. Beast was big, a lion of a man with sandy blond hair that he wore a little too long and eyes that were an extraordinary mix of amber and green. But he now sported a black eyepatch over one eye from an injury he must have received during the war. He'd always been intimidating and appeared even more so now. "It chose me."

"Love finds Little Goose?" He leaned his shoulder against one of the towering shelves and chuckled. "You do realize you will never find love in a book."

"How do you know? I'm going to buy it," she said, although she had not considered doing so until Beast mocked the notion. Nor could she afford the luxury of acquiring it. Nor did it matter the author was anonymous and its contents were probably a hoax. "I'm determined, and there is nothing you can say to talk me out of it."

"Nothing?" Beast slipped the book out of her hands. "Then let me have the honor."

"What are you doing?" She reached for the book, but he raised it above his head so she had no chance of grabbing it. He was an oaf, even for a duke. She supposed she ought to have addressed him as Your Grace, but he'd always been Beast to her and he did not seem to take offense.

"Stop hopping up and down," he said with a chuckle when she jumped to try to take it from his raised hand. "I'm buying it for you."

"You are not. I'll pay for it myself." But her face suffused with color as she reached into her reticule and came up with a mere two ha'pennies. "I seem to have forgotten–"

"Goose," he said quietly, his voice deep and rumbling, and no longer filled with amusement, "let me take care of this. I owe you at least this for teasing you. I insist."

"But–"

"I believe a duke outranks a little goose."

She sighed again. "If you must."

"I must." He tossed her a most appealing smile, which was quite something, for Beast rarely smiled. It softened his features when he did, but she dared not tell him so. He took her arm to escort her to the front of the shop where a gray-haired, slightly disheveled Mr. Gresham was busily sorting through his newest arrivals. Beast paid and waited for the bookseller to wrap her purchase and then his. "How are you getting home? And why are you in the streets of London on your own?" he asked, suddenly realizing she had no chaperone or footmen to accompany her.

"Um, I'm meeting Poppy and Penelope at Blakney's bake shop. I'll ride home in Penelope's carriage."

"I just left Penelope and Nathaniel at the Sherbourne town-house. Poppy was visiting them." He was no longer smirking but frowning at her. "What's going on, Goose? You've never lied to me before."

Her face suffused with heat. "Nothing."

"You are a terrible liar. I'm taking you home. And don't even think to protest. I'm not leaving you to make your own way back to Mayfair."

Olivia was too overset to toss back a retort. As Beast had remarked, she'd never lied to him before, and the fact that she had done so now rattled her perhaps more than it had him. Her situation was dire, but that was no excuse for her behavior.

"Thank you, Beast." She was tired and it was a long walk home. In truth, she wanted to rest her head against his massive shoulder and cry. She wanted to forget about the Season and finding a husband.

But a husband of her own choosing was what she desperately needed.

Perhaps *The Book of Love* would help her find one.

After all, there had to be a reason it fell on her head. Twice.

BEAST LIFTED GOOSE into his carriage and then climbed in after her, settling on the padded leather seat opposite hers. His friend, Nathaniel Sherbourne, the Earl of Welles, had mentioned things were amiss in the Gosling household. He had only to look into her troubled gaze to know that Nathaniel's assessment had been correct.

The ginger-haired moppet with sparkling, dark blue eyes who used to race across the meadow between the Gosling country house and Sherbourne Manor had been a happy child. Olivia, as everyone else referred to her since it was her given name, was still a beautiful girl with lush curls. But there was no longer a sparkle in her eyes. They were the color of sapphires and ought to have been gleaming like precious gemstones. Instead, they were dull and sad.

He leaned forward as his carriage slowly made its way through the busy London streets. "How is your family?" It seemed a harmless enough question, one that he hoped would give him some helpful answers.

She clasped her hands together and nibbled her lip. "Don't you know? Of course not. You only returned to England a few days ago, after years of fighting on the Continent. My parents are gone."

Damn. Why hadn't anyone told him? Perhaps he'd been too busy receiving congratulations on his heroic return from battle to spare any of his friends a quiet moment, even his best friend, Nathaniel. Beast's ducal title alone was enough to have every eligible young woman and her matchmaking relations make a beeline for him the moment he stepped foot off the ship that had brought him back to England from France.

He was alone with Goose now and meant to find out the truth regarding her situation. He covered her hands with one of his. "I'm sorry. I hadn't heard. Is there anything I can do for you?"

She cast him a wistful smile. "No, but thank you for asking."

She turned away to gaze out the carriage window, purposely hoping to put an end to his questions. He was just getting started. "Who has guardianship over you?"

She sighed.

"Goose, you know I'll get the answers from Nathaniel and Penelope. But I'd rather have them from you."

She turned to face him, her gorgeous eyes narrowed in suspicion. "What does it matter? There's nothing you can do about it."

"I'm a duke. One who happens to be almost as popular as Wellington at the moment. I can do anything I want. Including chew up your guardian and spit his guts out in the gutter."

Dimples appeared in her cheeks as she smiled.

Mother in heaven. The girl was pretty.

"It won't be necessary."

He shifted his large frame against the black leather squabs, leaning back to better study her. By the look of her, his help was entirely necessary. "Nathaniel has invited me to Sherbourne Manor for the week. Thad will be joining us. You remember Thaddius MacLauren, don't you?"

She nodded. "Yes, Laird of Caithness."

"I hear Penelope has invited you and Poppy as well. It will be like old times. I assume you are going."

This time, she shook her head in dismay. "No. You see…"

"Goose, has your guardian forbidden you to go?" He tried to speak softly to hide his mounting outrage, not quite sure why he suddenly felt so protective of the girl. Or rather, why he still felt so protective of her after all these years. The memory of her tumbling into the Sherbourne pond and striking her head on a protruding log amid the grassy shallows remained vivid.

He'd pulled her out and revived her, then tended to her bloodied forehead. He'd never saved a life before. Of course, he'd saved many since then because of the blasted war. But he'd never forgotten his Little Goose and was not about to do so now.

She did not appear eager for his help, yet she was so obviously in need of it.

The pulse at the base of her slender throat began to beat madly. "He wants me in London. We haven't opened up our country house, and I am not about to ask him to bother just for me."

"That is utter nonsense. You'll stay with Penelope and Nathaniel at Sherbourne Manor. Nathaniel is the Earl of Welles, and you've been a long-time friend to his sister. Your guardian can have no objection. No need to open up Gosling Hall. Thad and I will be staying with Nathaniel as well."

She rolled her eyes. "All the more reason why I should not go. We're not little girls anymore. What will everyone think? Penelope, Poppy, and me under the same roof as the three of you? We'll be ruined. Worse, you will be forced to marry us to save our reputations. Will you toss our names into a hat and each take a turn drawing one out? Although Nathaniel can't very well marry his own sister. You'll have to work around that."

"It is quite a dilemma. Indeed, how will we ever solve the problem?" He raised an eyebrow to emphasize his sarcasm. "My aunt and Nathaniel's aunt will be joining us. I expect there will be assorted guests coming and going throughout the week as well. We three gentlemen shall not be left alone with you ladies. See? Our happy state of bachelorhood is in no peril. Nor is your virtuous reputation."

He leaned forward again. "Who is your guardian?"

She pursed her lips to mark her displeasure, but it did nothing to detract from the lovely fullness of her lips that drooped slightly at the corners in a sensual pout.

Sensual?

When had his Little Goose ever been that? She waddled when she ran. She had freckles on her nose. Yet, he had to admit that she was no longer a skinny, gangly little thing. *No, indeed.* His Goose was rather nicely shaped.

"Francis Gosling," she blurted, thankfully distracting him from the errant path of his thoughts. "He's a distant cousin of my father's. Viscount Gosling now that my father has passed away. He inherited everything, including Gosling Hall."

Beast frowned. "Did your father make no provision for you?"

She shrugged. "Neither he nor my mother expected to die so young."

"No one ever does. But one prepares for it anyway." He shifted against the constraints of his carriage. "I don't like it. This doesn't sound right to me."

She clasped her hands tightly together, an almost impossible task since she'd already had her fingers entwined in a death grip. "It may not be right, but this is the way it is. My father was never known for his business acumen. Apparently, the Gosling holdings were in disarray when his cousin took over. He took great pains to let me know just how badly they were left. He views me as an added burden. There. Now you know all there is to know about me. These last two years have not been pleasant."

"What about now that you are in your debut Season? Surely–"

"Beast," she said in a heart-wrenching whisper, "I have no dowry to tempt a man, and Viscount Gosling has made it clear he does not intend to spend so much as a shilling on me. What's the point? Who will have me?" Her fingers unclenched and she absently curled one hand around a corner of the velvet window curtain to draw it back further. She gazed out the window and opened her mouth to say more to him. At least, he thought she was about to speak to him, but she must have changed her mind and decided to merely stare at the passing throng instead.

After a long moment, she emitted a soft breath and turned back to face him. "He has plans for me. I'm not certain what they are."

He growled softly. "I don't like the sound of that."

"But you don't have a say, do you?"

He was about to toss out the duke card again, but saved his breath. Yes, he was a high-ranking duke. The Beastling title was a proud and distinguished one dating back to the Norman conquest. But his status mattered little. To meddle in her affairs meant marrying the girl himself or agreeing to sponsor her Season, which would only bring about scandal. Everyone would wonder at the reason for it and presume he'd taken her on as his mistress or planned to take her as that once she was married off to some hapless simpleton. "I suppose I don't."

"You needn't fret, Beast. I'm not your responsibility." She gazed down at the package in her hand and smiled wistfully. "I think there's a reason this book dropped on my head. I'm going to read it this evening. *The Book of Love.* It must mean something."

He suddenly tensed. *Good heavens!* He was a dolt. He ought to have read at least a passage out of it before purchasing it for her. What if the book was all about the act of making love? The various positions. The exotic accessories one might... bollocks! He'd never hear the end of it from Nathaniel and Thad.

"Goose, let me have a look at it."

He reached for the package but she shrank back and clasped it to her bosom. "You are not taking it from me."

He ran a hand roughly through his hair. "I won't... well, perhaps I will. You see, its contents might not be what you think. There might be drawings... unseemly ones. And language that an innocent such as yourself should not... hell, Goose. Give me the book."

"No. Are you blushing?" She gave a sincerely hearty laugh. "I never thought I'd live to see the day. This is priceless. You ought to see the look on your face."

"Give me the book. I will not be accused of corrupting your morals. You are an innocent."

She tipped her chin up in defiance. "Perhaps, but I am not a child."

"Indeed, you are not. Your body proves that."

Her eyes widened and she gasped. "You noticed?"

She seemed delighted rather than appalled. He was horrified that he'd allowed the thought to slip out. "I may have only one functioning eye at the moment, but I see very well out of it. You are not sufficiently wise to the ways of the world to be trusted with that book."

She was smiling at him now, a big, dimpled smile. Obviously, she found his consternation quite amusing. But her humor lasted only a moment and she turned thoughtful once more. "Beast, did it hurt very much when you lost your eye? Does it still hurt?"

"It did at first. But it isn't lost for certain. It may heal in time and I'll have some of my vision back. For the last question, no. It does not hurt me any longer."

"I'm glad." Her lips quivered and her eyes turned watery as though she was struggling to hold back tears. For him?

Well, despite her impertinence, she'd always had a tender heart. Ridiculously tender at times. He thought back to the long-ago summer before he'd gone off to fight in the war. He, Nathaniel, and Thad had decided they needed a swim in the pond at Sherbourne Manor. The day had been particularly hot, so they'd strolled down to the crystal pool, a trio of arrogant university boys who thought nothing of taking off their boots and clothes, and jumping naked into the water.

The girls had been ten years old at the time and were supposed to be napping or doing whatever genteel task young girls were supposed to do at that time of the day. But they must have slipped out of the house. Not surprising, for they were often up to mischief. Whatever the reason, the little nuisances came upon them cavorting in the water. Thankfully, the water hid much of their bodies from view. But another moment or two and they would have been caught bare-arsed on the shore.

Their nakedness left them at a disadvantage.

The girls took immediate advantage. Penelope and Poppy had thought it great fun to run off with Thad and Nathaniel's clothes, leaving only their boots behind. Goose hadn't the heart for such mischief and left his clothes exactly where he had dropped them. He'd waded out of the pond once the girls had run off only to find his trousers, shirt, vest, and cravat meticulously folded in a neat pile next to his boots.

Her way of repaying him for saving her life, no doubt.

He'd dressed and gone back to the main house to retrieve clothes for his friends. Poppy and Penelope had been sent to their rooms without supper, and Goose–being Goose–had gone upstairs with them in a show of support, even though it meant she would also forfeit her supper.

Bollocks, the girl was maddening.

His carriage suddenly jerked to a halt, reminding him they'd traveled through the Strand, skirted along the park, and had now arrived at the Gosling townhouse off Audley Street. Goose hopped out of the carriage the moment his footman opened the door and lowered the steps, no doubt hoping to make it into her house with that wretched book before he could stop her.

He caught up to her in two strides.

"Oh, Beast," she said with an exasperated huff. "I promise not to read it if it's lewd. There, are you satisfied? Do stop fussing or you'll draw my guardian's attention to this very book that you're hoping no one will see. You'll just have to trust me."

He growled softly in displeasure.

"Stop frowning at me. Do you know you resemble a lion when you frown? And do stop growling at me, too. It only proves my point. You *are* a lion."

She had a way of talking to him that he'd never allow from anyone else. *Lion, indeed!* "Very well, keep the book. But you will join us at Sherbourne Manor for the week. You'll ride out with Penelope and Poppy in Nathaniel's carriage." He picked her up to move her out of the way, for she'd strategically set herself between him and the front door.

The Gosling butler opened it to let them in.

Beast strode in. "Where is Lord Gosling?"

"In his study, Your Grace. I shall let him know at once that—"

"I'll announce myself. I know the way." He'd been familiar enough with this house in his younger days. Little had changed. "Gosling, I'd like a word with you."

He strode into the study, ignoring the man's open-mouthed look of surprise, and shut the door before Goose had a chance to follow him in. This was between him and her odious guardian. The man needed to know he was back in town and would be watching him. If he dared raise a hand to the girl, he'd strike him dead. "My aunt requests the company of your ward at Sherbourne Manor this week."

There was no need to explain who his aunt was, everyone knew Matilda, Duchess of Hartford, one of Society's most powerful matrons. "The Earl of Welles will have his carriage brought around tomorrow morning at ten o'clock precisely to pick her up and bring her there."

"Really, Hartford! This is too much. You can't just barge in here and expect me to give Olivia over to you." But his eyes turned beady, as though considering what he could gain by doing just that. "She has appointments. Obligations. It will cost me dearly to get her out of them."

He arched an eyebrow. By God, was the man putting her up for auction to the highest bidder? "Cost you? How?"

"In good will, of course. That's all. I meant nothing more by it."

Beast knew he was lying, for Gosling was beginning to sweat and fidget. "Then I'm certain everyone will understand when you explain the change in plans."

"It isn't possible!"

He leaned across Gosling's desk, his gaze fierce and unforgiving. "Reschedule them."

"But… but… Lord Marston…"

"That old goat? What does he want with Olivia?" The possibility that Gosling would allow such a man anywhere near her curled his stomach. "You will lose a lot more if you ignore my aunt's wishes." *Mercy!* Now he had to explain this to Matilda. And bring her along to Sherbourne Manor. And explain to Nathaniel why his Aunt Lavinia also had to join them.

He groaned inwardly.

He was going to an awful lot of fuss over Goose.

And Lord help him if that book did contain lewd drawings.

He'd never hear the end of it.

He strode out of Gosling's study shaking his head. Goose was standing by the door, her eyes wide and her mouth pursed. He turned to her, still wondering why he was going to such lengths over a ginger-haired girl he hadn't seen in almost ten years who still had freckles on her nose and little ears that curled up at the top. "It's all arranged. Nathaniel's carriage will come around at ten o'clock tomorrow morning to pick you up. Be ready."

She said nothing for the longest moment.

"Goose, don't you want to be at Sherbourne Manor?"

"More than anything in the world." Her eyes shimmered with tears, but he knew the girl was too proud to cry in front of him. She nodded and cast him a fragile smile that shot straight to his heart. "Thank you, Beast. I don't know how you managed it, but I'll be ready."

He nodded. "Send word to me if your guardian gives you any trouble. Any at all."

She placed a gentle hand upon his cheek. "It's so very nice to have you back."

"It's good to be back." In truth, it hadn't been until the very moment he'd entered Gresham's bookshop and seen Goose. The sight of her rubbing her head, and then admonishing the book when it fell back on her head, had brought innocence and laughter back into his life.

He hadn't realized how badly he'd missed those simple pleasures.

Or how badly he'd missed his Little Goose.

CHAPTER TWO

"I'M SO GLAD Lord Gosling had a change of heart and allowed you to join us," Penelope Sherbourne said, sliding over to make room for Olivia in the Sherbourne carriage the following morning. The sun was shining brightly against a vibrant blue sky, the rare sort of sky only seen after a torrential rain when there wasn't a drop of water left to spill. Perhaps it only seemed beautiful to Olivia because she was happier than she'd been in months.

"It wouldn't have been the same without you, Olivia." The third member of their trio, Poppy Farthingale, said in agreement as the footman folded up the steps and shut the door. "It'll be such fun now that you're with us."

She cast each friend a smile as the carriage rolled away from the Gosling townhouse, wending its way out of London toward the Cotswolds and the charming town of Wellesford. Penelope had grown up at Sherbourne Manor while she had resided across the meadow at Gosling Hall. "I'm looking forward to it."

Had Beast not barged into her guardian's study and frightened the man out of his wits with his roars and growls, she would not have been permitted to go. She'd called Beast a lion yesterday and that's exactly what he was. Her very own fierce, brave lion.

Once out of sight of the Gosling townhouse, she eased back and smoothed out her travel outfit, a pewter-gray gown of muslin with a charcoal gray pelisse to match. Neither her gown nor her short boots were the height of fashion, but Penelope and Poppy were true and loyal. They would never hurt her feelings by casting a disparaging remark upon the faded elegance of her clothes.

"What's that in your hand?" Poppy asked.

Olivia smiled. "It's a book. But not just any book. It fell on my head yesterday, a sure sign that I was meant to have it." Her friends bobbed their heads and leaned closer for a better view of the red, leather-bound tome. The boldness of the red had faded over the years. Perhaps it had been exposed to the sun at one time, but it was still quite impressive. "It's called *The Book of Love*. I stayed up all night reading it."

Poppy's big, blue eyes rounded in delight. "How exciting. Is it one of those wickedly steamy–"

"Olivia would never read that sort of book." Penelope emitted a trill of laughter. "But I would." Grinning, she reached over and took it from Olivia's hands. "Are there any naughty drawings?"

"Penelope! Honestly. Do you think I'd carry it about so openly if there were? No, it's quite scientific."

"Oh." Both her friends muttered in disappointment and sank back in their seats. Penelope handed the book over to her. "That's no fun."

"Actually, it is quite fascinating." Olivia flipped it open and began to read a passage. "Love does not come from the heart but from the brain. It is the brain that sends signals throughout the body, telling you what to feel. Therefore, to stimulate a man's arousal–"

Poppy gasped. "That is utterly unseemly and shocking. Olivia, whatever possessed you to bring this indecent… goodness, do read on."

"It isn't indecent at all. It's scientific," Olivia insisted and took up where she'd left off. "Therefore, to stimulate a man's arousal response, one must arouse his sense receptacles in a pleasing way. By touch, taste, sight, smell, and hearing." She glanced at her friends. "Do you understand?"

"Not a bit of it," Poppy replied. "What are sense receptacles?"

"Those little parts of our body that make us tingle when we are excited about something or someone. But a man's sense receptacles do not operate in quite the same way as ours do. Nor does a man's brain. It is very different from our own."

Penelope snorted. "That much is obvious. Our brains function. Theirs do not."

Olivia giggled as she glanced down at the page, and then she lifted her head to look meaningfully at her companions. "What this author suggests is that a man's brain functions on two levels. The low and the high. The simple and complex. When a man's brain is at its lowest function, he is only thinking of sex."

Penelope rolled her eyes.

Poppy blushed.

"It is his simple brain at work, the one formed thousands of years ago at the dawn of Creation when men first walked about the primeval earth. Very little thought occurs when the man's sexual urges are aroused. Perhaps no thought at all. But that is good. It is evidence of his compelling need to breed heirs with any fertile female he comes across."

"But what about love?" Penelope asked.

"Love is a higher function of the brain. The important function that makes a man feel the need to protect his family. Wife and offspring. Otherwise, he'd merely spill his seed and then move on, leaving them to be eaten by wolves."

Poppy gazed at her in horror. "How ghastly."

"But that is why man has been given a higher brain, to enable him to love. However, before he reaches that upper function of intelligence, the man must first be attracted to us on the simple brain level."

Poppy shook her head and sighed. "And we do that by arousing his senses? Taste, touch, and so on."

Penelope gave a snorting grunt of disbelief. "It cannot possibly be that easy or women would have been using this advice for thousands of years."

Olivia snapped the book shut. "Oh, I think it is quite a delicate and difficult matter. The slightest wrong step and the man will be lost forever. I've made a short list of those I would accept as a husband. Do you have gentlemen in mind?"

Both of her friends nodded.

"I think the Earl of Wycke is rather nice," Penelope said. "So is Marquis Bellhampton. I haven't actually spoken to either man yet, but I've observed them from a distance and they seem pleasant enough."

Poppy cleared her throat. "My cousins, Rose and Laurel, made excellent matches for themselves. Viscount Chatham and Baron Moray. But I hardly dare look that high for myself. Violet and I," she said, referring to her younger sister, "are not descended from anyone important either from my mother's lineage or my father's. I doubt I will tempt any nobleman to fall in love with me. Let me give it some thought, Olivia. Perhaps a second son of good moral character. I recently read that Captain Arthur Rawlings, a younger son of the Marquis of Hawkes, served with distinction at the battle of Waterloo. He was recently knighted. I think he might be someone of interest."

Olivia reached forward to pat Poppy's hand. "But that's just the point. This book will allow us to aim as high as we wish. With a little practice and scientific testing, we ought to be able to make any man fall in love with us. Why settle for a knight when you can have a king?"

Penelope regarded her cynically. "With a little practice? We can have any man of our choosing? All well and good, but who are we going to practice on? My little cousin, Phillip, is the devil's own spawn, and besides, he's only eight years old. Who can we possibly get to–"

Olivia stared at her friend, worried that she'd suddenly stopped talking and was now making strange groaning sounds.

"How silly of me," Penelope said after a long moment, shaking her head and laughing heartily. "We'll have an entire week with the perfect low-brain functioning specimens. My brother and his friends."

"Nathaniel?" Poppy muttered.

The carriage struck a rut in the road and sent them all bouncing off their seats.

Penelope was the first to recover her balance and settle back. "Yes, my brother. And Thad. And Beast. They'll be with us at Sherbourne Manor. Oh, I can't wait to get started. Do let me experiment on Thad. He's such a thickheaded, Scottish dolt. If I can arouse his uncouth, stubborn sense receptacles and turn him into a fawning beau, then I will succeed with any man."

"Beast frightens me, so I'll use Nathaniel." Poppy gazed hesitantly at Olivia and then Penelope. "Oh, dear. I don't mean 'use' him, exactly. That sounds so cold and deceiving. He's safer, that's all. Besides, he's the only gentleman, other than Beast and Thad, of course, that I know outside of my own family. Do we let them in on our plan?"

"No!" Penelope replied. "They mustn't know or it will skew the experiments."

Olivia's heart beat a little faster. "That means I'll have to try out these theories on Beast. What if they don't work?"

Penelope shrugged. "Then where's the harm? He'll never know the difference."

Olivia wasn't completely convinced, but Penelope's answer did seem logical. "Oh, dear heavens! What if my trials do work?" She refused to consider the possibility. Beast would never fall into that lower state of sexual arousal over her, much less fall in love with her, which required his brain to revert to a higher brain function.

He was sinfully handsome, a much-decorated war hero, and a duke. From a line of wealthy and powerful dukes of Hartford. She'd read the gossip rags. He could aim for a marriage within the royal family. Any royal family throughout Europe. Why would he marry a goose when he could have a princess? And yet, if she managed to manipulate his brain so that he did fall in love with her, then marriage to Beast would be the answer to all her problems.

No, it is deceitful.

He deserved a love match… or at the very least, a marriage of his own conscious choosing.

She placed a hand over her heart to calm its rapid beating. Was she making too much of this? One week was not enough time to conduct all the necessary experiments. There were bound to be missteps.

"Are we in agreement?" Penelope asked.

"Yes." Olivia stuck out her hand and waited for her friends to place theirs on top of hers. "One for all and all for one. Penelope experiments on Thad. Poppy on Nathaniel. And I have Beast. I think we ought to start off cautiously. One man at a time. I've already read the book, so let me go first. I'll test Beast's sense receptacles. I'll start with something easy. Something he isn't likely to notice."

Penelope tipped her head, now curious. "Such as?"

"I don't know yet. Let's set a plan of action together. I'll carry it out and then report my findings to you at the end of each day. But it is vitally important you also observe Beast and let me know your thoughts. If something appears to be working, I must be told at once."

Penelope laughed softly. "Oh, I think if something works on Beast, you'll know. We won't have to tell you anything."

Olivia frowned, suddenly worried about the possibilities. "What do you mean?"

"Beast is a war hero. A man of action. If aroused, he'll do something about it," Poppy said.

"What do you think he'll do?" Olivia's thoughts began to whirl madly in her head.

Penelope laughed again. "Oh, my. Olivia, you look like you're about to faint. I didn't mean anything too awful. Perhaps kiss you, for starters."

"Kiss me? For starters?" She fanned herself with her hand.

"And then what?"

Poppy giggled. "Sweep you into his arms, carry you to his bedchamber, and toss you onto his bed while he whips off his shirt and achingly vows that he cannot live another moment without you."

Olivia breathed a sigh of relief. "Oh, for pity's sake, Poppy. We are talking about Beast, not some silly boy. Besides, he won't dare do anything while his bombazine-clad, dragon aunt is at Sherbourne with us."

Poppy grinned. "Are you sure?"

BEAST STOOD ON the front steps of Sherbourne Manor with his friends, Nathaniel and Thad, looking out across its expansive grounds. His gaze followed theirs toward the distant pond where Nathaniel's young cousin, Phillip, was tossing pebbles at the ducks in the water. Their angry quacks reached Beast's ears and should have caught the attention of the three girls huddled together on the trunk of a fallen oak beside the tranquil pool.

But Goose and her friends were too engrossed in that idiotic book. They ignored Phillip. And ignored the angry ducks that were now chasing him away from the pond and into the nearby meadow. "That damn *Book of Love*."

He rued the day he'd purchased it for Goose.

"What did you say?" Nathaniel asked.

"Nothing." He didn't dare tell his friends. Not before he got his hands on the book and made certain it did not contain anything obscene. Nathaniel would pound his face to dust for corrupting those innocents and he would not raise a hand to defend himself. "I'll go see what they are doing."

"Don't bother," Nathaniel said. "I'm sure it's harmless fun. Loopy and her friends aren't little girls anymore. They don't need looking after."

"Och," Thad said with a groaning laugh. "It's the big girls that are the trouble. I'll go with you, Beast."

Nathaniel shook his head and sighed. "Very well, I'll go, too. I'd better save Pip before the ducks do him permanent damage. Not that he doesn't deserve it."

By the time they'd walked down to the pond, Nathaniel's sister had caught up to their impish cousin and was walking hand in hand with him back toward the pond. Phillip, known casually as Pip, had been Nathaniel's ward for about a year now. Thad lifted the boy onto his shoulders, which thrilled the imp to no end and also served the purpose of keeping him from running off again. But Penelope was frowning at Thad.

For the life of him, Beast could not understand why. Thad hadn't said a word to her. Apparently, Thad was wondering the same. "Och, Loopy. What did I do to vex ye this time? Ye look like one of those ducks got their beak stuck up your backside."

Penelope gasped. "And you look like the backside of a duck, you big Scottish oaf. Don't call me Loopy."

Nathaniel laughed. "Come along, Poppy. We'd better walk ahead before they bite our heads off, too."

Which left Beast standing beside Olivia. She had her hands behind her back, obviously attempting to hide the book from him. "Beast, thank you again for making this visit possible. You were brilliant yesterday. Fiery and frightening. You had Lord Gosling quaking in his boots. I wouldn't be here if not for you."

Beast frowned. "He won't make you suffer for spending the week here, will he?"

"No. He wouldn't dare. Let's not speak of him. I'd much rather enjoy the lovely day."

"Very well, but I'm going to insist on seeing that book." He held out his hand to receive it, but she shook her head and took a step back.

"I promise to show it to you at the end of the week."

"Are you negotiating with me?"

She tipped her chin up. "Yes, I am. I think I am being quite reasonable."

"Why won't you show it to me now?"

She smiled at him, an adorably sweet and thoroughly enchanting smile. "Because I enjoy teasing you."

He laughed.

"And it contains secrets that only a woman should know. Things not appropriate for a bachelor to read."

He ought to have simply taken the blasted thing from her hands. If it was not suitable material for him to read, then it could not possibly be suitable for her. But something stopped him. He wasn't certain why, only that the sun was shining on Goose's red hair and there was a happy sparkle in her eyes. When he'd met her yesterday, they'd been clouded with worries and burdens a debutante should not have had placed upon her shoulders. "Very well. End of the week it is, for now."

"Thank you, Beast." Obviously surprised by his easy capitulation, she tossed him another sparkling smile and ran ahead to catch up to Poppy and Nathaniel. Lord, she still ran like a little goose.

He didn't know why he found that so charming.

CHAPTER THREE

"COME GIVE US a kiss, Olivia." Penelope's aunt, Lady Lavinia Sherbourne, held up her cheek to receive her greeting. Olivia then greeted Beast's aunt, Matilda, with much more formality, giving a curtsy as they were introduced and holding her breath while the dowager duchess eyed her speculatively.

They were in the summer salon that overlooked the Sherbourne garden, the two dowagers looking quite regal in their matching red silk wing chairs that were placed side by side. But Lavinia had a warm smile for Olivia as she continued to engage her in conversation. "We've hardly seen you since the new Lord Gosling closed up Gosling Hall. The mornings always seemed brighter when I watched you run across the meadow between our homes and burst onto our terrace to join us for eggs and kippers."

Olivia smiled. "Our morning routine. You, me, and Penelope. I miss those days, too."

"Don't forget me," Poppy said, giving Lady Lavinia a hug. "Our home wasn't as close by, but I would join you on the weekends."

"Poppy, dearest. I would never forget you." Lady Lavinia cast each of them a tender smile. "And now look at the three of you, all grown up and quite beautiful."

Penelope shook her head and laughed. "I doubt Nathaniel and his friends think so. I'm sure they still consider us nuisances.

Their tastes run to more sophisticated ladies of the *ton*."

Beast's aunt, Matilda, who had appeared quite stern and imposing at first, quickly jumped into the conversation. "Those boys don't know what they want." Once again, she studied Olivia with a speculative eye. "You're the one my nephew calls Goose, are you not?"

Olivia's cheeks heated as she cast her a wincing smile. "Yes, unfortunately he seems determined to call me that even though I am now in my debut Season. He claims I still run like a little goose."

"Well, at least he's taken notice of you. He hasn't shown interest in any young lady since his return to England. He's already been introduced to many of the highest rank and all quite beautiful."

Olivia's stomach sank into her toes. "Yes, yes. Of course, he is a favorite of the royal family and I'm sure they'd like to see him marry well. Perhaps one of their own cousins. I suppose you would, too."

She cast a glance in Beast's direction and her expression turned tender and quite doting. "I would like to see him marry happily."

Beast, looking elegant as ever and dangerously mysterious with the black eyepatch over his injured eye, strode forward as his aunt spoke those words. He frowned at all of them. "Sorry to disappoint you. No plans to marry. Not now. Not in the foreseeable future. Perhaps not ever. So let's move on to another topic. Lovely weather we're having, isn't it? Thad's lumbago is acting up. He believes we'll have rain tomorrow."

Matilda rolled her eyes. "My dear boy, if that is the quality of conversation we're to have all week, then I shall pack up my gowns and have your carriage brought around to take me home at once."

He planted a noisy kiss on his aunt's cheek. "Empty threat. I know you adore me. You may have others convinced that you're a dragon, but I know you are a tender lamb."

And Beast was a magnificent lion.

Olivia sighed over the loving way he teased and cajoled his aunt. The man was capable of affection. Deep, abiding affection toward those he cared for. It made her realize just how empty and devoid of it she'd been these past two years. Some people managed quite well in a quiet household where no one laughed or hugged or cared about another's thoughts.

But she was not one of those people.

She craved silliness and chatter and hugs for no reason. Those were the best, for they reflected happiness and sprang from all good places in the heart.

Beast suddenly turned to her, as though he sensed the path of her thoughts. What was he going to do?

He arched an eyebrow and the edges of his mouth curled up in the hint of a grin. "What are your thoughts on the weather, Goose?"

She shook her head and laughed. "Your aunt now has a firm grip on her walking cane and shall club you over the head if you persist in talking about the dullest topic in existence. But I will say if the rain holds off, Pip and I plan to go to the meadow after breakfast tomorrow in search of butterflies."

"Would you care to join us, Your Grace?" Pip asked. "We have nets, and Olivia brought me a sketch book so we can draw pictures of all the varieties we see. I would rather catch spiders and snakes, but she's afraid of them. So, it's butterflies for us."

Olivia smiled at Penelope's young cousin who was hopping beside her and looked about ready to rip off his cravat and collar and toss them to Lavinia's lapdog, Periwinkle, to chew on. "I'll compromise. Perhaps afterward, we shall go by the pond and look for tadpoles."

Pip rolled his eyes. "Fine."

Beast shook his head. "I have to ride back to London in the morning. Perhaps another time."

Olivia turned to him in surprise. "You're leaving?"

"Only for the day. I'll be back shortly after supper. At least, I hope Prinny won't require me to stay longer. He's hosting a luncheon in my honor."

"And I wasn't invited?" Nathaniel teased. "After all, I am an earl."

Beast emitted a soft rumble of laughter, his voice deep and resonant. "Dukes only, I'm afraid. You and Thad don't qualify."

Thad gave a derisive snort. "Are they still intent on introducing you to that Austrian princess?"

"A real princess? Will that make you king of Austria?" Pip asked, his eyes wide and approving.

Nathaniel laughed. "He'd merely be Prince Consort. Will you invite us to your castle on the Danube after the wedding?"

"How many bairns will they expect you to sire?" Thad's grin was wide and mocking.

Beast shot both of them a glower. "When did you turn into gossiping, old hens? It's a meal, that's all. No wedding. No bride. No leaving England."

Pip looked crestfallen. "Then you won't be king?"

Beast ruffled his hair playfully. "No. Not even close."

"What if you're ordered to marry the Austrian princess?" Olivia found herself breathlessly blurting. "What will you do then?"

More to the point, what would *she* do? It wasn't merely a matter of losing her test specimen. She felt a sudden and deep sense of loss over possibly losing *him*. But he'd hardly been in her life. Only a few summers when she'd been a little girl. Lovely summers, to be sure. But they were so long ago. And then a chance meeting yesterday.

Why was Beast so important to her?

"Goose, enough. I am not marrying anyone. The royal family will not force me to do anything I don't wish to do."

Her heart was pounding fiercely and her body began to tremble, but she fought off her momentary weakness and quickly regained her composure. "Will you tell us all about it when you return?"

He shrugged. "Some of it."

She nodded, afraid to say more. Perhaps she had not quite regained control of her feelings. In truth, her heart pounded even faster now. Beast was staring at her. Did he know she was falling to pieces? She was trying very hard to appear calm on the surface.

His gaze continued to bore into her, that black eyepatch and the dark superfine of his jacket as he turned his broad shoulders to face her, were all she saw. She was caught up in his lion gaze, in the turbulent swirls of his amber-green eyes. Then she thought she might be dizzy because she heard a ringing in her ears.

Beast grinned. "The dinner bell, Goose."

Oh, he must think her an utter nitwit. "Of course, it is." Knowing Beast would have to lead his aunt into the dining room, she turned to Pip. "Will you be my escort?"

The boy nodded. "How long do I have to sit there and pretend to enjoy myself?"

"A long time, I'm afraid. But you'll have me for company and you can talk to me all about your spiders and snakes. I promise not to cringe."

"Perhaps Cook has whipped up some boiled snakes and roasted spiders for our supper," Beast remarked.

The boy's eyes brightened. "That would be spectacular! Olivia, have you ever eaten a spider?"

"No." She gave a mock shiver. "Have you?"

He shook his head. "Not yet."

Oh, dear. Olivia hoped she hadn't put any ideas into the boy's already too fertile mind. "Don't you dare attempt it. Some of them are poisonous."

Pip dismissed her warning. "Not around here, they're not. Our meadow spiders are harmless."

"Perhaps," Beast said, "but you don't know what they've eaten. What's being dissolved in a spider's digestive juices may not be harmless to you."

Beast's aunt groaned. "I forbid further discussion on this topic as well. You are all ruining my appetite."

Moments later, they entered the dining room with its dark wood floors and tall windows that allowed in ample light. They sat down around the mahogany table that could easily accommodate twenty. Crystal glasses, elegant china, and gleaming silverware adorned a crisp, white tablecloth trimmed in delicate French lace.

They ate a supper of roast goose, which in Olivia's mind was almost as bad as speaking of spiders, for Pip had now taken up calling her Goose and was making jokes about how delicious her sister, said roast goose, tasted. That would have been harmless enough had he not made comments about sticking a fork in her and seeing how she tasted.

Olivia looked upon him appalled when he actually poked his fork lightly into her arm and then began to lick it with zeal. Her eyes rounded in horror when he muttered "yum" and "delicious" and began to make awful slurping and gobbling sounds. All three grown men were now snorting and chortling. Although Beast, to his credit, was rather quiet after his initial choking cough. He merely stared at her down the table in a way that had her body tingling with excitement.

That look!

Even with one good eye and the other hidden behind the eyepatch, there was something in his gaze that aroused *her*. Had he read *The Book of Love*? Was he using it to… no, he was too much of a gentleman to seduce her. And too accomplished and sophisticated to seriously consider her as a prospective wife.

"That will be quite enough," Lavinia intoned. "You rascals are not too big to take to the woodshed for a sound thrashing. At least the boy is innocently teasing Olivia. I know what your polluted minds are thinking. Leave the poor girl alone. Pip, one more word out of you and I shall feed you to the spiders."

"That won't be so bad. At least I wouldn't have to sit here wrapped up tight as a mummy. How can anyone breathe wearing these cravats? I'd rather eat alone in my room."

Olivia's heart tugged. "You don't mean that, Pip. Don't you

wish for company?"

He gave a wounded shrug. "It doesn't matter."

She sighed. "I'll share supper with you tomorrow evening."

"And I'll share it with you the following evening," Poppy said. "With Nathaniel's permission, I'll bring my cousin, Charles, with me next time. He loves to play marbles, and while he's a few years younger than you, I think you'll find him to be lots of fun."

Now Nathaniel was giving Poppy the same look Beast had given her. "That's an excellent idea, Poppy. You and your cousin are always welcome here."

Were these men starting to take notice of them? But they hadn't done anything yet. Or had they inadvertently been arousing their lower brain senses? She had to speak to Penelope and Poppy before they retired to bed. This was a most exciting observation and she couldn't wait to share it with them.

When supper was over, Pip tore out of the dining room, peeling off his cravat as he ran upstairs. The men retired to the study for a glass of port, and the ladies retired to the salon. The older women settled in their wing chairs and had a glass of sherry served to them.

"That was a sweet thing you did for the boy, Olivia," Beast's aunt remarked, casting her an unexpectedly warm smile.

Olivia tried to make light of it. She'd often felt lonely in the new Lord Gosling's household and truly understood Pip's own emptiness. His parents had died, and while Penelope, Lavinia, and Nathaniel were warm and loving toward the boy, she knew he had to be struggling over their loss. Nothing could replace a mother's kiss or the solid security of having one's father at home.

Penelope and Nathaniel had experienced a similar loss, but they'd had each other to turn to in their grief. She liked that they'd always been close. That's what families were supposed to be. That's what she wanted to find when she married, a man with plenty of warmth and cheer in his heart. "I think he'll enjoy the company of someone his own age much more, but Pip and I get along well enough. I hope he won't find me too boring while we are off chasing butterflies. By the time supper comes around, he might feign a headache and beg me to leave."

Lavinia reached over and patted her hand. "My dear, I'm sure he'll have a lovely time with you. And I think the grown men will be quite jealous."

Olivia laughed. "I cannot imagine any of those three picking up butterfly nets and joining us while we flit across the meadow."

"Indeed, not," Penelope said. "They're no better than Huns. They'd crush anything that had the misfortune to be caught under their big, booted feet. But let's not speak of those simpletons right now." She cast Olivia a conspiratorial look to signify they'd meet in Penelope's room later to discuss their initial findings. "I hear the men leaving the study. Shall we move to the music room? Olivia, will you play for us?"

Olivia nodded, for she enjoyed playing the piano and often used it to escape the boredom of the new Lord Gosling's house. She'd always think of him as that, for her father had been the real Lord Gosling, true and honorable in every sense. His distant cousin was a toad. A mean one at that, for he'd sold her piano a few months ago and taken great pleasure in her distress. "I'd love to."

They all moved into the music room, the men joining them and giving no protest when told they'd have to delay their evening card game a little while longer, for Olivia was about to give a recital.

Beast folded his arms across his chest and arched an eyebrow. "You still play?"

She nodded. "Always. I enjoy it."

"Until a few months ago when her ogre of a guardian sold her piano," Penelope said, frowning at her brother.

Nathaniel shook his head in confusion. "Why are you angry with me? I didn't give it away."

"You should have said something to the man. Threatened to beat him within an inch of his life. You know how much that piano meant to Olivia."

"No, Penelope." Olivia regarded her in dismay. "Please don't make more of it than it is. I could have said something to Lord Gosling. It wasn't your brother's place to–"

"I'll take care of it when I'm in town tomorrow." Beast spoke softly, but a shiver ran up Olivia's spine. Beneath the quiet calm was a lion who would rip apart Lord Gosling if he refused to restore it. Goodness, she liked that.

Not that she wished physical harm to Lord Gosling.

But she liked that he was in mortal fear of Beast.

She would have her piano back. "Thank you, Beast. I mean, Your Grace. I mean…" She sighed. "Thank you."

He made no response and took a seat beside his aunt to await the start of her concert. No doubt, he considered the matter settled and a foregone conclusion that he would restore the instrument to its rightful place.

Olivia sank onto the piano stool and lightly tested the ivory keys. The piano was in tune. Recently tuned, for the heat and dampness would have affected the purity of the notes otherwise. She started with a Scottish lilt that had Thad grinning in approval. "The lass knows her music."

Then she moved on to a haunting sonata that she'd learned only last year. Since Lavinia and Matilda were gently weeping by the end of it, she decided to finish her recital with a merry, country air.

When she'd finished, graciously accepting the enthusiastic cheers from Poppy and Penelope, the quieter cheers from Lavinia and Matilda, and hoots and howls from Thad and Nathaniel, she offered to play something more conducive to dancing.

Only then did she notice that Beast had slipped out of the room.

Where was he?

"You may play for us tomorrow, Olivia," Lavinia intoned. "We've all had a long day of travel. Matilda and I will retire to our chambers. Girls, you must now do the same. We'll leave the men to their card game."

Olivia's heart sank. It was true. Without proper chaperones, they could not be allowed to remain with the men. But it would also allow them to meet in Penelope's room and formulate their plans. "Very well," she said, motioning to her friends.

Nathaniel and Thad bid them goodnight.

Where was Beast?

She hoped she'd see him before he rode off tomorrow morning. Perhaps she would manage one test, a simple one, before then.

CHAPTER FOUR

Beast stood on the terrace listening to the strains of a lively country tune that Olivia played effortlessly. Night had fallen and the moon was shining overhead, hanging upon the sky like an enormous silver ball. Thousands of stars twinkled against the black sky. He leaned forward and rested his elbows atop the stone balustrade, determined to calm his rage.

That walking slime, Gosling, had purposely taken Olivia's piano away from her. He'd stolen her joy and her music. What did he intend to steal next?

He growled softly, that last thought enraging him further. She was *his* Little Goose. No one was going to hurt her while he was around to protect her.

"Beast, there you are. Why did you slip away from my concert?" He'd been so lost in his thoughts he hadn't noticed the music had stopped. He turned to the sound of Goose's soft voice and met her endearing grin. "Has my playing gotten that bad over the years?"

She was purposely trying to make light of her loss, but he would not allow it.

"Why did you let him take away your piano?" He knew he sounded angry, and was incensed on her behalf. Why hadn't she put up a fight? Even as the thought came into his mind, he knew it was unreasonable. How could she have stopped her guardian? She had no rights to assert in a court of law. The loathsome man hadn't beaten her. He'd taken her into his home, albeit treating her as an unwanted burden. He'd done the minimum required of a guardian toward his charge. "Sorry, I know it wasn't your fault."

It was not in Goose's nature to be combative, and even if it were, where would it have gotten her? She was a little thing and her shouts of protest and outrage might have brought her a sound thrashing instead of the return of her precious instrument.

She moved closer to him, obviously not intimidated by his frowning countenance. "Beast, why are you working yourself into a state over my circumstances? I could have objected and made a fuss, but I simply didn't care. It isn't my home any longer. I won't pretend that it didn't hurt. But it is nothing I won't get over in time. In any event, I've made plans of my own."

He tensed. "What sort of plans?"

She tipped her head up to meet his steady gaze. "I intend to be married by the end of the Season. I'll no longer be his responsibility."

Her answer only increased his tension. "So, you'd marry anyone just to get away from Gosling?"

Her eyes rounded in surprise. "No! How could you ever suggest such a thing? I am going to marry for love."

"Who are you in love with?" And why did he have the sudden urge to rip that man apart? Goose in love? It wasn't possible.

She cleared her throat and looked downward a moment before returning her gaze to his. "No one yet. That's why I needed the book. You know, the one you bought for me."

He groaned. "Don't remind me."

"Beast," she said, emitting a sigh, "I need to figure this out quickly. There's nothing lewd or remotely indecent in those pages. While Penelope, Poppy, and I have laughed over some of the observations written, it is actually a very thoughtful discussion about the elements of love. I can't share the ideas with you yet. It's important that I don't. I shouldn't be talking to you about it now."

"Why not?" He raked a hand through his hair. "You can tell me anything. Trust me to keep it in confidence, Goose."

"I know." She took a step away from him and turned to gaze at the moon and stars. "I appreciate your concern more than you will ever realize. But please don't ask me any more questions about it."

Hellfire. He had a thousand questions, a thousand concerns over this girl, and she was purposely keeping him at a distance. What was the matter with her? He was a powerful duke. He was not going to be pushed away until he was good and ready. He would walk away on his own terms and in his own time.

He raked a hand through his hair once more, irritated when she kept her gaze fixed heavenward. He was also not used to being ignored and he did not care for it one bit. "What if your plan fails? What if you don't find love?"

She shrugged her slender shoulders. "Then I shall find employment as a companion."

"Employment? Are you serious?" He wanted to growl in frustration. Goose had been born a viscount's daughter. A flighty, fool-of-a-viscount apparently, but a peer nonetheless. She wasn't meant to go into service in the household of some cantankerous, old battle-axe who would run her ragged with an endless stream of mindless chores.

She finally turned to him. "I'm not afraid of work, Beast."

But he was afraid for her. She was too beautiful ever to be safe in anyone's household. The men, most of them already married, would be sniffing around her like eager hounds after a fox. "Come to me first if you find yourself in need of employment."

She pursed her lips in thought, apparently not liking his suggestion if the frown on her face was any indication. "I am not your responsibility."

"Goose, there are times I wish to wring your pretty neck. I'm offering to help, that's all. In truth, you would be of great help to me. My aunt will soon be in need of a companion. I can see she likes you. It would be a perfect arrangement. She'd be in your gentle care and I wouldn't have to worry about her comfort."

Goose arched an eyebrow. "Are you making this up? Although your aunt uses a cane for support, she doesn't look frail. She's here with her maid who seems quite competent to attend to her every need."

"You wouldn't be serving as her maid. You'd be her companion, offering her intellectual stimulation and friendship during her waning years. She's growing older and her health can fail very quickly." Lord help him! Matilda was going to box his ears. "Where's the problem? You need a safe place to be and Matilda needs a trustworthy companion. I don't see how anyone loses in this proposition. Think about it. If you don't fall in love by the end of the Season—"

"And I find the need to leave Lord Gosling's residence?"

"Right, and that." He stifled the urge to growl again. That man deserved to be ripped apart. He might do it just for the fun of it. "Then come to me and I'll engage you as a companion for Matilda."

"Assuming Lord Gosling doesn't object. He's still my guardian."

This time, he did growl. "He won't. I'll make certain of it."

"OLIVIA, WHAT TOOK you so long?" Penelope whispered as she opened the door to her bedchamber and allowed her inside. Poppy was already there, seated on Penelope's bed with *The Book of Love* on her lap.

"Sorry, I had a chat with Beast." She sank onto the bright yellow counterpane beside Poppy, tucking her legs under her as she settled in to plot her next course of action. "What did I miss?"

Poppy handed her the book. "Nothing. We were waiting for you. What did you and Beast talk about? Were you arousing his sense receptacles? Was he responding?"

"No, nothing of the sort." She shook her head and sighed. "You know my situation with Lord Gosling."

Penelope joined them on her bed. "Indeed, we do. If it gets unbearable, I shall insist that Nathaniel take you in. You'll live with us for as long as you need."

"It won't be necessary. That's what Beast wanted to speak to me about. He said he would engage me as companion for Matilda, if it ever came to that."

Poppy's eyes rounded in surprise. "That's awfully generous of him."

"I know." Olivia pursed her lips in thought. "I almost feel guilty trying out these love... I'd hardly call them spells, but the point is to place a man under my spell. So, I suppose that is what I'd be doing with Beast."

The kinder he was toward her, the worse she felt about purposely enticing him, especially if her magical allure actually worked.

She opened the book. "Oh, dear."

It happened to open at the chapter discussing the sense of sight. She was going to turn the pages to find something else, for it seemed cruel to start there when Beast had only one good eye. But her heart beat slightly faster and her hand stilled on the page. Was her heart telling her to begin there? Or rather, was her brain sending signals to her heart not to turn the page?

Poppy shifted closer to peer at the book. "What's wrong, Olivia? The sense of sight? Is that where you're going to start with Beast?"

She nodded. "I don't see how I can avoid it. That sense is too important. According to this book, men look for beautiful women. They may define beauty differently, but there is one thing they all agree upon. The woman must appear to be a successful vessel for their sperm or they will immediately dismiss her in their minds, whether too old, too young, too frail, or too sickly. So, all men will first look for cues that a woman can provide him healthy offspring. At this first inspection, the color of her hair and eyes is not as important as the shape and symmetry of her body."

Poppy frowned. "What does that mean?"

Penelope rolled her eyes. "It means men look at a woman's breasts first."

Olivia grinned. "I suppose that does summarize this chapter. That's it in a nutshell, Poppy. If they like the look of her bosom, they will then move on to inspecting the rest of her. They can't help themselves. It is their lower brain function at work, the one designed purely for successful mating."

Poppy pursed her lips. "So, what are you going to do?"

"Right now, I believe Beast is rejecting me as a suitable mate because his mind still sees me as the Little Goose I was when we last met, the little ten-year-old he certainly would never touch."

"But you're all grown up now. We all are," Poppy said.

"And he realizes it. He even passed a casual remark about it to me, but he's fighting against his own mating urges. I need to break through the wall he's built around himself and lead his mind to accepting me as a potential mate."

"How? By exposing your bosom?" Poppy's eyes rounded in horror.

"Good heavens, no. I have no intention of removing my clothes and exposing myself. Besides, if he gets a good look and decides I'm lacking, then there is nothing to hold his interest. But we know the female bosom is important to a man. If I give Beast a mere hint of what lies beneath my clothing, his lower brain will compel him to keep looking until he makes his determination."

She paused to make certain her friends were following the path of her thoughts before continuing. "But there is an added benefit to allowing him only a peek."

"What's that?" Penelope asked.

"The brain tends to fill in parts the eyes perceive as missing. So, in catching a glimpse of the swell of my breast and frustrating his brain with respect to a full view of it, he will be forced to look again and again. In frustration, his brain will fill in what he wants to see... the lush breasts he desires. That action will reinforce his pleasure sensations. The hope is that his wall of resistance will crumble and he will come to a positive conclusion about my suitability as a mate, even though he has never been given more than a peek."

Her friends stared at her for the longest while. Stunned. Saying nothing. Then Penelope burst out laughing. "Oh, poor Beast! You must test this before he leaves tomorrow morning. He'll be thinking of you and paying no attention whatsoever to that haughty Austrian princess."

"Unless she tempts him similarly," Poppy said. "Then he'll be riding back to Sherbourne Manor thinking of her and not Olivia."

"Poppy, don't say that. He has to prefer Olivia."

Olivia rolled her eyes. "We'll learn something from tomorrow's experiment. He'll be back shortly after supper and we'll know for certain then."

Olivia was still contemplating her plan while she returned to her guest chamber and readied herself for bed. Penelope had assigned maids to assist each of them, and a local girl by the name of Betsy awaited her. "I'll need your assistance in dressing tomorrow morning, Betsy."

"Of course, m'lady. Is there a particular gown you'd like me to freshen?" The girl was about Olivia's age and quite cheerful, her dark curls bobbing as she scurried about the room attending to her duties.

"The blue muslin, if you please."

Betsy helped her to undress and don her nightrail. The girl liked to talk, so Olivia learned all about the young man Betsy hoped to marry, one of the local farmers, currently a tenant farmer on land belonging to the local magistrate, Mr. Baldridge. She was still chattering as she walked to the door to take the gown downstairs to air and press.

Once alone in the blessed quiet, Olivia brushed out her hair in preparation for bed. The room was warm so she opened the glass-paned doors that led out onto a small balcony overlooking the rear garden. A light breeze blew through her hair and caused her thin, cotton nightrail to billow and swirl around her hips and legs.

She inhaled deeply to take in the scent of roses and evening dew on the grass that carried on the wind.

The moon shone overhead, its rays falling across the garden in a silvery arc. Stars glittered in the sky. She closed her eyes and made a wish. *Please let me find love.*

There was something exhilarating about the country air, something natural and eternal. The earth, trees, plants, and animals. As a girl, she'd loved the summers spent at Gosling Hall, the flowers in bloom, deer in the meadow, and all the vibrant life that surrounded her. Gosling Hall was likely a ruin by now. The possibility saddened her. But she was determined to walk over there to inspect it before the week was out and they all returned to London.

Another scent caught her attention. Sandalwood. Beast's scent. She opened her eyes and saw a shadow move out from behind one of the oak trees. She recognized the muscled outline of Beast.

Had he seen her?

"Beast, is that you?"

He said nothing at first, merely prowling closer and looking like a lion about to pounce on its prey. An angry lion if his stance and suddenly fearsome scowl were any indication. "Where is your robe? Why aren't you wearing it?"

She looked down at herself, staring at her nightgown that now seemed impossibly thin. Could he see through it? "Why are you out here?"

"Why are you?" He turned the question back on her. "Damn it. Get inside. Go to bed, Goose. *Now.*"

Her heart raced, beating as fast as the flap of a hummingbird's wings. There was something gruff and barely restrained in the tone of his voice. She retreated indoors and leaped under her covers.

Only then did she realize she'd left the balcony doors open.

She was afraid to climb out of bed. What if he had climbed onto her balcony? What if he entered her bedchamber? *No.* Beast would never do that. And she did not want to close those doors. Her room was hot and needed to cool.

"Silly goose." Perhaps it was her body that needed cooling.

She had been jesting with her friends about the temptation of a woman's body upon the male brain, but women were also in danger of succumbing. And Beast was raw temptation. Although females did not respond in the same way as males, there was no doubt he was having an effect on her.

She shook her head and huddled beneath the crisp linens. She'd read the book and knew what to watch out for. Beast was only meant to be her test subject.

But her body felt an unexpected ache of longing.

In testing him, she was also making herself vulnerable to love.

This was a problem.

She had no intention of falling in love with Beast, but her own sense receptacles were stirring and in danger of being aroused. It couldn't be helped. Beast was big and strong. He was a wealthy duke. He was touchingly protective, just the sort of man who would keep her and their offspring from being eaten by wolves.

She wrapped her arms around her pillow, squeezing it tightly, as though it would also squeeze all thoughts of Beast out of her dreams.

But she couldn't be sure it would work.

She'd have to take extra care not to fall in love with her own test subject.

CHAPTER FIVE

WAS THERE ANYWHERE he could hide without Goose turning up and sending his body careening out of kilter? He was Alexander Beastling, Duke of Hartford, and he did not have to hide from anyone. Yet, this girl had him experiencing sensations he'd never felt before, ones that alarmed him. Perhaps frightened him. However, he would never admit his fear to anyone when he could hardly believe it himself.

He'd faced bayonets and cannonballs.

He'd faced death without so much as a quiver.

So why would the mere possibility of facing Goose send him into panic?

There was no denying the girl was having an effect on him and he did not care for it at all. He'd left his friends to their game of billiards, intending to take an innocent stroll in the garden to clear away those very thoughts of her.

And there she was again, a vision on her balcony, surrounded by candlelight and moonlight, her hair unbound and freely blowing in the wind, her thin nightgown hugging the curves of her body. Lord, her nightgown was thin.

To say she looked spectacular was an understatement.

She looked like an angel.

No longer his Little Goose.

The realization that he would lose her, that she would give her heart to someone else by the end of the Season, unsettled him. She was a young woman with a desire to marry, and despite her lack of dowry, she would receive several offers from gentlemen of good reputation. After all, bounders and cads would be sniffing after someone wealthy. Those who offered for Goose would want her for herself.

Why did he suddenly hate those men?

She would accept one of them in order to escape Lord Gosling's grim grasp. That's what worried him most, for she had compelling reason to marry. What if she forced herself to be with someone she could never love? It would be so easy to convince herself that love would grow in time. "Bah!"

It wasn't his place to meddle in her affairs.

He'd already done all he could. An offer of employment with Matilda and keeping a careful watch on that toad, Gosling, to make certain he did not mistreat her. If she married, his responsibility would be over. If she worked for Matilda, she'd be in safe surroundings and he needn't do anything more.

Thad and Nathaniel joined him outdoors.

"You're awfully quiet tonight," Nathaniel said.

He nodded. "Just needed a moment to myself. Prinny's luncheon is more than a mere meal to welcome back a few dukes who commended themselves well on the field of battle."

Thad grunted. "Of course, that Austrian princess."

Beast nodded. "He's made no secret of his wishes. And I've made no secret of mine. But he's Prinny, and I'm a mere duke. I'm bound to lose something no matter what I do. I need to figure out what I'm willing to give up and how to negotiate toward that end, assuming the need arises."

Nathaniel patted him on the shoulder. "Let's hope it doesn't."

They chatted a little while longer and then retired, each to their own quarters. Beast stripped off his clothes, tossed them over a chair for Nathaniel's valet to attend to in the morning, and fell into bed. But even though the windows had been open throughout the day and only shut as night fell, the room still felt stifling. He rose and strode to the window to open it, staring out as he did.

The wind caressed his skin as it swirled around his naked body.

The moon shone down across the open meadow.

His chamber was on the opposite side of the house from Goose's. She had a view of the garden at the rear of the manor. His room overlooked the front drive and distant pond and meadow. It had always been his assigned quarters whenever he stayed here.

He shook his head and grinned, suddenly remembering those long ago summer mornings, the sun shining against a bright blue sky and the skinny figure of his Little Goose running across the meadow between Gosling Hall and Sherbourne Manor in time to join Penelope and Lavinia for breakfast.

Blast! He was thinking of her again.

What was wrong with him?

He returned to bed, blaming his restlessness on Prinny's upcoming luncheon and not the heat stirred by the sight of a very grown up Goose standing on her balcony in nearly nothing but her lovely skin.

He was out of sorts by morning.

He growled when Nathaniel's valet knocked lightly at his door, seeking permission to take his clothes and polish his boots. "Enter at your own risk."

He then apologized to the poor man whose face had turned as white as the tufts of his thinning hair. "I'm not fit company this morning, Greville. You've done nothing wrong. Leave my boots. I'll have those polished by my own man when I reach London."

"Yes, Your Grace."

He quickly washed and shaved, then dressed casually for the ride to London. He wasn't in any particular hurry to leave Sherbourne Manor. It was only a three-hour carriage ride from town. He would be traveling on horseback, his trusted gelding Albion easily able to make it at a steady lope. The luncheon was at two o'clock in the afternoon.

He glanced at his pocket watch and noted it was barely seven in the morning.

He'd leave in an hour, arrive in London by late morning. Enough time to wash up again, take care of some Hartford business, and ride to St. James's Palace to mingle with the elite of England's elite. Indeed, the air would be quite rarified at this luncheon.

But he was hungry now.

Country living had a way of stirring one's appetite.

He strode downstairs and followed the scent of eggs, sausages, and fresh-brewed coffee to the dining room. To his surprise, Pip and Goose were already there, seated side by side at the table and engrossed in conversation.

He stifled a smile.

The pair were making plans for their butterfly hunt, no doubt. Two nets were leaning against the wall behind them. "Good morning," he said, striding directly to the buffet to fill his plate.

"Good morning, Your Grace," Pip said, sounding ever so sweet, but the boy was up to mischief. He'd once been a little boy himself and did not like that impish twinkle in Pip's eyes.

Goose cast him a gentle smile.

She looked quite pretty this morning, the ginger of her hair complimented by the blue of her gown. But there was something subtly different about her. He couldn't figure out what it was. No matter. It wasn't important.

But he could not resist another glance.

She looked good.

Really good.

He set his plate beside her and had no sooner turned to grab a cup to pour his own coffee, although it was usually the butler's duty to perform that chore, when Goose shrieked and jumped up from her chair, toppling it onto his boot and then tripping over it herself as she tried to push away from the table.

"Goose!" He reached out to catch her, his open palm closing

around something soft and round as she fell awkwardly into his arms.

Mother in heaven.

He'd caught her breast.

He released her as though he'd just touched fire and she tumbled to the floor. "Bollocks! Goose, I'm sorry. Are you all right?"

She shot Pip a murderous glance and then reached out her hand for Beast to assist her to her feet. "I'm fine. But that little devil put a spider in my eggs. He knows I'm afraid of them."

Beast took her hands in his and carefully helped her to her feet. He then turned toward the boy. "Pip," was all he managed in an angry grumble before the boy muttered "uh oh" and fled the dining room.

Beast was now left alone with Goose and four silent footmen who stood like statues, pretending they hadn't seen him fully cup her lush breast.

Or seen his body spasm in response, as though lightning had just shot through his fingers.

Or notice he now had his arm around Goose's waist, holding her body up against his while he tried to ignore that her breasts were madly heaving against his chest. "Beast, where is the spider? Did it crawl off my plate?"

She huddled closer to him, practically crawling up him in her desire to escape the eight-legged fiend.

He nodded to the footmen to clear her plate away and start hunting for the spider, and then returned to the task of calming her down. But he wasn't doing a good job of it, for he hadn't recovered from his own jolt of heat that still had his body shamelessly thrumming.

All because of that accidental touch.

He was definitely addled, because now he couldn't seem to look beyond the swell of her breasts.

She couldn't seem to stop heaving them at him.

Look at her face, you arse. It wasn't her fault she couldn't stop trembling or gulping magnificent breasts. *I mean breaths. Gulping magnificent breaths.*

"Goose, the spider's gone. Do you think you can calm down?"

She groaned and rested her forehead against his shoulder. "Of course. Give me a moment, Beast. My heart is still in my throat."

He wanted to point out that her heart was most definitely not in her throat. It was pumping wildly between her breasts, making it appear as though she'd increased three sizes *there* before his very eyes.

It seemed a tormenting eternity before she drew away and placed her hand lightly over her heart. "There. I think I'm all better now."

But he wasn't.

He'd just realized something devastating.

Something horrific.

Something unimaginable.

Goose had breasts.

And he liked them.

PIP APPROACHED OLIVIA cautiously as she stood on the front stairs of Sherbourne Manor watching Beast ride off. She turned to him and smiled. "You were perfect, Pip. And so was that spider. Wherever did you find it? Hopefully not in the house."

"I'm raising my price. I want a full shilling. Did you see the dark look on His Grace's face? He's going to take me to the woodshed and thrash me soundly the moment he returns."

"No, he won't. I'll make certain he doesn't. Come on, let's fetch the butterfly nets and go to the meadow." She glanced up at the sky. "We had better leave now. I think we'll have rain before long."

She thought of Beast, sparing him another glance and hoping he would reach London before the downpour came. She'd taken inexcusable advantage of his trust this morning and did not wish any more misery imposed on him. In truth, a few raindrops would be nothing to her deception. She truly felt badly about that.

But it had worked.

Quite spectacularly.

It was as though her bosom had suddenly become magnetic, for his hand had been drawn there and so had his gaze.

He forgot to look at her face.

At times, he forgot to breathe.

The Book of Love was powerful, indeed.

However, she was not going to let this surprising victory go to her head. It was merely the first step toward falling in love. She'd passed the low-brain function test, an important test necessary to crumble that wall he'd kept between them. But there was a lot more work to be done, for his Austrian princess would also pass this test.

She and Pip spent an hour in the meadow, but had to run back to the house when storm clouds suddenly gathered overhead and the wind picked up. The first drops fell as they were about to race indoors. "Just made it!" she said with a laugh and turned to Pip. "I'm still hungry. I hardly ate a bite before you dropped that spider in my eggs."

"I'm hungry, too." Pip nodded enthusiastically. "I'm always hungry. Penelope says it's because I'm growing. She thinks I'll be taller than Nathaniel."

"Yes, Pip. I think it's quite possible."

Both still breathless from their run, they joined the others in the dining room. Matilda and Lavinia were now awake and holding court around the table. Thad and Nathaniel were dressed casually, having just returned from their morning ride. Penelope and Poppy were about to serve themselves eggs from one of the silver salvers on the buffet.

She cast Pip a warning glance.

Although she'd put him up to the spider incident earlier, she had no idea where that spider was now and did not want Pip getting ideas about dropping it into Penelope's plate. She needn't have worried. Pip hurriedly ate two scones, then was ready to return to his playroom and work his mischief on his ever-patient governess, a fortyish Scottish woman by the name of Addie who was just the right mix of strict and tender.

Olivia hadn't changed out of her gown since the spider incident, but had added a fichu to cover her chest for the sake of modesty. *The Book of Love* was obviously potent, and she could not risk Nathaniel and Thad being caught in her womanly spell.

Nathaniel nursed his coffee, seeming to be in no hurry to leave the table. Indeed, no one appeared to be in a hurry this morning. "Goose, I thought I heard a commotion down here earlier. Did anything happen?"

"Not that I'm aware." She picked up her cup of hot cocoa and took a sip. Had the footmen tattled? She tried not to look guilty, but it was hard to remain unaffected when everyone was staring at her.

Penelope kicked her under the table.

She kicked her back twice. It was a childhood signal. Once for no. Twice for yes.

Penelope gasped. "Olivia, Poppy. I need your assistance. Aunt Lavinia, may we be excused?"

"I'm the earl here," Nathaniel grumbled. "You ought to be asking me."

Penelope rolled her eyes. "Fine. Lord Welles, we humbly ask to be excused. May we go?"

He cast Olivia a suspicious glance. "Very well. I suppose we'll figure out what you girls are up to soon enough."

Poppy stood up. "What makes you think we're up to something?"

Thad laughed. "You and Olivia are blushing. Loopy has that look again."

"What look?" Olivia asked.

"That duck-beak-stuck-up-her-arse look," Thad replied. "Now

she's shooting daggers at me. It's no good, Loopy. I know ye too well. Ye get indignant when ye've been caught doing something ye shouldn't be doing. We will find out eventually. Have no doubt."

Penelope stuck her chin up in the air.

Thad made a quacking sound.

Penelope inhaled sharply. "Come along girls. I'll not stand here and be insulted by this Scottish lout."

The three of them hurried out of the dining room and raced upstairs to Olivia's bedchamber where *The Book of Love* was safely tucked away in her fruitwood chest of drawers. "What were those two kicks about, Olivia? Does it mean you've had success with Beast?"

She nodded. "He…"

No. She couldn't tell them he'd accidentally closed his hand around her breast while trying to save her from falling. Nor did she mention he'd promptly dropped her thereafter. "He responded. I think I've overcome his resistance. But it's just the first step. Now, we must see what happens when he returns this evening. My success may only be temporary, not only because he might be attracted to the Austrian princess. It is also possible he'll revert to thinking of me as the little girl he knew all those years ago."

"I'm sure the book would say something about that if it were a possibility," Poppy remarked. "I think we should move on to step two."

"I agree," Penelope said. "What is it?"

"Well, assuming Beast has accepted me as a viable vessel to produce his offspring, then we must have him actually choose me. So now we have to move beyond the low-brain function and appeal to his more complex desires. When he sees me, he has to associate me with feelings of pleasure beyond his basic sexual urge." She tossed the book onto her bed and began to pace across her bedchamber. "Although that urge still remains important. He must continue to regard me as a potential vessel for his seed, but he must also learn to connect me with feelings of happiness and contentment."

"How?" Poppy opened the book and began to read at random.

"Well, I think we must question his Aunt Matilda. Find out what he likes to eat, his favorite entertainments, the type of women whose company he seems to enjoy. And I don't mean *those* sort of women. We need to learn all about the sort he would consider marrying. But she mustn't suspect we are snooping about her nephew."

"We can also question Nathaniel and Thad," Poppy suggested. "Spread the questions around. Each of us assigned to finding out specific information so we're not obvious about our intentions."

Penelope smiled in approval. "An excellent idea."

Olivia approved as well. "We have the afternoon to get this done. We ought to have little difficulty since it's raining. Nathaniel and Thad won't be running off to hunt or ride. So, let's make a chart of the questions to ask and who we ask."

"And let's decide which of us will question the men." Penelope joined Poppy on the bed and both began to leaf through the book. "I think Poppy should question Nathaniel. He's my brother and will only tell me to mind my own business if I approach him."

Poppy nodded. "Very well, but I think Olivia must question Thad. You have a way of goading him, Penelope. He'll never give you a straight answer."

"Nonsense. He's a big, dumb Scot. He is like a puppet. All I have to do is pull his strings and he'll give me the answers I need. Besides, Matilda seems to like Olivia. And if your circumstances require you to become her companion, wouldn't it be wise to get to know her better?" She came to Olivia's side and gave her a hug. "However, I am serious about my offer. If life is unbearable in Lord Gosling's home, then you must stay with me as my guest for as long as you need."

"Me, too," Poppy said. "There are so many Farthingales in

London, no one will notice one more. You can share a room with me and Violet. I assure you, my parents won't notice."

Olivia laughed. "Thank you. I'm hoping this book will work its magic and help me find the man of my dreams by the end of the Season. So, let's get to work. I'll question Matilda. She's obviously quite fond of Beast. I'll let her talk about him and gently guide the conversation to get the information I need. But I think we should ask the same questions of each of them, Nathaniel, Thad, and Matilda. This way, we can compare their answers."

Penelope returned to the bed and stretched out atop it, propping on one elbow. "Very well. This is your experiment, Olivia. And you have a better understanding of these ancient scientific findings. What are you going to ask Matilda first?"

Olivia nibbled her lip in thought. "Well, since the point is to have him fall in love with me, it seems logical to ask if he's ever been in love before. And if he has been, then I'd want to know all about the girl and what went wrong."

Poppy's eyes widened in alarm. "I never thought of that. Do you think Beast has ever been in love?"

Penelope made a soft, strangled sound. "Oh, Olivia. I forgot all about her. Yes, I think he was once. What are you going to do?"

CHAPTER SIX

BEAST HAD LEFT Sherbourne Manor early enough to avoid most of the rain, but his luck ran out on the outskirts of London. He tossed on his oilcloth and slowed his mount as the roads became thick with mud. Nonetheless, he still made good time and reached his townhouse before noon.

He left Albion in the care of his groom in the mews behind his home and then strode into the house and upstairs to his bedchamber. He called for his valet. "Collingsworth!"

The ever-efficient man who'd been in service to the dukes of Hartford for almost four decades promptly scurried in. "Your Grace, I've ordered a bath brought up and taken the liberty of asking Cook to prepare a tray of light refreshments for you. Your uniform has been cleaned and pressed, and I've set out your medals atop your bureau. Is there anything else I may do for you?"

Beast shook his head and laughed. "You've thought of everything, as always. What shall I ever do without you?"

His valet grinned. "Oh, I think you would manage quite well without me. But I'm relieved you find me indispensable. It's good to have you home again."

Beast sank onto a stool beside his bed in order to remove his boots.

Collingsworth immediately knelt beside him and tugged off the first boot. "I'll have those properly cleaned and polished in time for your engagement with the Prince Regent." He helped Beast off with the other one and then took the boots downstairs.

Beast waited until the bath had been brought up and filled with steaming water before stripping out of his clothes. He was alone now, and as he relaxed in the warm bath and rinsed off the dirt from his morning journey, he allowed his mind to wander back to Goose.

Why had his body responded so enthusiastically to her?

And why was it responding now to the mere memory of her soft breast cupped in the palm of his hand? That accidental touch had lasted less than a moment, but the *rightness* of it had felt eternal.

He shook off the ridiculous notion and climbed out of the tub.

Within the hour, he was groomed, dressed, and riding to St. James's for his audience with Prinny and the elite of Europe's royal families. He hoped Prinny had given up on a match between him and the Austrian princess, but as he entered the royal hall, he saw at once this was still foremost in his mind.

Beast was immediately introduced to the elegantly attired Princess Beatrix.

He bowed politely over her outstretched hand, surprised she was actually quite beautiful in a sophisticated way. But there was an upward tilt to her chin that made her appear to be looking down her nose at everyone.

She probably was.

Diamonds gleamed on her ears and around her slender neck, brilliant as ice crystals. Indeed, icy is how he would describe her. World-weary, as well. There wasn't a hint of innocence about her. He doubted she was still the young virgin ignorant of what took place in the marriage bed, although she and her staff would take pains to make it appear so. After all, the succession of kings was involved.

Beast was no foolscap.

This woman was not the sort to give her love to one man.

"Princess Beatrix, I hope you are enjoying your stay in London." Unfortunately, he was not the sort who could turn a blind eye to his wife's affairs. Nor was he the sort to turn to another woman once he was married. The dukes of Hartford tended to be faithful in their marriages. He could not speak for all of his male ancestors, but his father and grandfather had made enduring love matches and he expected to do the same.

"I am having a lovely time." Her eyes were a sharp, crystal blue and her hair was the golden color of honey. Her gown was stylish, emphasizing her nicely rounded bosom and trim hips. But there was a warmth lacking in her beauty. Beast did not blame her for it. She would not have been raised to believe in love. Her role was to strengthen alliances between countries and she seemed more than willing to undertake this duty.

To her credit, her language skills were excellent, far better than his. "It is a most pleasant town and almost as beautiful as Vienna."

Almost.

That word spoke volumes. He knew the princess intended to marry an Englishman and return home with the hapless dolt on a tether. He had no desire to be that dolt. He glanced at Prinny and arched a questioning eyebrow, the slight gesture conveying his displeasure. There were several peers of highest rank present who would not mind taking up residence outside of England. "I fear that London shall always be first in my heart."

Prinny coughed.

The princess cast him a wry smile. "A city is just a city. One's heart is given to its people. But I see your heart is already taken. By the people of England? Or is there one special person who controls it?"

"No one controls my heart." But Goose crept back into his thoughts. He tamped down the preposterous notion.

"Our dear Prinny has other guests to greet. So, I shall ask you to escort me as I walk about the room. We must get to know each other better."

It was the last thing Beast wanted.

But to deny her would cause an international incident. He held out his arm and led her off. "Have you met the other dukes?"

She laughed. "Wishing to be rid of me already? Why do you not want me as your wife? All the others are eager to make a match with me."

Bollocks, he'd stepped right into it. "I'm a soldier, not a statesman. I love England and have no wish to live outside of it. Nor can I ever see myself switching alliances. In truth, I will never agree to do it. Yet, it would be expected of me if I were to marry you. I am not a good fit for you."

"I think you would fit me quite well," she said, her manner now suggestive of relations that were quite outside the bounds of marriage. "I never thought you suitable as a husband either. You are too strong-willed and I would prefer a docile husband. But I require my lovers to be passionate and strong. You will do quite nicely while I'm here."

The only thing worse than marrying this princess was to be caught in her bedchamber *unmarried* to her. He did not care whether she wanted him for his body or whether this was merely a trick to force him into marriage. He was going to escape back to Sherbourne Manor as soon as this luncheon was over. "Unfortunately, that will not be possible either. Duty calls, and I must leave town this very afternoon." He bowed over her hand as Prinny and the Duke of Wellington approached.

Wellington muttered something about needing to discuss an important matter with him and drew him aside.

Beast tried to hide his relief but doubted he'd done a good job of it. He bowed once more over Princess Beatrix's hand. "I shall leave you in the excellent care of His Royal Highness. Excuse me."

Neither Prinny nor his Austrian princess was pleased with him, but he gave it no more thought. Wellington's brow was furrowed and he appeared to be worried about something. Beast understood how tenuous a peace existed at the moment. "Arthur, has something happened in France?"

"No, Alex." He cast Beast a wry grin. "But I know when one of my soldiers is in trouble. I thought I'd help you out."

Beast groaned. "Thank you."

However, his long-time friend and brother-in-arms still appeared worried. "The princess is beautiful. Every other man here wants her as his wife. Why don't you?"

Beast shrugged. "She isn't for me."

Wellington crossed his arms over his chest. "What sort of girl is?"

"I don't know. One who will be satisfied to have just one man in her bed, that man being me." But he said no more, for Wellington had his own marital concerns. "The dinner bell has chimed."

"Alex, I drew you aside for another reason. Give me a moment before we go in."

"Of course." But he eyed his friend warily. "What's on your mind?"

"Something I've discussed with others in the House of Lords. They've asked me to reach out to you."

"For what purpose?"

"We think you'll make an excellent statesman. You have the intelligence and agile wit to go far. The Austrian princess might not have been a wise idea on the part of Prinny, but there are several beautiful Englishwomen here who would suit your needs. Marry well and you might become England's next prime minister. I would back you wholeheartedly, as would most of the men in this room. Even Prinny."

Beast grinned. "Not Prinny. At least not right now. He's still peeved."

Beast managed to avoid rousing the royal ire for the remainder of the afternoon, and was just about to make his escape when he was collared once more by several high-ranking members of Parliament. "Glad you held firm on that Austrian nonsense, Hartford," the crusty Duke of Lotheil said, taking the lead among the peers. "We need you here in England."

He nodded.

"More to the point, we need you to take a leadership role. Help put the country back on its feet. Wellington is not the only one with popular appeal. Think about it, will you?"

"I'm flattered, gentlemen. I will give it serious thought."

He rode off, eager to leave London before Prinny changed his mind and came after him. He hadn't the chance to see about Goose's new piano, but he would take care of the problem next week when they were all back in London.

It was almost ten o'clock in the evening by the time he arrived at Sherbourne Manor still dressed in his full military regalia, for he had not only decided to skip the matter of the piano, but was also concerned about being home should Prinny decide he wanted something more of him. He did not wish to be anywhere in London, if that were the case. The prince could be stubborn when fixed on an idea, and he did not want a royal messenger finding him and ordering him back to the palace.

Nathaniel's butler admitted him into the house as he wearily strode up the front steps. "Your Grace, it's good to have you back. Everyone is in the music room."

"Thank you, Soames." He would have guessed as much on his own, for he heard the deep, male laughter of Nathaniel and Thad, and the lighter trills of female laughter emanating from the open doors. Goose was playing a lively country reel, he easily recognized her soft touch on the piano keys.

He was about to climb the stairs to wash the dirt off his face and change into more comfortable clothes, when Nathaniel spotted him. "Beast! Come in here."

Then Penelope and Poppy rushed out and each took one of his hands. "Do tell us all that happened this afternoon."

He spared a glance at Goose who remained quietly seated beside the piano, but her eyes were wide and curious, and although she did not get up to rush to his side as her friends had, she was tipped forward far enough to topple off the piano seat at the slightest gust of wind.

"Well? Are you betrothed or not?" Penelope asked, wasting no time in getting to the point.

"Not. Some English pizzle will be marrying the Austrian princess," he said, earning a severe rebuke from Matilda and Lavinia, for the girls should not have had to endure his coarse language. But he was out of sorts for more reasons than having an Austrian princess shoved at him.

His bigger concern was the quickening beat of his heart at the mere sight of Goose. She now had a lace fichu covering the swell of her bosom, but that only brought him back to this morning and the softness of her in his hand.

He refused to look upon her, instead, turning his attention to Poppy and Penelope. "Fortunately, the princess found me unsuitable." He did not know why he felt it so important to spill that news.

Thad laughed. "She found you unsuitable? Or was it the other way around?"

Beast shrugged. "I made it clear that my allegiance is to England only. Now that I've returned, nothing can tempt me away."

He hadn't meant to glance at Goose again, but found himself doing so. He saw relief wash over her innocently expressive face, and then she scooted off the piano seat to join her friends in standing beside him. She studied his chest full of medals and smiled. "Beast, you look quite impressive. What does each medal represent?"

Thad and Nathaniel chortled. "This one's for kissing Prinny's arse," said Nathaniel, which earned him a frown from Lavinia.

"The one with the fancy red silk ribbon is for being born a duke," Thad interjected. "And this one in the shape of a silver star is for not getting seasick on the boat home."

Beast shook his head and laughed. His friends were not going to acknowledge his accomplishments on the field of battle, something he might have resented had they not fought as valiantly and earned their own medals. "I'll tell you another time,

Goose. If you will excuse me, I'll wash up and join you shortly."

He strode out of the room and hurried upstairs to change into more comfortable clothes. When he returned downstairs, Goose was back at the piano playing another country lilt as her friends danced with Thad and Nathaniel.

Beast sank into a chair beside Matilda, knowing his aunt would have questions for him once the music stopped. But sitting beside her also gave him a clear view of Goose, and he found his gaze straying to her more often than he cared to admit. When the dance ended, everyone gathered around him once more to hear about his afternoon.

His aunt regarded him with a keen eye. "The Austrian princess is no longer a concern, but something else appears to be troubling you. What else happened?"

He shrugged, but ultimately decided to speak frankly since the rumors would soon be circulating around London anyway. "Several members of the House of Lords approached me about taking a prominent position in government."

"How prominent?" Goose asked, her beautiful eyes widening. It irked him that the word 'beautiful' seemed to pop into his head whenever the girl was around him.

He shrugged again. "Possibly prime minister, but that is a long way off. I'm a soldier, not a diplomat. I doubt I am suited to the role."

"A man can do anything with the proper wife," Matilda intoned. "I suppose that was part of the discussion as well. An advantageous marriage to a well-connected family?"

"Yes. But as I said, that is a long way off."

Penelope frowned at him. "You can't possibly consider marrying for reasons other than love."

"Loopy," Thad said in a low, warning tone. "He'll make his decision in his own good time. It isn't any of our business."

Nathaniel promptly agreed. "This is the real world, Penelope. Romantic notions do not always have a place here."

Goose shot to her feet and her hands curled into fists at her sides. "Yes, they do. It is the power of love that leads to greatness, not the power of connections or wealth or… would you be happy without love, Beast?"

Lord, could she hide nothing of her feelings? She looked so downcast and disappointed at the notion he might marry for practical reasons. What concern was it of hers? "Sit down, Goose. I've made no decisions."

He shot her a look that conveyed he certainly would not be confiding his decision in her. Perhaps he should not have been so irritated with her. But he did not want her believing love was the answer to his problems *or* hers. Certainly not hers. *The Book of Love* was giving her ideas, none of them good.

He slapped his hands on his thighs. "I'm starved. Is there any food left over? Or has Thad devoured it all?"

"There may be a few crumbs left," Nathaniel chortled. "I'm sure we can find something in the kitchen for you."

Rather than disturb his staff, Nathaniel motioned for Beast and Thad to follow him into the kitchen. "Cook will be angry, but there's no point in summoning her when we can manage on our own."

They excused themselves and left the women to their discussion. Matilda cast him a disapproving glower as he rose. He ignored her, for he was not going to sit there and spew his guts about love or marriage when he had no idea what he was going to do beyond filling his empty belly.

He felt Goose's disappointed gaze on him as he strode out with his friends. He could have dealt with her anger, but that look of hurt on her face simply tore at his insides.

He shrugged off any concerns about her with a silent oath. He did not answer to Goose. He answered to no one other than the royal family, and grudgingly to them.

What did he owe the girl? In truth, he hardly knew her. That she held a soft spot in his heart signified nothing. She was young and defenseless and deserved better than to be under the thumb of an unfeeling guardian.

It was flattering to be considered as a prospect for high position in government. He wasn't certain this was meant to be his path in life, but it certainly merited consideration. He knew he was a leader. He'd led men in battle, issuing orders and knowing they would promptly be obeyed, for their lives depended on their trusting him.

But Parliament was a very different field of battle, each man thinking of his own political needs, some of which would be opposite his. Soldiers were a band of brothers, as Shakespeare had so aptly and eloquently written in his play. However, those in politics were little more than warring factions out for their own cutthroat interests.

Another consideration was the sort of woman who would make a good wife for a prominent political figure. He would require someone cunning who understood the true nature of men and the lengths to which a man would go in order to have his way. A good political wife would use her feminine wiles to exert pressure on important family connections and anyone else needed to achieve her husband's desired ends.

A good political wife would be ruthless when necessary.

Goose was the opposite of ruthless. She and her romantic notions of love and honor, of sacrifice and compassion, would be a liability to him.

He silently chided himself.

Why was he thinking of her?

Especially now that she'd irked him with her talk of love. He wanted to shake the girl and warn her of the perils of trusting in that dangerous feeling. Giving your heart to someone and having it stomped on because they did not return your affection was not a pleasant experience. He certainly did not want Goose to go through that heartbreak.

Not his Goose.

While he, Thad, and Nathaniel tore into the leftover mutton, he resolved to take the girl under his supervision and teach her some caution. For someone who'd experienced neglect and no love since the death of her parents, she was incredibly naive. Impossibly hopeful. He did not want her getting into trouble because she was too willing to open her heart.

"Beast, have you heard a word I've said?" Nathaniel asked, passing him another slice of mutton since he'd devoured the first serving in two bites.

He set down his knife and fork. "What? No. Did you say something?"

His friend sighed. "Since you dismissed the Austrian princess as a candidate for wife, I merely asked if there was anyone else you might consider?"

Beast shook his head. "I haven't given it a thought. I've been home less than a week. Why is everyone pushing me to marry?"

Thad raised his hands in mock surrender. "Not me. I haven't said a word. Och, I think ye ought to enjoy yourself now that you're home. The lassies can wait until next Season. We all need to have a little fun before we settle down."

Nathaniel frowned. "But the opportunity to be backed as prime minister may never present itself again. Will you simply pass it up?"

"No, but neither will I be rushed into a decision. That's why I'm glad to be here and not caught up in the London whirl. I need time to think."

Nathaniel shook his head and groaned lightly. "Oh, I doubt the girls will allow you time for that. While you were away, they were busily questioning us about your past loves and whether you had ever proposed to a woman."

Beast arched an eyebrow in surprise. "Why would they ask that of you?"

Thad grabbed another slice of mutton and shrugged. "I'm sure it has to do with that book they've been carrying around all day. They're up to something and it involves you."

Beast drank down the last of his ale. "What did you tell them?"

"Everything but the truth." Thad laughed. "We made up tales

about the women you've loved."

"More than one?" Beast groaned. "But I've never been in love. Closest I've ever gotten was Millicent Westwood, and that was a boyhood infatuation I grew out of within two weeks of meeting her."

"We know that," Nathaniel said, "but the girls don't. My sister thinks she was your first love and that you proposed to her. So Thad embellished a bit. A lot, actually." He shook his head and grinned. "When Poppy started asking me the same questions, I told her about the second girl you loved, a tall, large-breasted brunette with emerald-green eyes. Your third love was a tall blonde with big breasts, by the way."

Beast set down his knife and fork and pushed his plate away. "No wonder they believe that's all we have on the brain. What else did you tell them?"

Thad winced. "We may have mentioned you enjoy the scent of gardenias."

"Bollocks, I detest that odor. Makes my eyes water. Makes me sneeze." Beast groaned again. "What did you tell them that for? I'll kick your arses to the meadow and back if they come downstairs tomorrow doused in that perfume."

Thad and Nathaniel burst out laughing.

"Och, Beast. It's harmless enough, and where are they going to find that scent, anyway? They'd have to go to London, to one of those fancy lady shops. Dinna concern yerself about that. They'll be headed up to Loopy's room by now to plot their next strategy. That's what you ought to be worrying about."

He shook his head and sighed.

If Goose walked down to the breakfast table tomorrow morning with her chest stuffed with cotton to enhance the size of her breasts and reeking of gardenias, he was going to shred that book to pieces.

CHAPTER SEVEN

"BEAST CAN'T ABIDE gardenias," Olivia said, settling on Penelope's bed and furrowing her brow as her frustration mounted. She and her friends had come upstairs shortly after the men had excused themselves to raid the kitchen. "Don't you remember our last summer here before the three of them went off to war?"

"Vividly." Penelope shook her head. "But I don't recall any gardenia incident."

"Perhaps it happened before your family arrived." Olivia pursed her lips in thought. "Do you recall my parents had hosted an afternoon tea at Gosling Hall? Or that Lady Plimpton was wearing gardenia-scented perfume? She'd doused herself with it. As she approached Beast, his eyes began to water and he coughed. Then he sneezed. And he wouldn't stop sneezing. He had to run out of our salon and stand outside on our terrace taking in great gulps of air."

Poppy settled beside her, tucking her bare feet under herself and smoothing out her nightrail. They'd all taken a moment to change out of their gowns and into their bedclothes before meeting back in Penelope's bedchamber. "Oh, dear. Obviously, Nathaniel and Thad have lied to us. The information they gave us is useless. I hope Matilda's information is more reliable. What did she tell you, Olivia?"

"Not much, unfortunately. She claims Beast has never been in love."

"Never?" Poppy sighed. "Then how are we to know what sort of woman tempts him?"

Olivia opened *The Book of Love* and began to idly scan through it. "Perhaps it doesn't matter. The point of this book is any female with an understanding of the male mind and its obsession with procreation can make the male of her choice fall in love with her."

Poppy stared at the book a moment before returning her gaze to Olivia. "But we don't understand the workings of Beast's mind. Wasn't that the point of questioning his friends and family?"

"Yes, but we know his friends, despite being well into their twenties and expected to behave like responsible adults, have the maturity and wit of ten-year-old boys."

Poppy arched an eyebrow. "And?"

"Can Beast be any different? They are his best friends, after all." Olivia snapped the book shut. "We are going to treat them like the nitwit boys they are."

"How?"

"It is obvious they are still thinking with their low functioning brains, so that is what we must continue to target."

Poppy nodded. "So, we must aim low."

"And not move on to assaulting their five senses yet?" Penelope pursed her lips. "Too bad. My brother hates liver. I would have had Cook serve him a plate of raw, bloody liver for breakfast tomorrow morning. We could have planned something for Thad, too. However, Thad will be more difficult. The dolt will eat anything that doesn't eat him first. As for scents, he's a Highlander and probably sleeps with his sheep. His nose must be made of cast iron."

Poppy sighed. "Why are you always so mean to Thad? He detests jellied eels, Olivia. We all know that."

"Perfect." Penelope smiled. "I hope the Sherbourne kitchen is well stocked because that's what will be staring back at him on his breakfast plate."

"Those tricks will never do," Olivia said. "No liver. No eels. And no wet, stinky sheep. Beast cannot associate me with foul scents or unpleasant foods. I must arouse his sense receptacles in a good way. We go back to step one and appeal to his lowest and most primal brain function."

Poppy sighed. "Are we going to talk about our bosoms again?"

"It's the only thing they think about," Penelope muttered. "What choice do we have?"

"As we know from reading the book, men look at a woman's body when their brains are in that mindless state of finding the perfect vessel into which to spill their seed. Thad and Nathaniel's comments about large-breasted women only confirms this book accurately depicts the one constant on a male's brain."

Poppy leaned closer. "And?"

"Beast is going to get an eyeful of my breasts."

Penelope and Poppy hopped off the bed. "What? You're going to show him…"

"No! Of course not. I would never be so obvious as to bare myself! All I am saying is we've obviously jumped prematurely into the next phase and must retrench. I assure you, he is going to walk out of that breakfast room aching for a look at my endowments."

"How are you going to manage that?" Penelope's eyes were wide in curiosity.

"With a little jostling and jiggling."

"I haven't a clue what you mean by that," Poppy said, "but I'm in. What can I do to help?"

"Count me in, too. My brother and Thad need to be brought to their knees. How dare they lie to us!"

Poppy pursed her lips. "But aren't we being deceitful with them, too?"

"Of course. What has that to do with anything?" No one ever looked finer when indignant than Penelope, and she did not disappoint. She tossed back her long, dark braid and her eyes were magnificently blazing. "My brother and his loutish Scottish friend are about to be roasted. The battle is on. Beast is going to fall madly in love with Olivia. All of her. Not just her jiggled and jostled breasts."

BEAST'S TWO FRIENDS were already downstairs and lingering over their cups of coffee when Beast strode into the dining room the following morning. It was early, barely after sunrise, and they were all going for a ride. Since no butler or footmen were around to serve them, and the silver urn stood on the buffet along with the usual eggs, kippers, and assortment of jellied meats, he grabbed his cup and poured himself some coffee before sinking into a chair across the table from them.

"Why are you both looking so morose? Thad, what's wrong with you? You've hardly touched your food."

"Och, I'm wondering if we weren't too hard on the lassies yesterday. After all, Goose needs to find someone to love in order to get herself out of her guardian's house before the end of the Season. Perhaps we ought to have helped her instead of lying through our teeth."

"We weren't subtle about it," Nathaniel said, staring down at his untouched plate. "I'm sure she caught on to our teasing. What do you think she'll do?"

Thad shrugged. "Goose is a sweet girl. She isn't who I'm worried about. It's Loopy who will swoop down on us like the Angel of Vengeance. Your sister can be scary at times, Nathaniel."

Beast laughed, but his battle instincts were on alert. He knew it was ridiculous to fear what Goose might do. As Thad said, she was sweet and innocent. But lately, his thoughts about her had been neither sweet nor innocent.

She was doing something to him. Rousing his lust and his protective instincts. He wasn't used to responding this way toward anyone. He'd felt lustful urges before. He'd felt protective toward those he loved before. Never had he felt both urges at the same time.

Never.

And it worried him.

He glanced at Nathaniel and then at Thad. Both men looked disgruntled. Thad muttered an oath in Gaelic as he set down his almost empty cup. "We have to help Goose."

"I agree," Nathaniel said.

Beast frowned. "What we have to do is get that book out of their sticky, little hands." As he pushed back his chair and was about to rise, the girls walked in. "Bollocks," he muttered as he and his friends rose to politely assist them into their seats.

Penelope and Poppy looked quite fetching in their day gowns. Goose looked... his heart slammed into his chest. "What in blazes?"

"Good morning, Your Grace," she said and gracefully glided into the chair beside his as though nothing was amiss.

He tried to respond with an equally casual 'good morning', but his jaw seemed to be locked in the open position and he could not move his mouth to shut it. She'd stuffed something into her bosom, a subtle enhancement that might have gone unnoticed to the casual eye. But he was too familiar with the shape of her body to be fooled. She'd done something to enlarge her heavenly endowments, for they were bigger and uplifted, and... he was making an ass out of himself by staring at her chest.

Thad and Nathaniel began to laugh hysterically. "Goose, watch where you point those things! You might poke out Beast's one good eye."

Perhaps not so subtle if his friends had noticed, too.

He curled his hands into fists, not liking that both of them were leering at the girl. This was Goose. His Goose. It mattered not that she was purposely provoking their responses. "You've had your jest at our expense. Now go upstairs and change out of that... whatever you stuffed yourself with before Lavinia and

Matilda come downstairs."

Lord, he did not want to be explaining this to either of those dowagers.

Goose cast him a dimpled smile that he found quite irritating. "What are you talking about? This is all me. Perhaps with a little bit of a lift here and a boost there. But that's all."

He swallowed hard, his traitorous mind and body recalling the softness of her. "Goose, I get it. I know what Thad and Nathaniel told you when you questioned them. And now you're getting back at them."

Her eyes rounded in innocence and she still wore that annoying smile. "Oh, no, Beast. I don't care about them. It's you I'm purposely manipulating."

"Me?" It took him a moment to get over his initial surprise, for his brain was working very slowly just now. He managed to shake his head and laugh. "Why? And why warn me of your intentions if that is your plan?"

"Because I won't ever lie to you again. I did the one time in your carriage a few days ago and it tore me apart. I hope you know that."

He should not have found her admission endearing. Had she been in his class on ancient Roman military battles, he would have flunked her. What fool would ever signal his tactics to the enemy?

But he liked she would always be honest with him.

Damn it.

He was the fool. She was openly declaring her intention to best him. In effect, showing absolutely no respect for his battle prowess and already treating him like a vanquished foe. Was she that confident?

"Oh, and I ordered something special for you for breakfast." She reached for the bell and summoned a footman who must have been waiting just outside the door, for the man walked in carrying a silver tray. Its contents were hidden under a gleaming silver lid.

Beast eyed her warily. "What is it?"

Her smile was once again dimpled and syrupy sweet. "Lift the lid and see for yourself."

"Och, Beast. Dinna do it. The thing might blow up in your face." But Thad was grinning inanely and so was Nathaniel, each casting him a look that confirmed his Goose was winning this round.

Goose touched her hand lightly to his as though consoling him. "Don't listen to them. You know I'd never do anything to hurt you."

Of course he knew it. She was the little girl who'd neatly folded his clothes instead of running away with them. She was the dewy-eyed young woman who believed love could be found in a book.

He lifted the lid just enough to peek under it.

"What is it?" Nathaniel asked.

He pulled the lid off completely. "Breast of goose," he said, staring down at his plate.

His friends burst out laughing, finding the jest at his expense quite hilarious. He would have been laughing, too, if he weren't the butt of the joke. "Point made, Goose. Go back upstairs and change into something less provocative."

He expected a gloating, triumphant look from the girl, for she'd certainly gotten the better of him. But this was softhearted Goose. She looked flustered and remorseful she might have made a fool of him. "Thad and Nathaniel lied to us and made up these ridiculous stories about the sort of women you loved. I really meant to tease them. Well, really tease all of you. But I'm sorry, Beast. I never meant to be cruel. Never to you. Please don't be angry with me."

His blood began to heat. He wasn't angry so much as sudden-ly feeling ridiculously protective of the girl. He wanted to take her in his arms and tell her... he wasn't certain what he wanted to tell her, for she had him quite off stride at the moment. He hadn't taken offense. He liked she wasn't afraid to tease him or his friends.

"You see, *The Book of Love* says–"

"That damn book of spells again."

"It's scientific. I've told you. There are no spells in it."

He drew her up beside him. "Scientific, my arse. Your... damn it, Goose. Your chest is spilling out of that gown."

Now he was sounding like an old goat.

"How is that possible? I'm wearing a day gown and covered up to my neck. But you can't draw your gaze away, can you?" Her eyes suddenly widened and she cast him a genuinely surprised smile. "You responded just as the book predicted."

Feminine laughter and masculine chortles filled his ears. He was betrayed not only by his mind and body, but by his traitorous friends as well.

He raked a hand through his hair. "Am I to be your test frog for the week? Is this how I'm to be repaid for my friendship?"

She gave a wincing nod. "It sounds awful when you put it that way. I'd rather think of it as–"

"Spare me the details." He took her by the shoulders and turned her to face the door. "You're going upstairs. You're going to take out whatever the hell you stuffed in *there,* and then come back downstairs with that book. You have five minutes to make yourself decent before I come up after you."

Lord, was he considering standing for the office of prime minister? He couldn't even handle Goose.

She fled the room, grinning.

Penelope and Poppy ran after her.

"Bollocks," he muttered, casting his friends a scathing glance.

Thad grinned and tossed him an imaginary ball.

"What are you doing?"

"Giving ye back yer eyeballs. They popped out of their sockets and rolled onto the floor when Goose walked in with her majestic assets on grand display." He grinned again and tossed him another imaginary ball. "And that one's your tongue. I almost tripped over it when it flapped to the floor."

He turned accusingly to Nathaniel. "Were you looking at her, too?"

"Don't growl at me, Beast. I couldn't help it. None of us could. Wasn't that the point of her experiment?" He shook his head and laughed. "Are we men truly that shallow? Is that all we think about?"

"Of course not." He growled again and began to pace. "We are honorable and wise." Although he was feeling rather stupid at the moment. "We are trustworthy. But other men are not. Goose is playing with fire and I don't want to see her burned."

"Nor do we," Thad admitted. "What do you want us to do?"

"Help me put a stop to her ridiculous experiments." But Goose was now inspired by her victory and she was also desperate to find love before the Season was over. She would never agree to give up on her quest.

His blood was still a hot boil when Goose returned downstairs with her book in hand. "Come with me," he growled, taking her by the elbow without awaiting her response.

She frowned at him and resisted. "Where are we going?"

"To the shade tree near the pond."

She eyed him warily. "Why?"

He stared at the book and then at her. Lord, she had a beautiful face. When had that happened? And why was he only noticing it now? "You're going to teach me all about love."

CHAPTER EIGHT

"Wait, Beast. Slow down." Olivia was trying her best to keep up with him, but his strides were twice the length of hers, and he was wearing trousers that hugged his muscled thighs while she had on a muslin gown that kept twisting around her legs. "You're walking too fast for me."

He'd kept a gentle grip on her arm as he drew her along the familiar path toward the pond. Were she not in such a rush, she would have stopped to admire the soft morning light that fell across the meadow and glistened over the water. Were she not breathless, she would have paused to inhale the fresh country air and knelt to take in the sweet scent of dew that clung to the flowers growing wild along the path. "Don't think to toss the book into the pond. I'll jump in after it."

He stopped to stare at her with marked impatience. "Can you swim?"

"No, my parents thought it best never to teach me. They didn't want me to go in the pond again after the day I fell in and hit my head. I expect I would have died if you hadn't been there to rescue me." She tipped her chin up in defiance. "So, you had better be prepared to dive in to save me again if you throw that book into the water."

He ran a hand raggedly through his hair. "Goose, you are being ridiculous."

"I'm being the only way I know how to be. And I'd hardly call my attempt to find love and happiness ridiculous. Don't you want it for yourself? Why can't I have the same? The only difference is that I must find it now. I don't have the luxury of waiting for it to find me."

He walked ahead in silence, and she hurried to keep up with him, hoping her words had penetrated enough to keep him from doing damage to the book.

She'd never forgive him if he did.

To her relief, he motioned for her to sit on the fallen log that rested beside the water's edge and then surprised her by handing over the book. "Let's set some ground rules," he said, his jaw clenched and muscles tense as he began to pace in front of her like a restless, prowling lion. "First rule, I'm not to be used as your test frog."

"You were never that."

He cast her a dubious glance. "Then what would you call what you were doing to me?"

She sighed. "Please sit down and stop scowling at me. I'll tell you whatever it is you wish to know. I've already said I will never lie to you."

He emitted a soft growl to mark his displeasure, but did as she asked. "Start talking," he said, stretching out on the grass beside her and propping himself up on his elbows.

She nodded, wishing he wasn't so angry with her, for he looked big and wonderful and made her wish desperately that this book was magical. She needed to find a good man and make him fall in love with her. More important, she needed not to fall in love with Beast while going about it.

He was a war hero. He was a wealthy and powerful duke who might very well be England's next prime minister. He was sought after by royal princesses. "You are not a mere test frog. You are the knight in shining armor that every girl dreams about."

The notion appeared to surprise him. "Goose…"

"Well, you are. Isn't it obvious? Women adore you and men

worship you." She emitted a ragged breath. "You have all the best qualities a girl would seek in a husband."

"That's news to me." He arched an eyebrow in obvious amusement, but allowed her to continue.

"I'm not trying to trick you into a marriage proposal. I respect you too much to ever do that. Besides, I know it is an impossibility. You can reach for the stars. I can only hope to escape my goose pen. However, if the science in this book helps me gain your notice and makes you like me even a little, then it will work on any man. You are the paragon. The unattainable grail."

He groaned. "That is utter nonsense. I am a one-eyed warhorse with a surly nature and a disdain for Society's vapid entertainments. Parties bore me. I hate dancing. And I'm too blunt for my own good. Most women are afraid of me."

"That's because you're big and rugged and always growl at them with marked impatience. But if you were to soften your growl and smile on occasion, you'd be devastating to any young woman's heart."

He laughed. "But then I'd be someone other than myself."

She shook her head and laughed along with him. "Oh, Beast. You're perfect as you are. I know it, but you refuse to show your true self to others. I suppose it is your natural wariness, your desire not to reveal too much of yourself until you are ready to trust."

"Goose, enough about me. It's you who needs my help."

She rolled her eyes. "I needed a big fat miracle to drop on my lap. In truth, it dropped on my head, didn't it? And then you magically appeared in the bookshop. I'm enjoying this week because of you. I would have been stuck in London with Lord Gosling and the unsavory men he seems to have gathered around him. I am forever in your debt for coming to my rescue. You are an essential part of my miracle. You and the book. I need you both. So please don't toss it into the water. Or rip it to shreds. Or burn it."

"Is my intention so obvious?"

"Yes. I know you detest what I am doing. But let me explain it to your satisfaction and then we'll move on to the next part of this experiment. You see..." She paused and swallowed hard, the little pulse at the base of her neck beating more rapidly as she considered her next words. Goodness, how was she to discuss male urges without her skin flushing with embarrassment? "You see, men are different from women."

He arched an eyebrow. "I've noticed."

"Er, yes. You certainly have." She smiled at him, but it quickly faded when he did not smile back. Obviously, Beast was not amused. "And that was precisely my first task, to get you to notice me as a woman and not as a little girl. You see, men look to women to procreate."

He sat up. "Goose!"

She frowned at him. "Well, they do. Every female is a potential vessel into which a healthy male intends to spill his seed."

He sank back and groaned. "This is preposterous."

"Let me finish. You'll see the truth of it when I'm done." She closed her eyes as she began to speak, for Beast was angry and casting her that fierce, hungry lion look again. "When a man looks at a woman, he is making a series of quick assessments regarding her ability to bear his children. Is she too old? Too young? Too frail?" She opened her eyes to check his response and frowned at him when she saw he was about to protest. He shook his head and simply allowed her to continue. "And while a man will ultimately peruse a woman's entire body, his first gaze is on her... breasts."

"Why?"

"Because they are the source of life, the source of milk for his newborn children. So, if he does not like the look of her, um... *those*, then he will pass her over as a suitable mate."

"So, by stuffing your bosom, your purpose was to make me notice your chest?"

She nodded. "You'd taken notice yesterday morning after the spider incident, but I needed to reinforce your approval by that silly trick this morning. And I didn't stuff my gown with anything."

"You didn't?" He appeared stunned. "Are you saying that was all you?"

"Yes. I just had on a different corset, one made of stiff whalebone that pushed me up, and then I tightened it until I could hardly breathe. It was most uncomfortable. Rest assured, I will not be doing that again any time soon."

"Mother in heaven," he murmured.

"By your response these past two mornings, I've learned two very important things. First, that you have found me to be a suitable vessel for your seed."

He groaned. "Stop talking like that. You are not a damn urn."

"And second, you *want* to spill your seed into me."

He shot to his feet. "Goose–"

She remained seated on the log, trying to appear calm although she wasn't at all. Her hands tightened on the book. If he meant to toss it into the water, he'd have to toss her in, too. She wasn't letting go of the book. "Sit down, Beast. Let me finish. I've now described your simple brain response. But now we must move on to the hard part, your complex brain. This is where I need your cooperation."

She looked up at him, hoping he'd sink back onto the grass, but he stood before her with his arms folded across his powerful chest, looking impossibly magnificent. "Please, I cannot do this alone."

He began to pace in front of her, once again a big, angry lion on the prowl. "And how am I supposed to cooperate?"

"By allowing me to experiment with your five senses. Sight, touch, taste, hearing, and scent."

Thankfully, he stopped prowling and knelt beside her. "Why?"

"Because I have to know what works and what doesn't work. Your simple brain has accepted me, we know that. But it has also accepted hundreds of other women."

"Hundreds?"

She nodded. "Perhaps thousands."

"Blast it, Goose! What sort of man do you think I am?"

She frowned at him. "The best sort. I'm not suggesting that you acted upon the urging of your simple brain every time a suitable woman passed your way. But it is also obvious your complex brain has rejected every woman so far. You are not married. Nor are you courting anyone." She inhaled sharply, realizing she'd made an assumption that might not be correct. Just because he'd rejected the Austrian princess didn't mean he wasn't interested in someone else. "You aren't courting anyone, are you?"

He eyed her warily. "No, I'm not."

Nor did he have any intention to, judging by his unamused tone. "This is why you are so perfect for these experiments. Since your complex brain has rejected everyone, it is my goal to have you accept me. In order to accomplish that goal, you have to find me uniquely suited to you. Indeed, so unique that no other female will do for you. I must become the most desirable reproductive vessel of your acquaintance."

"Stop referring to yourself as that."

She frowned at him again. "Fine. Forget about the vessel business. I must become the most desirable woman of your acquaintance. But how do I do that?"

He arched his one good eyebrow, the one not covered by his eyepatch. "Is that a question I'm supposed to answer?"

"No, it is merely conjecture. *The Book of Love* claims a male will take that next step and consider the female suitable as his chosen mate, meaning marriage, once a deeper connection is made between him and the object of his desire. I don't necessarily have to be regarded as beautiful by everyone, just you. You are the only man whose opinion matters. You are the one who must look at me and think that I am beautiful in your eyes."

"Or in my case, in my one good eye."

She sighed, wishing his tone wasn't so flippant. It was proof of his disdain for the scientific ideas in the book. Well, she hadn't expected him to be an easy subject. "My voice doesn't have to be particularly lilting or musical, but you must consider it pleasing to your ears. Same for my scent, it must arouse the pleasure sensations in your body."

"Pleasure sensations? Arousal? Goose, if that book describes the act of sex, I *am* going to toss it into the pond."

"It does nothing of the sort. It is *scientific*. I'll have to purchase quite another sort of book if I want to learn about the act of sex. Perhaps Miss Billings will have what I need in her Wellesford bookshop," she said, referring to the little shop located in the closest town to Sherbourne Manor and Gosling Hall. It was run by a delightful young woman who was the new shopkeeper.

Wellesford was only a half-hour walk from here, and she hoped they might go tomorrow if the weather held up.

As he drew closer, his expression still thunderous, she scrambled to the edge of the log and protectively clasped the book to her chest again. She gave a little squeal as she slid along the rough bark, for splinters of wood jutted from it and pricked her derriere. Fortunately, none had dug deep enough to pierce beyond the muslin fabric of her gown into her undergarments. She easily brushed off the splinters with a few quick pats.

Beast chuckled. "Need help?"

"Stop being a beast and start cooperating." She gave her derriere a final pat and moved closer to him once more. "Where was I? Oh, yes. I've just mentioned the senses of sight, hearing, and scent. There's also the sense of touch. It is important that you take pleasure in the touch of my skin."

Still scowling at her, he took one of her hands in his and gently stroked his thumb over it. "You mean like this?"

She nodded, her throat suddenly dry. His touch was exceedingly pleasant, his hand warm and protectively enveloped around hers. Did her pleasure show? Could he feel the hot tingles spreading through her body? "It would be more effective if you stopped giving me that angry lion look."

His expression softened, but he did not release her hand. Indeed, he looked quite handsome with that seductive grin now on his face. "Better?" he asked, his voice a deep rumble that sent more tingles shooting through her body.

It wasn't fair. Obviously, he'd done this before. Flirted with women. But no one had ever flirted with her before. She wasn't prepared for the sudden pleasure to her own sense receptacles.

"And what of the taste of you?" He leaned forward ever so slowly, his lips tipped up to reveal his amusement.

"I suppose that means kissing." She licked her lips. "Why are you looking at me that way? How else can you taste me? I'm not a food to be eaten."

He emitted a soft growl. "There are other ways to taste a woman's body."

Her eyes widened in surprise. "There are? How?"

His smile broadened, but he emitted a groan that sounded remarkably like one of frustration. "I am not going to show you."

"But you must, Beast. Please. I have to learn this, and you're the only one I trust to teach me. We can take it in small measures and stop if the experiment seems to be going amiss. Or you can simply tell me. Or I can perform the experiment on you."

"You will do no such thing! You are not *performing* anything on me. Damn it, Goose. Are you purposely trying to rile me?"

Her breath caught. "No! I'm trying to be logical and reasonable about this. I'm trying to be honest with you and give you fair warning of what I plan to do. I'm trying to remain calm and hopeful when every part of me wants to cry in despair for the shambles that will become of my life if I don't do something to change my circumstances."

"Goose—"

She tried to draw her hand out of his, but he held firm. Not that she really wished to draw it away. His touch felt exquisite. "No, I won't be patted on the head and told I am being ridiculous. I have no one to protect me from Lord Gosling, so I must protect myself the only way I know how. I don't care if it seems foolish to you. All I'm asking is for your help. So, will you give it?"

He looked everywhere but at her and began to shift on his feet so that his response, when it finally came, was not at all comforting. "I will not consider any such thing unless my terms are strictly met. There's to be no touching," he said, overlooking the fact he was still holding her hand and running his thumb in lazy circles over it. "And there absolutely will be no tasting. Agreed?"

She furrowed her brow. "I don't know."

"What do you mean, you don't know?" He released her hand and now ran his own through his hair in obvious frustration and dismay. Honestly, the man was going to be bald by the time this week was through if he didn't stop doing that every time she irked him. She seemed to be doing that a lot. But it was his own fault for insisting on setting rules to all her experiments.

"How am I to get the desired results when you are forcing me to abide by rules that are likely to inhibit the very results I am hoping for? How can I experiment with the sense of touch when I am forbidden to touch you? Or taste when I am forbidden to? I'm still not certain how that sense works. I thought it was mostly about kissing and also about food. Are you suggesting it is something more?"

Now he was looking at her oddly, his gaze hot and smoldering. He was angry, to be sure. Yet, he was also feeling something else, hopefully remorse for being so difficult when all she needed was his cooperation.

No, that look had nothing to do with remorse.

That look turned her insides to liquid.

"Stop scowling at me. Why are you so adamantly resistant to the sense of taste? Is it dangerous? Indecent? It sounds like it might be." She gasped as a sudden shocking thought sprang into her mind. Did it involve him running his tongue over her skin? Good Lord! "Um, is it ticklish?"

She felt a light tug of her hand and realized it was somehow back in his, which made no sense. He was adamant about no touching. So what were they doing now? He leaned closer so that she felt the warmth of his breath against her lips. "Yes, it is dangerous. Yes, it could be indecent, depending on where I taste you. Yes, it could be ticklish, also depending on where I taste you."

"Mother in heaven," she whispered, her eyes widening in alarm. Not that she was afraid of him, but she was in mortal fear of what her traitorous body would allow him to do without protest. No wonder he was insisting on rules for these experiments.

He rose abruptly and resumed pacing in front of her. "Damn it, Goose. This is not a fit conversation for us to be having."

Her hand dropped to her side, but she still felt the warmth of his fingers where they had been caressing her skin. "It is unusual, I will admit. But surely we can approach it scientifically and not be caught up in the results of our experiments."

He gave a curt laugh and turned to stare at her. "You're jesting, right?"

"You know I am in earnest. Do stop prowling in front of me. Will you help me or not?"

"Not." He resumed his prowling.

She shot to her feet and marched over to him, tipping her chin up as she frowned at him. She'd poured out her heart to him, admitting her fear and desperation. How could he refuse her? "Then I will have to find another test subject. I mean, another paragon. I'll ask Nathaniel or Thad."

He gripped her shoulders and shook her gently. "Over my dead body."

"You are no longer involved in these experiments, so why should you care? If you don't like the thought of my using one of your friends, then I'll ask one of Poppy's cousins. Those Farthingale boys will do quite nicely."

He shook her again lightly. "I repeat, over my dead body."

She sighed. "Why are you being so difficult? If you won't do it, then I must find someone who will. Someone who won't scowl at me every time I open my soul to them."

"No one is going to touch you."

Her frown deepened. "Not if you glower at them the way you are presently glowering at me. Honestly, Beast. You really do look like a stalking brute."

"Give me that book."

She huffed and clasped it to her bosom. "Over *my* dead body. Two can play at this game. Although it is no game to me. I need to marry a good man who will protect me from the ills my odious guardian has in store for me. So, will you help me find that man or must I do it on my own? Because I am going to do it. With or without your help. What is your answer? Will you guide and protect me or must I stumble through this by myself? This is your last chance. No negotiation. Are you in or out?"

He ran a hand through his hair.

Honestly, did she overset him that badly? Then he deserved to be bald before the week was through.

His soft growl startled her back to attention. "Fine. I'll do it."

She let out the breath she hadn't realized she'd been holding. "Thank you. I–"

He held up a hand to cut off the pretty speech she'd intended to give him. "Don't."

"Why are you still so out of joint? This is all going to be carefully thought out and quite scientific."

He threw his head back and laughed. "Scientific?" He plucked the book from her hands and set it on the log before drawing her into a copse of trees beside the pond, to the exact spot where he, Thad, and Nathaniel used to disrobe before jumping into the water naked. It was hidden from view of the house and the local pathways. "This," he said in a husky murmur that had her heart thumping like an excited rabbit's… or perhaps an excited goose. "This is dangerous."

"What are you doing?"

"Teaching you the power of touch." Ever so slowly, he slipped his arms around her waist and drew her gently toward him. He did not force her up against his chest, but her body seemed to naturally go there of its own accord, as though instinctively responding to the heat and hardness of his body.

Her hands slid up his chest and came to rest against his muscled shoulders.

Merciful heavens!

This was so much better than reading a book.

"What are you thinking, Goose?"

"My thoughts?" She licked her lips. "In truth, I don't think I can put a coherent thought together at the moment."

He lowered his head so that his freshly shaven, but slightly bristle-rough cheek rested against her own smooth, blushing cheek. His lips pressed softly against her ear as he whispered, "What are you feeling?"

"Giddy," she admitted.

He placed a soft kiss at the base of her neck. "And now?"

"Oh. Very giddy," she whispered as her heart began to pound erratically and her blood began to heat. Every part of her ached with wanting him.

He chuckled, but only for a moment before his gaze turned scorching and he began to nibble kisses along her neck.

"Oh, my! What are you doing, Beast?" Suddenly, the pulse at the base of her throat was not the only pulse in her body that was throbbing.

His big hands, palms open and splayed across her back, began to roam higher. Lower. Everywhere. "Are we still experimenting?" she asked, her voice breathy and hoarse to her own ears.

"Yes. Do you wish to stop?"

"Good heavens, no." Her heart was still beating wildly as she met his gaze. "What is this delicious thing that's happening to me? I had no idea a touch could be so powerful."

"We've only just started."

She licked her lips again. "You mean there's more?"

He nodded. "This is merely a restrained beginning."

Overwhelmed by the flood of sensations washing over her

body, she said, "I know you're handsome. That's the sense of sight. I can feel the heat of your body against mine. Your hands and lips feel warm and wonderful on my skin. That's the sense of touch." She took a deep breath. "Sandalwood and leather. That's the sense of smell."

He laughed softly.

"There's an exciting rumble to your deep voice. The sense of hearing. That's four senses. Would you care to try the sense of taste?" Her own words surprised her. What was she doing? He was supposed to be the test subject, not she. But, praise heaven! She had no intention of stopping him now. Might as well jump in all the way. "What are we to taste?"

His voice was the dangerous purr of a lion. "Each other, of course."

She nodded. "I'm ready. I trust you. I know you'll never hurt me."

He lowered his lips to hers and showed her what he meant to do.

Mother in heaven! Mother in heaven! He was kissing her. Did he realize this was her first kiss? Her one and only ever. She was glad it was with Beast.

She pressed her body closer to his, not recognizing this wantonness in her and trying to make scientific sense of all the sensations exploding inside of her all at once. *Touch.* She ran her hands up the taut muscles of his granite-hard arms. *Scent.* She breathed in his male heat that mingled with the fragrance of his soap. *Sight.* No, she didn't need to open her eyes to know that Beast was exquisitely rugged and handsome. *Hearing.* She could hear nothing but the erratic pounding of her heart between her ears and the roar of pleasure coursing through her body.

And now his lips were pressed to her mouth and he was tasting her.

This is what he'd meant, for as she ground her lips to his, she could taste the coffee he'd had this morning. She also tasted the male heat of him, the pulsing urge controlled by his simple brain.

The one that drove him mindlessly to mate.

But she was the one driven mindless.

She was the one grinding her mouth against his with desperate urgency.

He appeared to be in full control, slowing her down as he probed and plundered her pliant mouth, his tongue gently parting her lips and skimming along her lower lip before delving in to mingle with her own tongue in a sensual dance.

She slid her hands up his chest and wrapped them around his neck. She never wanted to let him go. Perhaps he had no wish to let her go either, for he moaned low in his throat and lifted her up against him, never breaking their kiss. Her feet now dangled off the ground. Her breasts were pressed flat against his chest. Her legs were caught between his, and one of her thighs accidentally rubbed against the male part of him. It hardened and gave a little throb when she rubbed against it again.

He suddenly broke off the kiss and set her down, drawing his hands off her before she'd fully regained her balance. She grabbed onto his arm, but quickly released him. He was angry. At himself, no doubt. He'd taken this experiment too far and he knew it.

"Don't berate yourself, Beast. The kiss was splendid and it was important for me to know what a kiss felt like." She tried to sound calm, but her ragged breaths and the heave of her chest probably gave her away. Fortunately, he was not looking at her.

He was too busy pacing back and forth in front of her. Then he suddenly stopped and turned to stare at her. "What do you mean by that?"

She regarded him in confusion. "I don't know what you're asking."

He appeared slightly alarmed, but it couldn't be. Nothing scared Beast. He was a magnificent war hero who had faced death with pride and valor. "To know what a kiss felt like? Have you never been kissed before?"

"No. Never. Isn't it obvious?"

He groaned. "You ought to have given me fair warning."

She smiled at him. "You didn't give me time. Not that I would have mentioned it. I didn't want you *not* to do it. Honestly, Beast. This was the perfect experiment. Dangerous, to be sure. But you cut it off before it went too far. And now I finally understand the power of these sensations. They were just words in a book until you kissed me. Then everything became clear. You brought the words to life, gave them the meaning they deserved."

"It isn't going to happen again." He was growling again and pacing around her as though they were both locked in a cage and he was eyeing her for supper.

"It doesn't have to," she agreed. "I now understand what I have to do."

He inhaled sharply and turned to stare at her. "Do? You are not going to do anything."

"Not to you, of course. But I think you've shown me enough to try these out on a man I would consider marrying."

"Are you daft, Goose?"

She rolled her eyes. "I am not going to go about kissing every man I see."

"You are not going to do anything to any man. At all. Ever."

"Ever?" She turned away and marched back to the log, picking up the book and making certain to hold it close to her chest so he couldn't dispose of it. Although, after that kiss, he might not feel constrained about groping her in order to get the thing out of her grasp.

But no, Beast was ever the gentleman. She could see he was troubled by the result of his experiment. Well, he shouldn't have kissed her. He knew it was dangerous. He'd warned her about it himself.

And then he'd kissed her anyway.

"You can't take back the kiss or any of the sensations you made me feel," she insisted, now growing impatient with him. "Stop scowling."

He frowned at her before turning away to stare across the

pond. "I'm not scowling at you."

"Then stop scowling at yourself. You haven't ruined me." But she realized that was not so. Society would have considered her a soiled dove and no longer marriage worthy had they been caught. "No one saw us. Your bachelorhood is quite safe. So is my reputation."

She walked to his side when he did not respond.

He barely acknowledged her presence.

She sighed. "Will you never speak to me again? I don't know why I should be the one punished for what you did. You went about this experiment all wrong. Even I know that."

He arched an eyebrow in surprise. "How was it wrong?"

"That would be obvious if you'd read the book. But I'll tell you, since I've read it. These senses are powerful. They are like explosives in an untrained person's hands. You knew it, and yet you didn't hold back. You relied on your experience to summon the power of all five senses at once. And our kiss is what came out of it, one that completely overwhelmed my sense receptacles and yours as well. You hadn't expected that part or you would not be so overset now."

She paused a moment to study him, but he was still looking away. "You have only yourself to blame for treating this experiment like a battle assault and coming at me with all guns blazing. If you don't think I'm ready to try these experiments out on someone else, then I think we must take it slower. Arousing only one sense at a time. And you are not to use me as the test frog. You are the one to be tested."

He cast her the oddest look.

Wordlessly, he turned and walked back to the house.

"Does this mean you won't be my test frog?" She sank back onto the log still clutching the book and losing all hope when he refused to respond. "Well done, Goose. Now he'll never speak to you again."

But she knew it was more than that.

Beast was never merely a specimen to be poked and prodded

and studied.

He was the paragon. The grail. The knight in shining armor every girl wished for. He was the knight in shining armor who'd just kissed her.

Her eyes began to water.

And with that kiss, her knight in shining armor had stolen her heart.

She was falling in love with Beast. How was she to stop herself?

Did *The Book of Love* have an answer for that?

CHAPTER NINE

BEAST WAS HALFWAY back to the house when he realized Goose had not followed him. "Bollocks," he muttered, knowing he ought to leave well enough alone and march inside. But he couldn't allow matters to remain the way they'd been left between them.

He stopped and looked back.

She sat on the log, her face buried in her hands and her shoulders slumped. The sight of her looking so forlorn struck him with the piercing force of a lance through the heart. Why couldn't she be stomping and angry? Why couldn't she be cynical and manipulative? No, she had to be his Little Goose. Soft and vulnerable. In her innocence, trusting him so completely. And what had he done? Immediately crushed her heart.

"This is my fault." What had possessed him to kiss her? Of all the stupid things he'd ever done in his life, this had to rank among the stupidest.

He strode back to the pond and sank onto the log beside her. "Goose, don't cry."

She glanced up, obviously surprised he had returned, and then shook her head. "I'm not crying. I have no tears left inside me."

Great. She was the last person on earth he'd ever wish to hurt, and he'd just torn her heart to pieces. "What can I do to make amends?"

"Nothing."

"Goose–"

"Go away."

"Not a chance." He put his arm around her and drew her close. "Talk to me."

"I am talking. I'm telling you to go away."

He sighed. "That isn't going to happen."

"You can't do this to me, Beast. You can't kiss me and walk away. You can't kiss me and pretend it didn't happen. Or pretend I am not affected by it."

"You're right. I can't." He was beginning to develop a new respect for the prime ministers charged with running a country. He'd been a miserable failure at the simple task of guiding Goose. *Hah!* He'd led her straight down the path of ruin.

But she'd ruined him as well, for she hadn't been the only one stunned by these sensations. They were new to her, but not to him. However, he'd been unprepared for the impact they'd had on him. The look of her, with her big blue eyes and red hair and the light dusting of freckles across her pert nose. The honey sweetness of her lips. The scent of lavender on her silken skin.

He was as aroused as a rutting boar, wanting to explore every curve and hollow of her sinfully beautiful body with his hands and lips.

He stopped himself right there.

He was supposed to be the one calm and in control. Instead, he was hot and throbbing and dreaming up wild fantasies about his next taste of her. It wasn't going to happen. There would be no dallying with Goose. Either he resolved to marry her or keep his hands off her and help her find a proper husband. There was no middle ground.

Right now, it would have to be hands off.

He was just home from war.

He had yet to decide on the path his life was meant to take. What if that path had no place for Goose? She'd hardly been in his life before he'd bumped into her in the bookshop a few days ago.

He'd once rescued her from drowning, but he would have done that for anyone. It was not enough to toss caution to the wind and allow himself to be ruled by an unexpectedly hot desire for this girl. Lava-flowing, volcanically explosive desire that he didn't understand nor could he explain.

He would protect her from her vile guardian, of course.

But he would not give his heart free rein.

He withdrew his handkerchief from his breast pocket and handed it to her. "Dry your tears."

"I told you, I'm not crying."

Perhaps not, but her chin was wobbling and her eyes were filling with tears. He sat close but said nothing as she sighed and dabbed the cloth gently over her eyes. "I don't want to face anyone yet."

"We don't have to go back inside. We can stay out here all day if you wish. We've only gone through chapter one. Why don't you read the next few chapters to me? It's quite pleasant out here. There's a light breeze off the pond and we're sitting under a shade tree. We can stay out here into the evening, if you like."

He saw the glint of hope in her eyes. "We'll be summoned to lunch at midday."

He shrugged. "We'll come back out here afterward. Nothing untoward about that. Anyone can see us from the house and know we are simply reading."

This log and most of the pond were visible from the house. Poppy and Penelope probably had their faces pasted to the window right now. Perhaps Thad and Nathaniel were peering out as well.

Lord help him if Matilda and Lavinia were looking out from their bedchamber windows. What would they make of his spending hours in the company of Goose?

He'd come to Sherbourne Manor for the purpose of avoiding prying eyes, but it seemed this was to be his fate no matter where he went.

"Thank you, Beast."

He nodded, but her simple words of gratitude, which he did not deserve, managed to convey a wealth of emotion. He'd always felt protective of the girl, but now he felt possessive of her, too. *Mine. I want this girl. I want to mate with this girl.* She'd spoken of a man's simple brain. His was working furiously at the moment, for all he could think about was the desire to spill his seed inside of her.

Which would not happen, he was civilized enough to know better. But his brain was locked into that one simple thought. *She is mine. Mine.*

The beast in him wanted to claim her, to chase away any male who dared approach her. How was this helping Goose? How was this not going to leave him in agony every night?

"I think we must set aside the senses of touch and taste," she said. "They are obviously too dangerous to explore further."

He emitted a soft, beastly rumble. "Agreed."

She smiled at him.

Mine. Will kill any interlopers.

"The sense of sight is what I'd like to work on. After all, it is the first impression that is most important. Let's read that chapter first and then we can discuss how I might make a good first impression on a potential suitor."

Easy. You're beautiful.

"And about my gowns. I'd like a man's point of view on what colors might look most attractive on me."

Doesn't matter. The man will be wondering how best to take the gown off you.

"Do you think the style of my hair matters?"

No. The man will be looking at your breasts.

"Beast, what do you think?"

That he needed an ice bath. That he needed lightning to strike him and fry his brain. Goose was not an object. She was not an urn or vessel. And he was not a simpleton who thought of nothing but sex. And yet, here he was, thinking of Goose and the incredible sex he knew they would have if her response to his kiss was any indication.

Of course, it was that damn jest this morning. Breast of goose carried in on a silver salver and set before him. His brain had made the connection and it was forever branded into his skull. Was there something to this book? "A splendid idea. Let's concentrate on the look of love."

"SHALL I READ or would you prefer to read?" Olivia asked Beast, who was once more stretched out on the grass, his hands propped behind his head. One leg was bent at the knee, so that he looked quite casual as he prepared to learn all about the next chapter.

"You read it, Goose." His eyes were closed, and she worried he might fall asleep as she droned on about the differences in what males and females looked for in a mate. As for her, she'd found the topic fascinating and knew it would never put her to sleep.

She settled on the grass beside him, sitting next to his big, prone body. Although it was still early morning, the sun had already warmed the grass beneath them, and she felt it seep through her gown. She also felt the delicious heat emanating from his body, but she forced herself not to think about that.

"The description we form in our minds of our perfect mate begins early in our lives, even before we've made the distinction between parental love, friendship, and romantic love. It is not unusual for a young girl to look at her father, the giver of love and protection, and decide she wants to marry him."

Beast grinned. "Did you do that, Goose?"

"Yes." She shook her head and laughed lightly. "I thought my father was the most wonderful man in the world. But as I matured, I realized he was not mine to have, nor would I want him in any romantic way."

"I should hope not."

She gave a little shudder. "Thankfully, the process of distinguishing between blood relations and suitable marriage prospects is something our brain seems to naturally protect against." She sighed and read on. "At five years old, we adore our fathers, but at ten years old, we understand we must search elsewhere for the man of our dreams." She paused to smile at Beast. "This is about the time I found my knight in shining armor. You."

"Me?" He seemed genuinely surprised. "Is that why you, Poppy, and Penelope were always trailing after us when you were little girls?"

"Yes, although we did not understand what we were doing at the time. To us, you were these strange and splendid creatures. We were fascinated by the three of you. Your behavior, your freedom, your natural confidence. We were always chaperoned and admonished to behave as proper young ladies. But you were wild and reckless young men. The world was open to you and you took full advantage. We had no such opportunity. We were confined to the parlor and forced to take lessons on needlepoint and etiquette."

"That sounds boring."

"It was. So we watched you, and giggled when you drank to the point that you crawled home too drunk to make it up the stairs. But somehow, you three always managed to make it back home in one piece. You were big and muscled and seemed to grasp life with both hands. On occasion, one of you would be sporting a black eye, but we knew that whichever taproom drunkard had attacked you, he would have wound up on the losing end of the fight."

Beast winced. "We did some stupid things back then."

"But you were happy. You laughed heartily. You ate just as heartily. We were taught to pick at our food, that young ladies should always be dainty. But you three were like feasting wolves."

"We were growing boys."

Olivia laughed. "And we noticed. We used to spy on you

sometimes when you went to the pond to swim."

He sat upright, but seemed more embarrassed than surprised. "Bollocks, we only knew of that one time when Poppy and Penelope stole Nathaniel and Thad's clothes. How often were you by the pond and how much did you see?"

She blushed. "Not very often. We were little girls and watched closely. But occasionally we managed to sneak away. At those times we saw… everything."

"Everything?" He appeared to be deciding whether to laugh or scold her.

"Yes," she said in a rush before he decided on the latter. "Every blessed thing. You were muscled and naked and not built like us, but we didn't understand what we were looking at back then, or the purpose for the differences in our bodies."

He sank back and groaned. "And now you do?"

Her cheeks suddenly felt as though they'd caught fire. "Well… yes. One does not forget such a sight. And one occasionally comes across farm animals doing…" Her voice trailed off. She'd said quite enough.

Probably too much.

He stayed silent for a long, uncomfortable moment, so Olivia decided to fill in the void by continuing to prattle. "It was innocent. No one was harmed. And it served an important function in the formation of our ideas of the perfect man. In this respect, women also make instinctive assessments of a suitable mate. Since we need you to love and protect not only us but our offspring, we look for more than a beautiful body. We look for strength and power. We want a man with muscles. But we are also realistic. The more power a man has, the less important his muscles. So, a wealthy and powerful duke can be weak and puny, can be wizened and drooling, and he will still be attractive to women."

Beast snorted in disdain. "Greedy women."

"Perhaps, some. But even a weak and wizened duke can be genuinely attractive to those women who are in desperate need of protection and want their offspring to survive what would otherwise be a very harsh life."

He sat up again. "Are you that desperate, Goose?"

She arched an eyebrow. "No. At least, not yet. Hopefully, I never will be. But I'm not all that realistic, am I? I still believe in holding out for romantic love, no matter how desperate my circumstances may become. I want to marry for love. But I don't know, Beast." She set the book down as her hands began to shake. "Lord Gosling has brought some rather unpleasant men around to our townhouse. All of them *gentlemen* in the *ton* sense of the word. But they are not gentlemen in my eyes. Some of them look at me in a slimy way."

All mirth fled his features and he suddenly became the protective beast she'd grown to admire. "Goose, promise me you will come to me at the first hint of trouble. I don't want you to be brave and try to handle this alone. There's no need. I'm willing to help you. Promise you'll come to me first."

"Beast—"

"I don't want you to be worried you might impose on me. You won't ever make yourself a nuisance to me. I'll never forgive myself if any harm befell you. Just say the word, and I'll set you up as companion to Matilda. I'll do it right now. You never have to go back to your guardian again."

"No, Beast. The scandal would ruin you."

He gave a soft, lion growl. "Do you think I care?"

She nodded. "You should. Setting me up as companion to your aunt would ruin your chances for the great career everyone believes you will have. All you have to do is avoid scandal. But if you do this for me, malicious tongues will wag. No, your reputation must remain untarnished and you must marry the right girl."

"And who says you are not that girl?"

"Everyone." She shook her head and emitted a mirthless laugh. "I'm a penniless ward. I have no powerful connections. I don't even have a suitable wardrobe for the Season."

"I'll buy you a new wardrobe." He was up and prowling in front of her again. "The best silks and satins. What else do you need?"

She rose and put out a hand to hold him still. "Stop it, Beast. Then no one will wonder whether or not I'm your aunt's companion. They'll know I'm not. They'll believe you've taken me on as your mistress."

"Damn it, Goose."

"There's no sense fretting about it. But this is why you're my knight in shining armor. You're big and powerful and protective. You're the man who has filled my dreams ever since I was a little girl. I just didn't understand the significance until I'd read this book. But what I am interested in now is making myself the object of a suitable husband's dreams. How do I do that, Beast? What sort of man do you think will want me?"

CHAPTER TEN

M ERCIFUL HEAVEN.

What sort of man would want Goose?

The question plagued Beast that night and into the following day as he and his friends, and Olivia and her friends, and Pip walked into the quaint village of Wellesford. It was late morning, the sun was shining, and a light breeze rustled through the silvery-green leaves that shaded the road.

Any man in his right mind would want her. *He* wanted her, to his dismay. What was wrong with him? He was no untried boy excited for his first taste of a woman. But there was a quiet allure about Goose that could not be denied and it had nothing to do with the irksome book she held so dear.

He was relieved that she, Poppy, and Penelope were walking ahead of him and his friends. Pip walked with the men, behaving for the most part because he did not want to irritate them and be foisted back on the women who seemed far more capable of taking care of the boy. Not that they did not look out for Pip or include him in their conversation, they did.

But Goose, Poppy, and Penelope seemed to have eyes in the back of their heads and knew the moment Pip began to stray off the road or pause to poke a stick into a foxhole.

Nathaniel caught Beast studying Goose's backside when she bent over Pip to draw him away from his latest misadventure, a nest of garden snakes amid the underbrush along the side of the road.

Nathaniel cast him a smug grin. "Enjoying the scenery, Beast? She has very pretty tail feathers, hasn't she?"

"Shut up," he grumbled. "Just making sure Goose did not get herself caught up in something dangerous while rescuing Pip."

His friend's grin broadened. "Are you sure you're not the one in need of rescuing?"

Beast shook his head and sighed. "From Goose? I think I'm safe enough." He winked at her when she strode back to their side with Pip in tow, looking like a victorious army general.

She cast him a dimpled smile.

A few of her curls had come loose in the breeze. One dangled over her forehead. Beast reached out to brush it back in place. His hand grazed her cheek as he did so, his knuckles skimming along her warm skin.

"Oh, dear. I should have pinned it better." She put her hands to her hair and began to fuss with it. "I had better fix it before we reach town."

"You look fine. Just needs a tuck behind your ears."

She had asked for his help in making her the object of a man's dreams. In truth, she needed no help at all.

What man could resist her? She'd worried about the fashion of her gown and style of her hair. All irrelevant. In his dreams, he'd be slipping the gown off her body within seconds of getting her alone. As for the style of her hair, he'd be pulling the pins out of that lush mane and running his fingers through her cascade of curls.

He might notice her inviting smile or the sparkle in her eyes, but mostly, he'd be taking in her naked body and hoping he could hold himself together long enough to pleasure her instead of succumbing to his own release.

He shook out of the wayward thought.

He should not dream of Goose in that way. He dared not dream of her at all. He could not afford to when he still had to think of his future. She had admonished him about it yesterday.

Still, he did not like to think it would be one in which she had no place.

The sun had shifted and was now glistening on Goose's hair. She'd started out wearing a bonnet, as had Poppy and Penelope, but all three had removed them once out of sight of the house, claiming they preferred the feel of the sun and wind in their hair. "Move into the shade, Goose. I don't think sunburned is a good look for you, not to mention, it is painful."

She scrambled closer to him and gave him a playful poke. "Move over. I'll walk in your big, hulking shadow."

He grinned as she fell into step beside him, but he switched sides so she mostly walked in the shade of the trees that stood along the road's edge. She had a light spring in her step, and it warmed his heart to see her happy. He worried about what next week would bring for her, but he still had several days to think about that and come up with a workable plan.

They reached town without further incident, although Pip had picked up a rock and tried to knock a bird's nest out of a tree in front of the magistrate's house. Fortunately, he missed and the rock sailed over the branch, clattering harmlessly against the whitewashed wall. A little more to the right and it would have broken Magistrate Baldridge's parlor window.

Goose rolled her big blue eyes and shook her head in dismay. "At least there was no beehive in that tree or we'd all be running for our lives, chased by a swarm of angry bees."

When the lad attempted to dart into the woods, this time to chase squirrels, Thad grabbed him and lifted him onto his shoulders. "Up ye go, Pip. Ye'll serve as pirate lookout. Let us know when ye see any. Ye're to sound the warning if there are any marauders lurking in the hedgerows to attack us."

That earned Thad a rare smile from Penelope who fell into step beside him.

Nathaniel and Poppy lagged behind, apparently engaged in their own conversation.

Beast didn't mind. It allowed him to concentrate on Goose

without comment from anyone. They walked in companionable silence past rows of neatly maintained thatched-roof homes, most with an abundance of red, purple, and pink flowers spilling out of window planters and arched over trellises or merely planted in their front walks.

When they reached the center of town, Thad set Pip down to wreak havoc on the unsuspecting population. Goose quickly took up the slack and grabbed the boy's hand to march him toward the shops. Penelope and Poppy joined them, leaving Beast and his friends to saunter to the Golden Hart tavern where they could enjoy a pint while waiting for them to finish their shopping.

Beast worried that Goose might feel disappointed not having funds to purchase so much as a ribbon for herself, but Nathaniel seemed to read his mind. "My credit is good here," he said with a wry smile. "After all, I own this town. I told Poppy that they should all purchase whatever they like and put it on my account."

Beast nodded.

Thad raised his tankard of ale in silent salute. "Should have thought of it myself, but Pip was busy yanking on my hair and kicking his feet into my ribs. I was concentrating on getting into town in one piece."

When the shoppers returned, Nathaniel ordered lemonade for them. Beast noticed that all had returned with packages in hand except for Goose. "Did you not find something you liked?"

She cast him a cheerful smile. "Lots, but I don't really need anything."

When she finished her lemonade and a light repast that Nathaniel had ordered for all of them, Beast rose and nudged her to her feet. "Come with me."

"Where are we going?" She pursed her lips and frowned, obviously confused by his intentions.

"To find you something you don't need."

She sighed and shook her head, casting him a particularly sweet smile. "Beast, it isn't necessary."

"I know. I didn't say it was." He held out his arm and waited for her to take it. He didn't know why the fact she'd returned with nothing rankled him so badly. She did not appear to be bothered by it, which rankled him all the more.

Was she now used to receiving nothing?

"You are quite an odd fellow. Do you know that?" But she went with him, no doubt worried he would make a fuss if she continued to resist his offer. Perhaps she'd noticed the determined frown on his face and realized that further protest was useless. He'd taken charge and was not allowing her to return to Sherbourne Manor empty handed. "So, you're going to buy me my favorite thing I don't want?"

"That you don't need," he corrected. "Surely, there are a few items that caught your eye."

"Well, there is a particularly scandalous book Miss Billings has hidden behind her counter–"

"No books." He chuckled, knowing she was teasing him.

In the end, he bought her a hot cross bun from the bakeshop, liking that the baker, a portly fellow by the name of Reginald Clyde, was genuinely delighted to see Goose. "We missed the sight of yer smiling face, Miss Gosling. Are ye here to stay for the summer?"

"I wish I were, Mr. Clyde. But it is only for the week and then back to London for me."

The man nodded. "Well, 'tis a shame we won't see more of ye. Did our hearts good to see ye and Miss Penelope and Miss Poppy come around. Ye're nice girls. Quality and it shows. Right, Yer Grace?"

"Quite right, Mr. Clyde." Beast purchased a dozen more buns for their afternoon tea because he saw that Goose enjoyed them. He felt a pang of regret she hadn't chosen something more permanent, something to remember him by. A pin, a ribbon. A simple locket.

But she had taken pure delight when biting into the sticky confection. The sparkle in her eyes and grin on her face was a pleasure he would not soon forget. However, he resolved to come back into town another day and choose a gift for her that would last beyond five minutes. Of course, he'd also select items for Penelope and Poppy to avoid tongues wagging. He expected Goose would know it was for her.

"That *tasted* delicious," Goose said, tossing him an impish smirk as they all walked back to Sherbourne Manor later that afternoon.

He groaned. "We are not talking about that wretched book."

She gazed up at him innocently. "I was merely discussing the treat you bought me. It *looked* delicious, too. And *smelled* heavenly. Ooh, and the *touch* of that sticky bun on my fingers was—"

She laughingly gave a startled cry in his ear when he picked her up and strode toward the pond. They had turned up the drive to the manor and were near it now. "Beast! Put me down. Don't you dare toss me in!"

She wrapped her arms around his neck and clung tightly to him as they reached the water's edge. "You know I can't swim."

"Will you stop talking about the five senses?"

"I only mentioned four. I never got to the sense of hearing. Although, I suppose my shrieking in your ear counts." She laughed, apparently not the least concerned he would follow through on his threat to toss her into the water. She knew he never would.

He stepped away from the edge and was about to set her down, but she held on to him a moment longer. "Thank you for a perfect day, Beast." She kissed him on the cheek, a light, lingering kiss that was neither sensual nor provocative, but managed to set him on fire anyway.

"It was a good day." He put her down as the others approached, paying little attention to any of them, for his mind was on the past. He could not recall a nicer day in years. Indeed, he'd have to go back as far as his last summer here to remember a day as fine, and Goose had been a part of it back then as well.

He watched her run back to the house with Penelope and

Poppy.

Lord, she still ran like a little goose.

He grinned.

Pip tugged on his hand to gain his attention. "Why didn't you throw her in? I was sure you were going to do it."

"No, that would have scared her. She can't swim. I only meant to tease her, not make her cry. She knew I would never do anything to harm her. She–" She trusted him to protect her.

Pip shook his head. "She ought to learn to swim."

"Perhaps I'll teach her someday." He ran a hand through his hair as the mere thought of holding her warm, naked body against him in the water began to set him on fire again. He had to stop thinking of Goose that way.

That damn book.

"Come on, Pip. Let's go back to the house."

The boy nodded. "I like Goose. Do you think her guardian is going to hurt her?"

He placed a comforting arm over the boy's shoulder. "No, I won't ever let him."

OLIVIA AWOKE EARLY the following day and leaped out of bed. "I hope I haven't missed it."

She hastily washed and dressed, then made her way downstairs as quietly as possible, wincing when the front door groaned as she eased it open.

She hadn't missed it!

She paused on the front steps, the perfect perch to watch the fiery sunrise over the pond and meadow. Usually, they were shrouded in mist at this early hour, but not this morning. There was a lovely quiet to the dawn, a peaceful silence that would soon be broken as others began to stir.

However, all was not completely silent. She listened to the

leaves rustling in the breeze and the soft tweet of birds nestled in the trees. A few butterflies flitted from bush to bush, their golden wings hardly flapping as they glided on the wind.

She shaded her eyes with one hand and glanced up to stare at the white tufts of clouds floating overhead against a sky of rich magenta streaked with deep pinks, purples, and bursts of orange. Those brilliant colors would soon give way to shades of blue.

Her gaze then shifted to the pond, for the sun's rays glistened on the water like diamonds caught in firelight. "Splendid," she muttered and took a deep breath. "Oh, I'm going to miss this."

She decided to walk to the pond, but had not taken a single step before she noticed someone come out of the trees where the men removed their clothes to go for a swim.

Obviously, one of them had taken a morning dip.

And he hadn't bothered to don his shirt, thinking he was alone at this early hour, so he'd left it dangling casually over his shoulder. Her heart skipped a beat upon recognizing Beast striding toward her, his splendid warrior body on grand display.

There was something about Beast that made her heart flutter and her breath catch. He was rugged perfection. Broad shoulders, trim waist, and muscled arms. But there was more to him than merely the fine cut of his figure, or the gleaming waves of his golden hair. He continued toward the house under the soft rays of morning sunlight, unaware she was watching him.

She stood in place, waiting for him to notice her.

He hadn't looked up and seemed lost in his own thoughts, and while she stood too far away to clearly see his eyes, she'd looked into them often enough to know there was a compelling beauty and intelligence reflected in their amber-green depths.

"Beast, your eyepatch," she said in a whisper, nibbling her lip in consternation. He always wore it to cover his one bad eye. But he wasn't wearing it now. No doubt, because he expected no one to be about at this hour.

Should she slip back inside the house? Pretend she hadn't seen him?

The decision was taken from her when he chose that moment to glance up.

"No help for it now," she muttered, remaining on the front steps and watching as he strode toward her. She could not tell if he was frowning or smiling, but he did not appear angry when he finally reached her side.

Her breaths had been erratic when she'd first spotted him. Now, she was unable to breathe at all. *Mercy.* His hair was wet and beads of water were trailing down his neck and across his exquisitely broad chest. The gold hairs along his chest were also damp, as was the bronzed skin along his muscled shoulders. "What are you doing up at this hour, Goose?"

He did not appear at all embarrassed to be caught without his shirt or his eyepatch.

She felt a blaze of heat run up her cheeks, for she could not tear her gaze away from him. His lips softly curled into a smile, revealing he knew it.

"Um," she replied, not so cleverly.

She was standing on the first step, but still had to look up to meet his gaze. She made the mistake of casting a glimpse downward, her eyes drawn to the light dusting of golden hair that began at his chest and tapered as it disappeared below his navel and into his trousers. Fortunately, he hadn't noticed her gawking since he'd been donning his shirt and had it over his head at the time.

She was struggling not to make a dithering fool of herself. "Um, I love the sunrise. My... um, room at Gosling Hall overlooked the meadow. I would wake up with the sun each morning and toss open my window to peer out at the grazing deer and the birds chattering in the trees. The deer should be coming out to forage at any moment. Ah, and here are the first. A doe and her two yearlings."

He grinned at her, obviously amused by her discomfort and then followed her gaze toward the meadow. "Have you been back to your home since Lord Gosling took guardianship over you?"

"No." She recovered a bit of her composure now that he was not looking directly at her. "I miss it. I've wanted to walk over there ever since we arrived, but I'm afraid of what I might find. He dismissed the staff so there's been no upkeep for the last two years."

"That's a shame."

"Oh, Beast, why do some men act the way they do? It would have cost him so little to maintain a groundskeeper and small staff."

"I know," he said gently, his gaze still fixed on the nearby meadow. "I have no answer for that. Some men are just too petty and mean to see beyond their own selfish interests."

"I heard endless lectures on why he had to stint because my father hadn't properly managed our funds. I really miss the place. It held such happy memories for me. I might go over there after breakfast."

He nodded. "I'll go with you."

"Thank you, I'd appreciate your company. But you don't have to."

He laughed softly. "Yes, I do. Those tricks you've learned from that damn book may have roused my sense receptacles… in a good way… too good at times. But it also works in the opposite direction. Your guardian has roused my ire and I mean to do something about it."

Her eyes widened in surprise. "What are you going to do?"

Although he knew she was staring at him, he kept his gaze on the meadow. "It depends."

"On what?"

He finally turned toward her. "On what he's done to hurt you. If he's allowed the house to fall into ruin merely to spite you…"

"Don't worry about me, Beast. He can take away my piano. He can neglect my house. But he can't take away who I am or what I feel inside." She smiled at him and hesitantly reached out to touch his cheek just below his injured eye.

"Don't, Goose." He stopped her hand by gently wrapping it in his before she could do what she'd intended. "I didn't think anyone would be up yet. I left my eyepatch in my bedchamber. Don't stare. I know it looks hideous."

"I'm sorry. It wasn't my intention to make you uncomfortable. It's a terrible injury, but it is also a part of you, so how can it ever be hideous to me?" She eased her hand out of his and placed it against his cheek, careful not to touch the area near his wounded eye. "You are a most magnificent beast. One I care for dearly."

She thought he'd draw her hand away again, but instead, he turned his face so his lips touched the palm of her hand.

He placed a light kiss against her palm.

Then another on the inside of her wrist.

Her legs turned liquid and her body began to tingle. She was eager for more, but that was all he did before pulling away and taking a step back to study her.

"That felt nice, Beast."

He arched an eyebrow and cast her a rueful smile. "Too nice. I shouldn't have done that. We agreed the senses of touch and taste were too dangerous."

She laughed and shook her head. "So is the look of you. My heart is fluttering. But I suppose you have that effect on all women. You certainly knew what you were doing when you kissed my palm and wrist."

He climbed onto the first step so they were now on even footing. He was a full head taller and so much broader in the shoulders. Despite being of average height, she felt small next to him. His arms were as solid as granite. What would it feel like to trail her fingers over the hard muscles and experience that forbidden sensation of touch?

No, better not. Her sense receptacles were already ridiculously aroused after the intoxicating way he'd just touched her.

"I don't know how I affect other women. It doesn't matter.

You are not like any other, Goose. Don't ever think you are just one of the crowd." He tucked a finger under her chin and tipped her head up to meet his gaze. "Any man of worth will recognize the quality in you instantly. You don't need to arouse a man's sense receptacles with any tricks from that book. Just be yourself and you will set male hearts aflutter."

"Is yours fluttering now?"

He cast her a wry smile. "No. My heart never flutters. I suppose that's why I make a very poor test frog. Although you seem to have had some victories over me."

"I hardly think those count since I was only appealing to your baser, male brain function. Those tests would have worked on any man. I haven't had any success yet appealing to the part of your brain that controls falling in love."

"Ah, the higher brain function. The one that forms the deep and lasting connections. Are you sure?"

She regarded him curiously. "About you falling in love with me?" She laughed softly. "I think we can agree there is no danger of that."

"You're overlooking the fact that I kissed your hand."

"In a lovely and seductive way," she said with a nod. "How is it different from the way you'd kiss any other woman?"

"No different, I suppose. But there's no one like you, Goose. If I gave my sense receptacles free rein, I'd kiss you. And keep on kissing you."

Her eyes rounded in surprise. "You would?"

He nodded.

"I wouldn't stop you."

He cast her a mock look of horror. "Then I had better stop myself. Once I get started, there's no telling where those kisses will lead."

Someplace wonderful, she expected.

To her great disappointment, he drew away and climbed the remaining two steps into the house. "I'll see you at breakfast."

She waited for him to disappear inside before setting off for the meadow. However, she remained on the edges, not wishing to disturb the deer as they now emerged from the woods between Sherbourne Manor and Gosling Hall and wandered through the tall grass to munch on shrubs.

A majestic buck joined the others.

He reminded her of Beast, the way he watched protectively over those in his herd. This buck, she presumed, had mated with each of the four does, and the young deer were all his offspring. It brought to mind the description of males in *The Book of Love*, spreading their seed wide. Did this male love one doe in particular?

She was fascinated by the nuances of their movements and lost track of time. She must have been standing out there longer than she'd realized, for Beast surprised her when he came back to her side. "Woolgathering, Goose?"

She shook her head in denial. "I was watching the deer, the way the dominant male interacted with the females in his herd."

Beast groaned. "That book again. Everyone's awake and gathering for breakfast. Care to join us?"

"I'll be along shortly. It's lovely out here." After a moment, she sighed and took his offered arm as they walked back to the house. Beast was dressed now and sported his eyepatch.

He was still the handsomest man she'd ever met.

What was she to do about that? How would she find a suitable husband when he was the man she dreamed about? "Beast," she said, nibbling her lip in thought, "if I were to kiss your hand the way you kissed mine, would you like it?"

He threw back his head and laughed. "Goose, you ask the oddest questions."

"Well, would you?"

"Not answering that."

"Why not?"

"Because it doesn't matter. We're not going to find out."

CHAPTER ELEVEN

O LIVIA SET OFF for Gosling Hall with Beast and Pip shortly after breakfast. Poppy had joined Lavinia and Matilda in the lady's salon to write letters to her family, while Penelope walked to town with Nathaniel and Thad to run errands in preparation for the dinner party they intended to hold on Saturday evening. Invitations had been sent to the local gentry, and Olivia looked forward to catching up with old friends.

Pip was his usual exuberant self, hopping and skipping beside her as they cut across the meadow and nearby woods that bordered Gosling Hall.

"Look, Olivia!" Pip cried. "I see your house."

She smiled and hurried forward with him, suppressing the pang of sadness that shot through her heart when the lovely, rambling manor that had once been her home came into view. It now resembled a faded, gray lady. Genteel. Elegant. But having seen better days.

The path from the woods led to the rear of the house and the formal rose garden that had once been the finest in the shire. The roses her mother had so proudly tended were now trampled and in disarray. A few sheep had wandered over from the neighboring farm to graze on the overgrown grasses and hedgerows. Several windows were broken, but the thatch roof appeared to have held up well.

She ought to have been relieved the house merely appeared

to be neglected and not utterly demolished.

Beast slid his arm around her waist, his touch warming her even as she gave a shiver of dismay. "It isn't so bad, Goose. No major damage to the exterior," he said, his thoughts mirroring hers. "Shall we go inside?"

She nodded. "I don't suppose Lord Gosling bothered to properly secure the house. I wonder what we'll find."

To her surprise, most of the rooms were as they had been left two years ago. She'd managed to close up a few before her prompt departure. All the furniture in the front salon and the tables, chairs, and buffet in the dining room were still covered in sheets, protecting them from dust and water leaks. But she hadn't had time to tend to the bedchambers upstairs before Lord Gosling had marched in, declared he was now in charge, coldly dismissed the staff, and taken her to London.

She'd discover their condition soon enough. But first, she continued to explore downstairs, wandering from room to room and soaking in the memories while Pip played outdoors, entertaining himself by running circles around the house.

"I can check on Pip if you prefer to do this alone," Beast said, stopping in the doorway of the dining room, obviously wanting to give her the space she needed to roam freely.

"No, the devil-child will be safe enough. I'll worry when he stops running and we can no longer hear him making noise." She tried to smile, but couldn't quite manage it. Her eyes began to water as longing and bittersweet memories came rushing forward. Her heart ached, but she was glad Beast was standing close by to lend support. She also liked that Pip was obviously unaffected and managing to amuse himself.

"Goose! Goose!" She turned toward the window and laughed as Pip made silly faces at her through the dusty panes. It reminded her of the joyful times and constant mirth that she'd experienced growing up here.

She waved at him and made a silly face back.

When he took off again to make another run around the

house, she ambled to the music room and carefully raised the white sheet covering the piano. As she did so, little motes of dust floated upward and danced amid the rays of sunlight. "It's only a little out of tune," she remarked, her fingers lightly playing the keys. "Which is not a problem since I sing a little out of tune anyway."

Beast joined her beside the piano. "Not a problem for me either. I have no ear for music."

She looked up in surprise, her heart melting a little at his affectionate grin. "You don't? Why did I not know of this before? My paragon has a weakness."

He folded his arms across his chest and rested his hip against the piano. "I'm sure I have many."

She laughed and shook her head. "I doubt it. But I like that the man of my dreams has at least one failing. I was beginning to despair you were perfect."

"Ah, then you will have many reasons not to despair. I am hardly that."

Pip banged on the window to attract her attention.

Olivia turned to the boy, frowning slightly when he motioned her closer. "Come here, Olivia. I have something to show you."

She crossed to the window, opened it, and immediately shrieked. "Pip! Don't eat that spider!" She grabbed his arm, afraid he intended to do just that. No, he couldn't be so stupid, could he?

The boy dangled the disgustingly big and furry thing over his open mouth, daring her to stop him, which she did because she didn't trust the boy to use his wits. But in struggling with him, the spider accidentally fell onto her shoulder and began to crawl down her arm.

She froze and her eyes widened in terror. "Is it poisonous? Will it kill me?"

She tried to still her panicked breaths, but couldn't. She felt the prickle of each spider leg as it marched over her. When it suddenly turned upward and began to crawl toward her neck, she felt as though her heart was about to burst. "Beast? Can you get it off me?"

He slowly reached out his hand. "Stand still. Close your eyes."

She did as he asked, soothed somewhat by his gentle, yet commanding tone. Still, the blood rushed to her head and there was a deafening roar between her ears. Then she felt something cold against her neck.

"Got it," Beast said in the next moment.

She opened her eyes and saw the spider had now crawled onto Beast's knife, the one he always kept tucked in the lip of his boot, but must have withdrawn to lure the spider toward its metallic shine.

Remaining remarkably calm, he stuck his arm out the window and shook the spider off the blade.

Pip raised his foot to stomp on it.

Olivia suddenly found her voice. "Don't kill it!"

Pip lowered his foot and watched the spider scamper away before he turned to her with trembling lips. "It was an accident," he said, his eyes beginning to fill with tears. "I didn't mean to drop it on you. Will you forgive me, Olivia?"

"Yes, of course. I shouldn't have grabbed your arm like that." Her voice sounded ragged, for she had yet to calm down. "But Pip, it might have killed you. What were you thinking? And where did you find it? You're lucky it didn't bite you. Come inside and let me give you a hug."

"All right." In the next moment, Pip made his presence known by slamming open the front door and rushing into the music room where she and Beast still stood beside the window. He flew into her arms and hugged her fiercely. "I only meant to tease you, never scare you."

"I know, Pip. You're forgiven." She playfully mussed his hair when he drew away. "But next time, I'm just going to let you eat it."

He gazed at her with youthful earnestness. "There won't be a next time, I promise."

She hated to see the boy so distraught. After all, she might have overreacted. The spider looked horrid and deadly, but it could have been harmless. However, by the look on Beast's face, she sensed that it was not harmless at all. "Yes, there will be a next time," she said, with a light, laughing groan. "Because that's what you do. Just promise me you'll think about the consequences before you act. And when you grow up and fall in love, you will not do any such thing to your sweetheart."

He sniffled and wiped his eyes with the sleeve of his jacket. "I promise."

"Come with me, Pip," Beast said, placing a hand firmly on the boy's shoulder.

Olivia's eyes widened in surprise. "What are you going to do?" She did not want Beast to punish him.

He arched an eyebrow. "Don't you trust me?"

"Mostly, yes. But it depends on what you intend to do to Pip."

"You needn't be so protective of the boy."

Pip tipped his head up and cast her a stoic look. "I made the mistake. I'll take what's coming to me. Don't defend me, Olivia."

Beast shook his head and led him into what used to be her father's library. The books were all in place upon the shelves, and both the books and shelves were covered in dust. He withdrew his handkerchief and wiped the spine of several books. "Choose one of these, Pip. I'm going to read it to you."

As the boy perused each one, Beast cast her a stern look, which she understood to mean that she wasn't to interfere. She had no intention of doing so, assuming that was all he meant to do. "Finish your tour of the house, Goose. We'll wait for you outside."

"And you're just going to read to him?" And not cosh the boy about the head with the book he chose?

He nodded. "At his age, it's safer if he reads about adventures rather than undertaking them."

She hoped her expression conveyed how wonderful she thought him, for he was a man used to war and the violent toll it had taken on so many good men. It would have taken nothing for him to raise his arm and strike the boy, but instead, he'd turned it into a moment of inspiration. By reading to him, he was sharing with Pip whatever adventure this lonely boy chose. "Thank you, Beast."

Pip giggled.

"What's so funny?" she asked.

"The look on your face. *Thank you, Beast*," he said, mimicking her in a high-pitched, breathless tone and batting his eyelashes. "You looked... goopy."

"I have no idea what you are talking about." But heat rose in her cheeks, for she understood quite well what he meant. She had been staring at Beast and her heart had simply melted. He was brave and handsome and wonderful.

And she was a goopy puddle.

BEAST HAD TRIED to maintain a straight face during the exchange between Goose and Pip, but couldn't hold back a grin. The two were quite a pair, Pip obviously adoring Goose and not quite understanding how to gain her notice other than scaring the wits out of her. And Goose obviously returning his affection, but in a protective, mothering way and not understanding that the boy worshiped her as a goddess.

Little Goose a goddess?

No, she was too warm and approachable ever to be considered that. And yet, she was beautiful in an untraditional way. Quite beautiful, actually.

Pip tugged on his hand. "Are you going to read to me?"

Beast shook back to attention. "Yes, let's sit on the front steps while Goose finishes inspecting her house."

Pip hopped beside him as they made their way down the hall toward the front door. "Why do you always call her Goose? Her name is Olivia. I think it's a pretty name."

He nodded. "It is."

"So why Goose?"

Beast shrugged. "I don't know. That's what I've always called her." But he knew it was more than that. To call her Olivia would force him to recognize that she was all grown up and tempting as blazes. He needed to keep her as Goose, at least until he made his decision about the course of his future. "Sit down and stop asking questions. I think you'll like this book. It's about a boy who pulls a sword out of a stone and becomes the next king of England."

Pip's eyes brightened. "Nathaniel says you could become the next king of England."

Beast shook his head and laughed. "No, I think there must be at least forty people ahead of me before that would ever happen."

"Nathaniel also says you could become our next prime minister, that no one is ahead of you for that."

Beast flipped open the book and stared at the first page. "Seems your cousin talks to you a lot."

Pip nodded. "He and Penelope always come up to tuck me into bed. Sometimes they stay and chat with me."

"Well, I've made no decision yet about political office." He began to read, wishing to give the boy no more chance to ask questions he had yet to answer for himself.

He'd read two chapters and was about to start on the third when Goose joined them. She sat on the step beside him and emitted a forlorn sigh. "What did you find, Goose?"

"Better than I hoped. Dust everywhere, but the furniture is all in place and nothing appears to be missing. I'll have to ask Nathaniel about it. I think he must be quietly watching over Gosling Hall or else thieves would have stolen everything of value by now. I wonder why he never said anything to me."

"Perhaps not to get your hopes up. He never mentioned it to me either."

She pursed her lips in thought, that fretful pout quite sensual, if one had a mind to kiss her, which he didn't. What he had was an *ache* to kiss her. But his intelligent brain, that higher functioning one she always spoke about, knew it would be too dangerous. "Do you mind if I take this book and finish reading it to Pip over the next few days?"

"Not at all," she said. "I think it's a wonderful idea."

Pip cleared his throat. "You're giving him that goopy look again."

Beast laughed and took her hand to help her up. Her cheeks were a bright pink, a sign of her embarrassment, but he rather enjoyed basking in her admiration. Her opinion mattered to him. Her smile mattered to him.

He spared a glance at the boy. "You'll appreciate those looks when you're older, Pip. It means the woman trusts and admires you for who you are and not for your wealth or title. It means she is one of the honest ones. Cherish that. Such women are few and far between."

"Are you going to marry her?"

Goose's cheeks turned to fire. "Pip! What a question! Of course, he isn't. He's fortieth in line to the Crown. He's possibly next in line for prime minister. He isn't going to offer for a goose."

She groaned and hurried off ahead of them to return to Sherbourne Manor.

Beast put a hand on Pip's shoulder, a companionable gesture designed to keep him from running beside Goose and oversetting her further with his questions. "Leave her alone, Pip. Young ladies are sensitive about matters of marriage." He knew by Goose's remark that she must have overheard his conversation with Pip through an open window upstairs while they were seated on the steps below waiting for her to finish inspecting the house.

What did it signify?

Probably nothing.

He and Pip hadn't spoken of anything out of the ordinary. Goose knew all about the choices he was facing. He'd made no secret of them. What she did not realize was the role she played in them. "Pip, have you ever heard the expression, silence is golden?"

"Nathaniel mutters it to me all the time."

Beast chuckled. "Do you understand what it means?"

The boy nodded.

"Have you ever considered keeping silent?"

"No. Have you ever considered marrying Goose?"

"No." But he silently chided himself for the thoughtless response. He ought to have taken his own advice and kept silent, but the boy would not have stopped asking him until he'd responded. He hadn't considered Goose before these past few days.

He wasn't a reckless youth who would toss all away for a *goopy* smile.

No matter that her smile seemed to light up his heart… and other parts of him not suitable for discussion.

He handed the boy the book and told him to take it up to his bedchamber for now. "I'll read more to you this evening. Keep it by your night table and let Addie know not to put it away."

Pip took off upstairs, managing to sound like a thundering herd of horses on a cavalry charge. Beast watched him until he disappeared from view, although the sound of his feet echoed throughout the house. He shrugged and turned to walk into the lady's salon, curious to locate Goose. But she wasn't in there with Poppy or the aunts.

"Is something wrong?" Matilda asked, looking up from her embroidery.

"No. Goose ran on ahead and I was just wondering where she was."

Lavinia sighed. "Returning to Gosling Hall must have upset her. Perhaps she went straight up to her bedchamber. I assume the elephant we heard banging up the stairs a moment ago was

Pip. How bad a ruin is Olivia's home?"

"Not nearly as bad as I feared. Genteel neglect is the more apt description. Has Nathaniel been watching over the property? It hasn't been plundered or looted. Someone must be protecting it."

"I hope he has been," Poppy said with obvious concern. She set down her quill pen and placed the stopper back on her inkpot. "I'll go see if she is in her room."

Lavinia waited until Poppy had left to respond. "Those girls are so dear to all of us in the Sherbourne family. Nathaniel has said nothing to me, but I would not be surprised if he has been quietly tending to it. We were all surprised when it was left to Lord Gosling. It isn't part of the entailed estate. Why would Olivia's father not have given it to her along with an income sufficient to maintain her and the property?"

Matilda shook her head and sighed. "Not all are as dutiful and attentive as the Hartford men. Beast's father would have protected her, had she been his daughter."

Lavinia frowned. "It is all so odd. Her father never struck me as the frivolous sort. Ah, well. Too late to do anything about it now."

Perhaps.

Beast should have taken the time to investigate her situation before returning here immediately after the Prince Regent's luncheon. He'd remedy that oversight now. He knew of a reliable Bow Street runner by the name of Homer Barrow. The man was excellent and trustworthy. He'd planned on calling upon him on their return to London, but why wait?

The sooner the man began to investigate, the better.

Beast's hand would be stronger when he called upon Lord Gosling if he had damaging information to hold over the man.

Poppy returned, her cheeks pink from hurrying up and down the stairs. "She isn't in her bedchamber. Where could she be? I don't think she returned to the house."

"I'll look for her." Beast gave a curt nod and strode out of the house, his gaze scanning the meadow. She wasn't there. He turned toward the pond.

There she was, seated on the grass under one of the large shade trees near the bank of the pond. He called her name softly as he came up beside her. "Goose."

She turned to the sound of his voice.

"Are you all right?" He knelt beside her.

She nodded. "A lot of memories, most of them joyful. They suddenly hit me like a big, crashing wave. It's a beautiful house, isn't it?"

He nodded in agreement.

"Why is it Lord Gosling hasn't let it to a family? For all his griping, the place would bring in a solid income."

"We'll look into it when we return to town. I'm sending word today to a Bow Street runner I know. Perhaps he'll have something to report to me by the time we are back in town."

"Beast, my head wants to protest and remind you that you have much more important matters to consider. But my heart is very grateful. I know I cannot fight him on my own, yet I don't wish to drag my friends into this untenable situation. I never considered myself a violent person, but I want to wrap my fingers around that toad's throat and keep squeezing until his eyes pop."

He laughed. "That's mild compared to what I wish to do to him."

"Promise me you won't damage your reputation in helping me. I'd never forgive myself if you harmed your chances because of me."

"I know, Goose. Let's take it a step at a time. I'm considered a fairly good tactician."

She wrapped her hands around her knees and cast him a dimpled smile. "I'm suddenly looking forward to doing battle with that loathsome man. I can't wait to see the apoplectic look on his face when he learns that England's favorite war hero is helping me out."

"Favorite? I think Wellington has that honor."

Her smile broadened and her gaze upon him was soft and tender. "Not in my eyes."

CHAPTER TWELVE

"PENELOPE, YOU'VE PUT together a grand affair," Olivia said as she, Penelope, and Poppy strolled from room to room to make certain all was in place for this evening's dinner party. Saturday had come too soon, and while Olivia looked forward to the evening, she also dreaded its end. Tomorrow would be a day for packing, and on Monday, they would all return to London.

Her stomach roiled at the thought, but she put aside her worries and resolved to enjoy the festivities that her friend had worked so hard to plan. They strolled into the dining room. "This table puts the elegance of any London supper table to shame." She gave a nod of approval, quite proud of her friend and all she'd accomplished in the matter of a few days. "I never realized you were so talented."

Penelope shook her head and laughed. "Organizing a party isn't so hard when one has a staff as capable as Nathaniel's. All I have to do is smile and take all the credit."

"We know you do much more than that. Still, we are very proud of you," Poppy said. "My goodness, all this grandeur makes one feel quite insignificant."

Olivia agreed, for the table groaned under the weight of polished silverware and silver trays, gleaming crystal glasses, delicate tureens, and a massive candelabra. The china plates were rimmed in lapis and gold and bore the crest of the earls of Welles in its center. Tall vases filled with pink roses had been set at precisely measured intervals along the table.

Penelope put her arms around both of them. "Enjoy your-selves tonight. We shall be among friends and good neighbors. In a few days we'll be back in London and tossed back into the frenzy of the marriage mart." She wrinkled her nose. "I wish there was a way for us to avoid being trotted out like fillies up for auctions at Tattersalls."

"Too bad we can't find men to marry around here," Poppy said. "Somehow, courtship feels more fun when among friends and familiar surroundings."

Olivia considered pointing out that Nathaniel and his friends were eligible bachelors, but since she had no intention of interfering with Beast's political prospects, and Poppy was still too timid about aiming for a husband with a title, and Penelope and Thad could not be in a room with each other for more than five minutes without declaring war, she simply kept silent.

"How do I look?" Poppy asked, smoothing out imaginary wrinkles in her gown.

She had on a gown of pale pink silk and her maid had wound pearls in her prettily styled dark hair. "You look beautiful," Olivia said.

Penelope agreed, but suddenly began to fuss as well. "What about me?"

Olivia cast her friend a warm smile. "Also, beautiful. The apricot silk of your gown brings out the natural creamy rose of your complexion as well as the auburn tones in your hair." Penelope's maid had fashioned her hair in a loosely upswept chignon held together by diamond clips.

"My turn now." Olivia glanced down at the robin-egg blue of her silk gown. "What do you think?" The gown was her most stylish, but it was still two years out of fashion by London standards. Thankfully, they were in the country now and she hoped the few changes she'd made, removing a frill here, sewing a touch of lace there, would not be seen as an obvious alteration. Her hair had been wound in an intricate twist at the nape of her neck that required no special adornments.

She hadn't any fancy clips or pins that would match her gown anyway.

"I think Beast will have a hard time taking his eyes off you," Penelope said, giving her a hug.

"No. I wasn't referring to him. He isn't…"

"He has to be," Poppy said with sudden urgency. "If he isn't, then that means *The Book of Love* hasn't worked. But it has to. It must."

Olivia tipped her head to glance at Poppy. "Why must it work on Beast? We all knew he was the impossible goal."

"But that's just it. Isn't this what we've all been working toward? If you can attain your impossible goal, then maybe there's hope for me." She began to wring her hands.

Olivia and Penelope exchanged glances. "What's going on, Poppy?"

"Nothing. At least, it's still nothing. But what if it could possibly be something? I just don't know. Never mind. It's hopeless anyway." She rushed out of the dining room.

"I'd better go see what's on her mind," Olivia said.

Penelope held her back "No, I'll go. In truth, I think this is my fault. I've been pushing her into aiming higher for a beau and I think I've overset her. I had better apologize."

Olivia remained in the dining room a moment longer, gazing at the settings and absently placing the guests in their proper chairs. Beast, of course, would be seated beside Lavinia since he was the highest-ranking male at the table. Penelope's brother, since he was Earl of Welles and host, would be seated at the head of the table. She and Poppy would wind up somewhere in the middle beside one of the local squires.

"There you are, Goose."

She turned to the familiar rumble of Beast's voice and caught her breath at the sight of him. "Beast, you look so handsome." The black of his eyepatch somehow enhanced his stature and he looked simply wonderful in his formal attire. The black jacket contrasted against the crisp white lawn fabric of his shirt. His tie was also a snowy white. He appeared daunting and magnificent.

He chuckled. "And you look dazzling, Miss Gosling. There's to be dancing after supper. Will you save one for me? The last one, I hope. It's to be a waltz."

She nodded. "I'd be delighted. You called me Miss Gosling."

The sound of her name on his lips felt quite nice. It mattered not a whit that it was the proper manner of address and meant nothing more. There was something in the way he'd spoken it, she could not get over the sense it did mean something more to him.

Perhaps this was the start of a higher brain connection. When had Beast ever addressed her as anything but Goose? Or Little Goose. She might fall into a swoon if he ever called her Olivia. "Why did you call me that?"

He cast her a devastating smile that sent tingles shooting up and down her body. She loved the way his lips curled upward in that slightly arrogant way. She'd save every dance for him if he asked. Of course, he'd only offered for the one, but ending the evening in his arms was quite something to look forward to. "Goose is an endearment for you that I'd rather not share with strangers."

"An endearment? I thought it was because I ran funny. I suppose I still do. You were mocking me."

His smile slipped. "Never... not even the first time I called you that. The name was always meant to be affectionate, never derisive or cruel." He ran a hand through his golden hair. "I never considered it would hurt your feelings."

She placed a hand on his arm. "It hasn't. I've always taken it the way you meant it. The same way I call you Beast. But I must remember to refer to you as Your Grace when we are in company." She pursed her lips as she studied him. "It feels odd, I will admit. You've always been Beast to me. But everyone knows you as the Duke of Hartford. Yet, you are so much more than a mere title."

She shook her head and grinned at him. "I hope you do not take the fact I never think of you as a duke as an insult. The man you are is what counts most, not the good fortune of your birth."

"To you it matters, but most young ladies and their social-climbing parents do not care about me beyond my title." He reached out and tweaked her chin. "I picked up something for you in town. Silk ribbons and hair clips for Penelope and Poppy, but this gift is for you."

She held her breath as he reached into the breast pocket of his jacket and removed what appeared to be a bracelet. Her eyes widened. "You didn't have to."

He nodded. "I know. It is something you do not need, but something you wanted. I noticed you looking at it the other day when we all walked into town."

She stared at it as he clasped it on her wrist. "You've added charms to it. A piano. A goose. A house... a beast. Oh, it's beautiful."

He tweaked her chin again. "Remember to save me that dance."

Mercy. It would be one of the highlights of her life. She was unlikely to forget it. Or him. Or this beautiful gift. Or a single moment of this evening. Or a single step of their waltz.

She hoped she wouldn't ruin it by stomping on his feet.

She'd never danced the waltz before nor taken lessons to learn it. Poppy and Penelope had tried to teach her a few steps the other day, but Penelope was the only one of them who'd actually waltzed with a man. Although stumbling around in circles with one's inebriated cousin hardly counted for anything, as far as Olivia was concerned.

As guests began to arrive and gather in the drawing room, Olivia had no further chance to speak to Beast. He was soon surrounded by an adoring throng comprised not only of determined mothers and their ingenue daughters, but men who were eager to hear all about his victories in battle.

She didn't mind.

He'd thought of her. He'd gone out of his way to purchase this gift for her. It was a simple bracelet, the charms made of etched tin. No diamonds or emeralds, nor rubies or sapphires. He knew she wouldn't care about those. It was the sentiment that mattered.

Each charm represented something significant in her life.

Overwhelmed and happy, Olivia busied herself greeting old friends who still resided in the neighborhood.

Lord and Lady Plimpton were among the first to arrive. Their daughters were a few years older than she and her friends. The last of the Plimpton girls had married last year. "It is so good to have you back with us," Lady Plimpton said, and Olivia was relieved to note she no longer wore the gardenia perfume that used to overpower Beast and chase him out of the house onto the balcony gasping for breath. "We were hoping you would return to Gosling Hall, my dear. But I suppose London holds more excitement for you."

"I would love to remain here, but unfortunately, the new Lord Gosling does not love the country. I suppose he will put the property up for sale eventually."

Lord Plimpton regarded her oddly. "Certainly not without your permission."

She cast him a mirthless smile. "If it were up to me, he never would receive it. But I doubt he'll ask me. Why would he? All of the Gosling holdings are his now."

"No, that can't be right." Lord Plimpton shook his head and frowned. "I was certain your father had made arrangements. We share a London solicitor, you see. Sir Winston Aubrey. A most reliable man. I ran into your father one day just coming out of Gray's Inn where Sir Winston has his chambers, and he mentioned..." He paused to glance at his wife in obvious consternation.

"What did he tell you?" Olivia's eyes rounded in surprise and her heartbeat quickened. "My lord, would you mind telling this to His Grace?" She glanced toward Beast who was surrounded by an even larger audience now. "Oh, dear. Perhaps not now. But after supper."

However, Beast happened to look over at her and must have seen the distress in her expression. He excused himself and headed straight toward her. And listened intently as Lord Plimpton told him all about his encounter with her father. The discussion was rapid, and since Olivia had stepped back with Lady Plimpton to allow the men privacy, she could not hear all of their words. A few caught her attention. "Inns of Court… Chancery… testament."

Olivia's heart remained firmly trapped in her throat throughout supper, for the dinner bell rang before she had the chance to talk to Beast and get his opinion on the matter. She hardly tasted the ten courses offered up for the festive meal, taking only a sip or two of the turtle soup everyone exclaimed was divine. The smoked ham and the lamb in a chestnut puree were set before her, but she left those meats untouched on her plate.

However, she noticed the goose in plum juices had been set near Beast. He grinned at her and cast her a discreet wink as he took a bite of the roast goose.

She waited patiently through the dessert course but not even she could resist the custard or the lemon cake. Then the ladies retired to the drawing room, the elder matrons having their sherry, while coffee and tea was offered to the younger ladies.

By the time she'd finished her tea, Olivia was tapping her foot impatiently. It felt as though eons had passed before the men finished their port and smokes and ambled in to join the ladies. Nathaniel cut quite the fine figure and caught the eye of every lady in the room, as did Thad when he entered shortly afterward.

Nathaniel and Thad escorted the ladies into the music room, which had been left bare of furniture to allow for the much-anticipated dancing. But while he and Thad joined in, Nathaniel opening the entertainment by leading Poppy onto the dance floor and Thad following with Penelope, Beast was nowhere to be found.

Where had he gone?

Oliva lagged behind and peeked into the card room where tables had been set up for those who preferred to play whist. Lord Plimpton was also missing, and she wondered if their absence was connected to their earlier discussion about her guardian.

She considered looking for Beast, but had no chance to slip away before Marcus Baldridge, the magistrate's son, claimed a dance. Then Lord Plimpton's visiting nephew, Captain Andrew Gordon, claimed the next. Thad claimed the third and Nathaniel claimed the fourth. The night was about to end. As the musicians struck up the refrains of a waltz, she realized this was the dance Beast had promised her, but he was nowhere in sight and obviously had forgotten. He wasn't with Lord Plimpton for the old lord was now back in the room and standing at his wife's side.

She tried to fight off her disappointment, tried to convince herself it did not matter. But it did. Dancing with Beast meant the world to her. Perhaps she was being unreasonable. After all, he'd given her a bracelet.

Unable to keep up a cheerful facade, she slipped out of the music room and wandered onto the terrace. Tears began to well in her eyes, but she wiped them away with her hand. She silently chided herself for behaving like a weepy hen. Or weepy goose. "There must be good reason. Beast wouldn't abandon me."

She resolved to distract herself by gazing at the stars that dotted the night sky. She knew a few of the constellations and spent her time trying to find each one. In truth, the stars were dazzling. But her heart still ached.

The party was about to end along with the waltz, for the hour was nearing midnight. A few of the guests were making motions to leave. Olivia knew she ought to return indoors, for it was time to bid everyone good evening. But she was still ridiculously overset and dared not risk everyone noticing.

She decided to remain where she was. The torches lining the terrace and garden paths gave off very little light, allowing her to hide, wobbly chin and sniffles, and no one would be the wiser.

"Goose? There you are. I've been looking all over for you."

She gasped and turned toward the sound of Beast's voice, not having heard his steps until he was already upon her. Was she that distracted? Or was it Beast's battle training that allowed him to come upon an enemy with stealth and catch him unaware?

"Sorry I'm late. After speaking to Lord Plimpton, I decided to send word immediately to my Bow Street runner about Gosling Hall and all that Lord Plimpton mentioned. It will give him a good start to his investigation."

"You were late because of me?" Her heart had been pounding with despair a moment ago and was now pounding with elation.

"Then I went upstairs to read to Pip. I had promised him earlier. The lad is still struggling with the loss of his parents. I could not bring myself to disappoint him. I knew you would understand. At least, I hoped you would. Am I forgiven? I'm sorry I missed our waltz."

She wanted to throw her arms around Beast and hug him fiercely. "Of course, you're forgiven. How could I ever fault you for being kind to Pip? I'm so glad you thought of him." She laughed lightly. "I was merely being petulant. I was certain you had forgotten about me. Utterly silly. You gave me a gift and I imagined… never mind. You didn't forget me."

He gave a seductive growl as he took her into his arms, slipping one arm around her waist and taking her hand in his. "No, Goose. Never."

Tingles of excitement threaded through her body. The heat of his touch seeped through her as well. She tried to remain calm and unaffected. But how could she when every pulse in her body was throbbing with excitement? "I'll have to thank both Lord and Lady Plimpton for the news they gave us. I don't wish to get my hopes up. It may come to nothing at all."

"We'll see." His warm breath blew against her ear as he bent closer. "My Bow Street runner will dig up whatever there is to be found. But let's give it no more thought. There's nothing to be done about it this evening. And I still owe you a dance."

She pursed her lips in confusion. "How? The waltz was the last of the evening. The musicians will have put away their instruments by now."

Yet, his arms remained around her. The heat of his touch turned her insides liquid. He cast her a smile that made every last bit of her melt. "We shall make our own music."

"We shall?" The Sherbourne music room had been crowded and too hot for her liking. But out here in Beast's arms, she knew she was standing in fire. Her body was lit up like a torch.

"Unless you don't wish to."

She laughed again. "Indeed, I strenuously object. Why ever would I wish to dance under the moonlight with the handsomest man at the party? The handsomest in all England."

He chuckled at her jest and drew her even closer.

She felt the warmth of the breeze on her cheeks and inhaled the scent of sandalwood on his skin. This was Beast's alluring scent. It now mingled with the summer air that was heavy with the scent of roses and grass and moist air from the North Sea.

As she continued to breathe him in, she began to feel light-headed.

He was rugged. Masculine. A hard-muscled, desirable male.

She closed her eyes and allowed him to expertly guide her through the steps, twirling her with such ease, she felt as though she were floating on a cloud. There was no orchestra playing. She merely danced to the music of her heart.

A proper young woman would have merely rested her hand on Beast's shoulder, but she needed to cling to his solid strength so he would not float away like a bubble. Not that there was anything light or flimsy about him. She did not want the beauty of this moment to burst, for she feared he wasn't real and would disappear if she ever opened her eyes.

He was the perfect dream.

His strength flowed through her. His touch felt like lightning against her fingers.

She lost herself in the enchanted moment.

When their pretend dance ended, she hoped he would lead her into the shadows to steal a lingering kiss, but they were not alone outdoors and she realized everyone on the terrace and others inside may have been watching them from the windows.

Of course, everyone watched Beast.

He was the person of interest.

He was England's hero.

She was irrelevant, although he did not make her feel that way at all.

He grinned at her. "I know what you're thinking, Goose."

"You do?"

He nodded, still holding her despite the fact they'd stopped dancing. "You're thinking this would be a perfect moment for me to steal a kiss from you."

She hoped the night would hide her blush. "I was thinking no such thing."

"Too bad, because that's exactly what I was planning to do."

She gazed up at him in surprise. "You were going to kiss me?"

He nodded. "But I shall scratch that plan since you aren't interested."

Her huff was mingled with laughter. "You give up awfully easily for a man who's proven his valor on the field of battle."

He cast her a smug grin. "Does that mean you've changed your mind?"

She looked around. People were now noticing they'd stopped dancing and he hadn't released her.

He gave her hand a light squeeze. "You're nibbling your lip and fretting. Don't worry, Goose. I'm only teasing you. When I kiss you, we shall be quite alone."

Her eyes rounded in surprise. "Then you haven't scratched your plan, after all?"

He held out his arm to escort her back inside. "No."

BEAST HAD KNOWN it was dangerous to dance with Goose on the terrace. No music. Just this delicious girl in his arms. And everyone watching, because everyone always watched him and he was growing tired of it.

Instead of behaving himself, he'd caused a stir by waltzing with Goose. That would give the gossips something to talk about. England's hero was now courting Lady Olivia Gosling. He wasn't, really… at least he wasn't certain what he was doing with Olivia beyond needing to be with her. Aching to be with her.

Aching to possess her, truth be told.

And not in any nice way, for the girl had a way of making him forget propriety and reason.

"Good night, Beast," she said, smiling up at him as the last of the guests departed. She tried to stifle a yawn, but her smile was sleepy, her eyes were drooping, and it was obvious she wanted nothing better than to lean her head against his shoulder and drop off to sleep.

On impulse, he put his arm around her. "I'll walk you upstairs."

She nodded. "Poppy has already retired. So have Lavinia and Matilda. I think Thad is helping Nathaniel and Penelope close up the house now that everyone's gone home."

"I'll have them leave the music room door unlatched. I'm going to take a walk around the grounds before I retire." He was still wound up and needed to relieve the coiled tension building inside of him before he did something stupid.

The damn *Book of Love* was working on him.

Goose had only to look at him and his heart soared.

Other parts of his body responded as well. But it wasn't merely her spectacular looks that set him off like a fireworks display. Everything about her drew him in deeper. Her kind and compassionate nature, her irritating hopefulness. Her appreciation of the smallest gestures. In typical Goose fashion, she'd forgiven him the moment he'd told her he'd been off writing to his Bow Street runner. When he'd also mentioned reading to Pip, her eyes had glowed with love.

Was it for him?

Or was the glow in those beautiful sapphire pools meant for Pip?

The girl was ridiculously soft-hearted, genuinely caring for the boy despite the spiders he kept dropping on her head.

Her breathy sigh brought him back to attention. "What is it, Goose?"

"There's a full moon tonight. The sight of it over the pond will be lovely. A big, silver ball reflecting off the dark water." She cleared her throat and stared at him as though waiting for him to respond.

He arched an eyebrow. "I'll see you in the morning."

"Of course. I hadn't meant to suggest I should accompany you." Heat shot into her cheeks.

"You hadn't?"

"No." She became flustered and her cheeks turned a deep shade of pink because that was exactly what she'd hoped to do and he knew it. And she knew that he knew it. "Our dance on the terrace had the guests abuzz. Being seen with you by the pond at midnight would wreak havoc on both our reputations. I'll make my own way upstairs. Enjoy your moonlight stroll."

She turned on her heels and fled up the stairs, her backside wiggling like the tail feathers on a goose.

She had beautiful tail feathers.

He sighed, knowing she'd misunderstood his hesitation.

He'd been raised as a gentleman, but the girl had a way of bringing out the uncivilized urges in him.

He would kiss her eventually.

It wouldn't be a prim or proper kiss.

Nor would it be just one kiss.

Nor would she be keeping her clothes on after he kissed her.

There was a strong possibility that his clothes would fly off, too.

CHAPTER THIRTEEN

*T*HIS IS A *night for dreams and fantasy.*

Olivia was not going to dwell on the fact that Beast had not wanted her to join him for his walk. Obviously, he had important matters on his mind and did not want her around to distract him.

He'd given her a bracelet and a dance under the moonlight. She hadn't the right to ask for more.

Since her maid could hardly keep her eyes open, Olivia dismissed her as soon as she'd helped her out of the lacings and ties of her gown. "I'll manage the rest, Betsy."

"Thank you, m'lady. In truth, I'm not used to keeping these late hours. I'm quite dead on my feet." But she waited until Olivia had slipped off her gown and then assured her that she'd freshen it in the morning and pack it up for her trip home. "Sweet dreams, m'lady."

"To you as well, Betsy." She maintained a smile until the girl left, but her heart was already aching. This perfect week was about to come to an end, and she dreaded the thought of returning to London and the toad who called himself her guardian.

She wasn't afraid of him, especially now that she had friends willing to help her, powerful friends who would keep him in line if he attempted to force her into marrying anyone not of her liking. He'd quaked in his boots when Beast had stormed into his study and demanded she accompany Matilda to Sherbourne Manor.

He'd faint when Beast returned her to the Gosling townhouse with a warning to treat her well or face the consequences. Beast's mere threat would be enough to make that toad behave.

But she disliked involving her friends in her situation.

The threat would be enough. She would work out the rest on her own as best as she could before turning to any of them for more help.

Olivia slipped off her stockings and camisole, then donned her nightgown. The thin linen felt cool upon her skin, not at all how she imagined Beast's hands would feel if he ever touched her in an intimate way. His hands would be big and warm, their touch fiery and sensual, evoking a passionate response from her.

She shook back to her senses.

She only knew about such things from what she'd read in books and in the way Beast had made her feel tonight and the time earlier in the week when he'd kissed her.

After removing the pins from her hair, she brushed it out and then braided it so that it fell in a long, loose braid down her back. Since her chamber was too warm, she crossed to the glass-paned doors that led onto her small balcony and opened them.

Her balcony overlooked the spot where she and Beast had been dancing a short while ago. She peered down, imagining their waltz all over again.

It could not have been more perfect.

Tears formed in her eyes.

She wiped them away with the back of her hand, but more tears took their place. These days at Sherbourne had been a dream come true. Would she ever know such happiness again?

"Goose, what's wrong? I thought you were going straight to sleep." Beast stepped out from the shadows below. He'd removed his jacket and cravat, and had them casually slung over his shoulder. "Are you crying?"

Her heart began to pound in panic. "You're still here. I

thought you were going to the pond."

"No, I merely intended to stroll around the garden. You're the one who suggested the pond. The moon is just as beautiful from here." He set his garments aside on the terrace balustrade and then surprised her by scaling the trellis that ran up the wall beside her window. He moved with the agile stealth of a wolf.

In the next moment, he hopped onto her balcony.

"Beast!" Her voice was a breathless whisper.

Mercy. What did he intend?

He touched a finger to her wet cheek. "Why the tears, Goose? Did you not enjoy the evening?"

"I loved it," she admitted, the delicacy of his touch heightening her agony. "But we return to town the day after tomorrow and… I'm not ready for this beautiful dream to end. But it must, for all dreams do no matter how hard one wishes otherwise." A mirthless laugh escaped her lips. "I've come out here every night before retiring to wish upon a star. I've wished upon the moon, too. I've even wished upon *The Book of Love.* Every time I opened it. If the book had ears, they'd be numb from my pleas by now."

"Goose… it doesn't have to end." His voice was rugged and raspy, holding the promise of something more than a dance, if she would allow it. What was he suggesting? Another kiss that would keep her going until she found the right man to marry?

The fierce look in Beast's eyes suggested he was offering something dangerous.

Yes, she'd allow it. She would allow anything with Beast. But what if they were found out? His reputation would be the one damaged by scandal. No one cared about her. "I won't have my situation made the subject of every gossip rag in London. I certainly won't have you implicated as my *benefactor.*" She wrapped her arms around herself, for she was now shivering despite the warmth of the night. She wasn't cold. She was scared about what might happen if she allowed him too close.

He noticed and took her into his arms. "Don't be stubborn, Goose. I told you I would help."

She pushed against his chest to move away. "Aren't you listening? You are the last person I will turn to for help. We've discussed this before. I won't involve my dearest friends in scandal."

He allowed her to slip out of his arms. Despite being a valiant warrior, force was never Beast's way. Not that he ever needed to use force to keep a girl in his arms. She was the only one foolish enough to push out of them.

"Goose, you know I don't care about that."

"But I care about it for you." She could see he was growing irritated and restless, but there was no room to prowl across her small balcony.

He ran a hand raggedly through his hair and pinned her with a glower. "Stop thinking of others and think of yourself. I don't need you to worry about what happens to me, or my political future. I can take care of myself."

"But I have the power to destroy your future and I will not have a hand in that." She ought to have sent him away, not only because it was improper to have him standing beside her, but because the desire he aroused in her was overwhelming and a bit frightening.

She had pushed out of his arms a moment ago, but that did not diminish her ache to be held in them, to lose herself in his touch and in his kisses.

He stirred her wanton impulses as no man ever could. "Beast, please go."

He cupped her face in his hands instead. "Stop thinking of me as England's next prime minister. If I wanted that, I'd be in London right now courting some duke's icy daughter and kissing every royal arse presented to me."

Despite her astonishment, she giggled. "You don't mean that."

He lowered his head to hers so that their lips were almost touching. "I don't do well with diplomacy. I've never felt the need to kiss anyone's arse, not even the royal ones. Although your tight, little tail feathers are quite tempting."

She inhaled lightly. "Be serious, Beast."

"I am. Quite serious." He still held her face gently in his hands. His lips were now so close to hers, she could almost taste the brandy he'd been drinking. The scent of it carried on his warm breath.

She licked her lips. "Then you've made your decision?"

"I think I made it the moment I tore out of London as though the devil were chasing me. I wanted to be here. I wanted..." He released her and turned away. "You're right. I had better go. Goodnight, Goose."

"Beast, wait." She reached out to stop him as he was about to swing his leg over the railing and descend the trellis. What was she doing? Hadn't she just asked him to leave? "You didn't finish the thought. What else did you want?"

His gaze was a mix of heat and smoldering desire. "Nothing remotely proper. Let me go before I do something we'll both regret."

"With me?"

He nodded. "With you. To you. I shouldn't have climbed up here."

She held on to him. Not that it would have done much good had he chosen to ignore her, for her hand was small and his muscles were large. She barely had her fingers wrapped around half of his rock-hard arm. "Then why did you?"

"Hell if I know." But he cast her a grim smile. "You were crying. I couldn't bear it. You were undressed. I couldn't bear that either. Your hair was down. I wanted to loosen the braid and run my fingers through your hair. I couldn't bear not touching you. I couldn't bear not kissing you."

She closed her eyes and emitted a breathy sigh. "No regrets, Beast. I shall never have any with you. I'm ready whenever you are."

"WHAT?" BEAST HADN'T had all that much brandy, certainly not enough to demolish his good sense. Goose was doing that all by herself. Ready? For whatever he meant to do to her? Was this a test out of *The Book of Love?*

Goose's eyes were closed.

She looked innocent and vulnerable.

She looked luscious.

"Damn it, Goose. Open your eyes." Her cheeks were still damp with tears. Her nightrail was too damn thin. He'd have it off her in seconds. Then what? Ravage her? Kiss every inch of her beautiful body? Then bid her good evening and go on his merry way?

"I don't want to open my eyes. I want the dream to continue."

"The dream or the tests described in *The Book of Love?*"

Her eyes popped open and she cast him a look of indignation. "I wasn't thinking of the book. Did you not just tell me to think of myself? Well, I am. I want to wring all I can out of this enchanted night, and that means kissing you. You are what made it perfect for me. The earth won't shatter over one harmless kiss. Nor will I."

Moonlight wrapped itself around her body, revealing her every curve as it shimmered through the sheer fabric of her nightgown. It shone upon her hair that fell in a long braid over her shoulder. His fingers itched to undo it. He dared not touch her, but her braid rested on the soft mound of her breast like a beacon of temptation.

One kiss? He could manage that.

Wordlessly, he lowered his lips to hers. It was the only part of her he dared touch. Her lips. Tasting their softness. Pressing lightly. Crushing lightly. Licking his tongue along her full, lower lip.

Dipping his tongue into her slightly parted mouth.

But his arms betrayed him and somehow wrapped around her so she was swallowed in his embrace.

He knew it was a mistake.

Her skin felt soft. Silky. He unwound her braid and ran his hands through the lush mane that now fell to her hips. He drew her closer, hard up against him so he felt the softness of her chest against the hard planes of his body, and felt the rapid beat of her heart against his own steadily beating one. *Merciful heaven.* She felt so good.

She tasted of honey.

He lifted her up against him, loving the way her hair spilled over them in fiery waves. Loving how she clung to him, moved with him, wrapped her arms around him.

He struggled to maintain control. All would be lost if he ever gave in to the staggering desire he felt for this girl. He would never steal Goose's innocence and walk away. If he bedded her, he would marry her.

It was as simple as that.

She was his to protect.

Lord, what was he doing to this precious girl?

He broke off the kiss with a ragged groan and stepped back.

Goose's eyes were still closed. One of the sleeves of her nightrail had slipped off her shoulder, exposing her creamy skin. He reached out, meaning to nudge the fabric back in place, but her skin was warm to the touch, and he couldn't seem to stop touching her. He found himself tugging it lower instead. It caught for a moment on the taut peak of her breast.

She inhaled sharply.

"Goose–"

"Don't stop," she said with a sultry moan that shattered the last of his resistance.

He drew the thin linen down to expose one soft breast. "Lord, you're beautiful." He cupped the lush mound, gently kneading and running his thumb across its rosy tip. "So beautiful."

He bent his head to taste her, suckling and swirling his tongue across the taut bud. Then his hands were all over her, cupping her breasts, cupping her buttocks to draw her up against him, sliding his hands along her supple body, and touching where he'd sworn never to touch.

What was he doing?

This had gone beyond a harmless kiss. His body was a powder keg of torment. Lord, help him! In her innocence, she had no understanding of what to do or what came next. He had only to slide his fingers between her thighs and show her.

So he did.

And watched as she gave herself over to this new pleasure, watched as she arched her back and tipped her head, and licked her lips. She moaned and purred like a kitten as she surrendered to him. "Beast?" Her breaths were short and rapid as she approached a peak she'd never reached before. "What is this magic?"

"You're the magic." He took the bud of her breast in his mouth and suckled it, losing himself in her heat and the womanly scent of arousal.

She was so close to her release now.

He dared not stop.

He'd taken her too far.

And then she emitted a soft gasping heave and clung to him as the powerful crest of her desire flooded her senses, enveloping her in one hot pounding wave after another.

He felt her response against his fingers.

"Sweet heaven," he murmured, drawing her tightly into his arms as she began to calm. He held her against his own pounding heart. He stroked her hair and kissed her softly on the lips when she looked up at him in wonder.

He held her and soothed her until she no longer trembled against him.

His own hands were now shaking from the force of his unsatisfied desire as he helped her put her nightrail back in order. He brushed back her hair, but made no attempt to help her braid it. Those glorious curls were in too much of a wild disarray. "I'm sorry, Goose. This wasn't supposed to happen. Not to you."

Her eyes were once more glistening. *Dear heaven!* Had he hurt her? No, she was smiling at him. "Oh, Beast. I'm glad it happened. Don't berate yourself. I encouraged you, didn't I?"

He glanced away and cursed softly. "I knew better."

"You stopped before any serious harm was done. I would not have let you go much farther."

His eyes widened in horror. "Not much… I would have been inside you next. There was no place else left to go. When would you have stopped me? After I'd ruined you?"

It wasn't a question he expected her to answer.

In his eyes, he'd already ruined her. That he had not spilled his seed inside of her, that there was no chance of her carrying his child, signified nothing.

She was no casual dalliance.

"I would not have allowed you to take the nightgown fully off me. For your sake, not mine," she said, casting him a wry grin. "I know you, Beast. You would have felt honor bound to marry me if all my clothes had come off."

The breath rushed out of him. "What makes you think I don't feel honor bound right now?" And why was he feeling the sudden urge to propose to this innocent? "Would you marry me if I asked you?"

She frowned at him. "Put it out of your mind at once. I will only marry for love. Not for pity. Not for convenience. I expect marriage to me would be most inconvenient for you. You need to think about proposing to someone important."

"Are you turning me down?" His body was on fire and lust was clouding his mind. Why else would he be peeved that she was refusing an offer he hadn't made? Or had he just asked her? *Bollocks*, he must have had more to drink than he realized.

Was he foxed?

He did not think so.

She sighed and shook her head. "Calm down, Beast. You haven't asked me. Nor do I want you to ask me while you are drunk."

"I'm not drunk."

"Fine, but I'd hardly call you sober. Nor are you in love with me, so let's stop this conversation right now." She placed her hand on his arm. "I'm glad you kissed me. It was magical. I'm glad you did more than kiss me. That was magical, too."

He arched an eyebrow and frowned. "I took advantage of you."

"Yes, and I did the same to you."

"Where does that leave us, Goose?"

"I don't know. In a nice place, I hope."

"A nice place?" He wanted to shake sense into the girl. "I behaved just like the mindless, thoughtless, low brain functioning specimens described in your damn book. You're not some convenient urn for my seed."

"Why are you so overset when I'm not?"

"You should be."

"Perhaps I will be in the morning, but I doubt it." She glanced up at the moon. "You had better go before I embarrass myself and beg you to stay."

He swung his legs over the railing. "This discussion isn't over."

He did not wait for her response before he descended the trellis onto solid ground. He needed solitude to think seriously about the girl who seemed capable of addling his senses at will. "We'll resume our chat in the morning."

She gave a placating nod. "Goodnight, Beast. Thank you for this evening. All of it."

He cursed softly and resumed his walk in the garden, refusing to look back for fear Goose was still watching him.

What was he to do about the girl?

He knew what he *wanted to do*… marry her.

He knew what he *had to do*... marry her.

Now all that was left was to convince Goose of it.

He strode indoors, secured the latch that had been left open for him, and then went to Nathaniel's study to pour himself another brandy before retiring. She'd accused him of being inebriated.

He wasn't.

But he fully intended to get fog-riddled, ass-faced drunk now.

He drained the glass he'd just poured for himself and then poured himself another. He needed to numb himself, to calm the fiery tumult raging in his body. He wasn't used to feeling out of control. Lord, it would have taken nothing for that last thread of restraint to snap. He had only to unbutton his trousers and plunge himself into Goose.

She wouldn't have stopped him.

She wouldn't have wanted him to stop.

That was the worst part. He'd almost irreparably hurt the very girl he'd meant to protect.

He sighed. Matters were moving too fast for his liking. He wasn't meant to become prime minister, he'd always known it. He'd basked in the glory for a few days, but the decision to keep out of politics was an easy one to make. The more troublesome decision was about this ginger-haired girl.

She was not the sort of girl he would normally have chased. Until Goose, his taste ran to sophisticated, cool beauties who had no expectations of marrying for love, were easily bought off with trinkets, some of them expensive, but none of them meaningful, and therefore had little effect on his heart.

But he'd crossed a line tonight, wanting her with a carnal heat that could not be dismissed or denied. Tonight, he'd wanted to marry her. Was it a passing fascination or something that would endure? He'd never been in love before and wasn't certain how one felt when in that state.

He drained his glass, feeling the smooth burn of the amber liquid as it slid down his throat. "Tomorrow," he muttered, setting down the empty glass before making his way to his chamber. The only sound to be heard was of the steps creaking under his weight as he climbed them.

A light breeze surrounded him as he entered his bedchamber. Nathaniel's valet had left his window open to allow in the cool night air. He undressed in the darkness and stretched out naked on his bed.

He closed his eyes and allowed the quiet to surround him.

It was a peaceful quiet, very different from the tense silence before a battle. He hadn't grown used to this sense of peace yet. After all those years of battle, nights were not restful for him.

Nor was he used to the *scent* of peace, of meadow grass and refreshing country air spilling into his chamber. It was a sweet scent, unlike that of gunpowder. Unlike that of death or infected wounds or rotting food.

He was still trying to adjust to this new life at home... or rather, the resumption of an old life he hardly remembered. Their meal this evening had been delicious and elegant. The house had sparkled and so had the women, their gowns and fine jewels shimmering in the glow of candlelight. The entertainment had been light and merry, the carefree sensation quite odd after years of warfare and constant danger.

He wasn't yet comfortable in this tranquil life.

But this would be his daily routine from now on, work in the mornings. Balls, dinner parties, and theater in the evenings. Undisturbed sleep... at least, until the next war broke out. It would, inevitably, for this was the way of men.

He might be considered too old to serve on the front lines by then.

He shrugged off these wandering thoughts.

His life was his own now. He could make of it whatever he wished. He had meant to enjoy himself, indulge in idle pleasures, including wanton pleasures of the flesh. Women were throwing themselves at him.

Settling on one woman had never been under consideration.

Goose had now set his plans awry.

He wanted only her.

Was it because he loved her?

He understood the need to protect her. He understood the sexual urges she aroused in him. It had nothing to do with the tricks she thought she was using out of *The Book of Love* that she toted around everywhere she went.

Although she'd read much of that book to him, these deeper feelings were still strange to him. He did not understand love yet, but knew he had to come around to accepting it because Goose would not have him unless he loved her.

How could he convince her when he wasn't certain of his feelings himself?

No, that wasn't quite right.

He opened his eyes and gazed into the empty darkness. He'd returned to England with an emptiness in his heart that Goose, by her mere presence, seemed to fill.

Was this love?

It had better be.

He was going to marry her.

She was not going to talk him out of it.

CHAPTER FOURTEEN

"WHERE'S GOOSE?" BEAST asked, striding into the dining room in time for breakfast the following morning and immediately noticing her absence. He'd taken his usual morning ride with Nathaniel and Thad, needing to clear his head that was still clogged with thoughts of the girl.

Being sober hadn't helped.

Perhaps seeing her now that he was no longer staggering and blurry-eyed would clear away his confusion. But where was she?

Lavinia and Matilda grinned at him.

He glanced around the table. Poppy was blushing and had a sweet smile on her face. Penelope was smirking at him. Even Thad and Nathaniel were eyeing him oddly. Good grief! Had Goose told them about last night?

Pip finally spoke up. "She walked to Gosling Hall."

"She'll be back soon," Penelope assured him. "We won't leave for church for another hour yet. She wanted to see it one last time before we all returned to London."

He frowned at Nathaniel. "And you let her go alone?"

Nathaniel and Thad both set down their napkins and rose. "We didn't know," Nathaniel said. "How could we when we were out riding with you and have only just sat down ourselves." He turned to Penelope. "Why didn't you go with her?"

"She refused our company," Poppy said.

"We wanted to, but she asked us not to follow her," Penelope added, now nibbling her lip and frowning as well. "She's been crossing the meadow between our homes for years without incident. Beast, why are you scowling? Do you think she's in any danger?"

"No," he admitted, but he still did not like that she was on her own. "I suppose knowing we're about to return her to her guardian has me on edge."

Matilda set down her teacup. "My boy, it has us all on edge. Lord Gosling sounds detestable."

Not to mention he was likely a thief, but Beast wasn't going to level the accusation until he had solid proof. "I'll go find her."

He strode out before anyone could offer to come along with him. In truth, it was better to meet Goose alone, for she was never one to hide her feelings. She was utterly dreadful at hiding them. Had she been at the table when he'd walked into the dining room, everyone would have known something had happened between them last night… and not just that dance.

Several deer were grazing in the meadow but leapt back into the woods as he marched toward Gosling Hall. The house was surrounded in an eerie mist as he approached. It was not unusual for this time of the morning, but since the mist had already lifted everywhere else, the fact that it seemed to linger around Gosling Hall set him on edge.

His heart began to pound. "Goose," he bellowed, not liking that the front door had been left open. He entered and began stalking through the halls. "Goose! Where are you?"

He heard light footsteps upstairs and then she appeared on the landing. "I'm right here. I was in my old bedchamber."

He took the stairs three at a time, foolishly needing a closer look at her to make certain she was all right. "Why did you come here alone? Anything might have happened to you."

She cast him an indulgent smile. "Lord Gosling won't come here. He hasn't thought of this place in the two years he's been my guardian. Why would anything change now?"

"Because he's worried that you're about to find out the truth.

That the place is yours. That perhaps much more was left to you than he ever let on. That he knows I will kill him for what he's put you through."

Her smile faded and her eyes widened in alarm. "The courts will take care of him if he's done me an injustice. I will not have you murdering anyone on my behalf. But thank you for offering."

He released his breath in frustration. "Damn it, Goose. How do you feel this morning?"

"Splendid. And you?" Her eyes were clear and sparkling, and the dimples in her cheeks were on full display. Her hair was drawn back in a loose bun at the nape of her neck and her little ears stuck out.

She wore a white day gown with a dark blue pelisse over it.

He never noticed what women wore. He'd never cared beyond wondering how quickly he could slip the gown off his quarry's body. It wouldn't take him long to strip Goose out of her clothes. He ached to see her naked. She had the prettiest body.

"Beast, why are you frowning at me?"

Because, damn it. I want to marry you. "I'm not. I'm frowning at myself."

"Are you still overset about what happened last night?" He tensed as she placed a hand on his arm. "Don't be. It was wonderful, everything I hoped it would be. Don't growl and say it was a mistake. How can something that makes me so happy be wrong?"

He growled anyway.

And said it was a mistake.

But it wasn't.

He'd known it from the moment he'd seen that book drop on her head in the London bookshop. Wasn't this the curse of the dukes of Hartford? Fall in love once and forever.

He was sober now.

He had his answer. He was a beast in love.

Yes, he loved this girl who looked beautiful even in the morning light. And in moonlight. Daylight. Overcast skies. It did not matter. "Goose, are you in love with me?"

She blushed. "I suppose you want the truth."

"It would be appreciated."

She shook her head. "I'd never lie to you. I suppose you know the answer already. Yes, I love you. Utterly and completely. You are every woman's grail."

"No, I don't want to be that. I'm just a man with faults and virtues just as any other. What I want to know is whether you love *me*, or are you merely in love with the idea of the duke who is a war hero?"

She nodded. "You, Beast. I've always had feelings for you. But they are so powerful now, they scare me. Love is a daunting proposition, isn't it? It muddles your head and jumbles your insides. I melt whenever I'm with you. I miss you whenever we're apart. That's why I cannot accept your offer to become your aunt's companion. I couldn't bear being close to you and knowing nothing would ever come of it."

"What makes you think I don't feel the same way about you?"

Her smile turned sardonic. "Because you have yet to declare it. If you truly love me, then why not just say so? I've just told you how I feel about you. What stopped you from simply responding with *I love you, too*? Or from taking me in your arms and kissing me passionately. You look like you want to run away."

He raked a hand through his hair. "I don't."

"Don't what? Don't love me? Or don't want to run away?"

His response was cut short when he heard Pip clamber into the house and stomp up the stairs calling for Goose. Penelope and Poppy must have accompanied the boy because cries of "Olivia" filled the air.

Thad and Nathaniel joined them, calling out his name.

Beast wasn't certain whether he was frustrated or relieved. Perhaps relieved. Goose was right. Had he been ready to make the commitment, he would have simply told her that he loved her.

He knew he loved her, so why hold back?

It wasn't a matter of falling under one of the spells in *The Book of Love*. It was her working her magic on him. The book only helped him to understand the science behind his response. But it did not make him respond to her in any way that was not of his own choosing.

"We're up here," Goose called out, hurrying from her bedchamber and running down the hall to the landing.

Pip was the first to make it up the stairs. He hugged her fiercely. "Olivia, I shouldn't have let you go alone. Your horrible guardian might have abducted you or killed you."

She laughed and looked over his head in bemusement as the others joined them on the now crowded landing. "Oh, Pip. Thank you for worrying about me. But I'm quite safe. My guardian is afraid of Beast. He won't go near him for fear Beast will bite his head off."

Pip laughed and turned to grin at Beast. "You do look like an angry lion. Are you afraid of him, Olivia?"

"Of Beast? Good heavens, no. He's my friend, as are all of you. Would any of you ever hurt me?"

Pip shook his head. "No."

"Neither would Beast. So, you see, I'm quite safe."

Nathaniel grinned and then cleared his throat. "Have you looked your fill?"

She nodded. "Yes, I'm quite finished here. Thank you for looking after the place, Nathaniel. I know it was you, so don't bother to deny it. Shall we return to Sherbourne?"

The girls and Pip strolled on ahead, but Beast held back his friends. "What's wrong?" Nathaniel asked.

"I'm going to have another look around the grounds of Gosling Hall. Something is out of place, but I can't figure out what it is. It's just a feeling I have."

Thad arched an eyebrow. "Do ye think Gosling's here?"

"I'll tell my staff to be on the lookout for any strangers,"

Nathaniel said with deepening concern.

Beast nodded. "Don't let Goose go anywhere unattended."

Nathaniel glanced toward his sister and her friends. "Shall we mention something to the girls? They ought to be made aware of any lurking danger."

"Yes, but try not to scare them. It may be nothing at all. I'm only going by the stiffening hairs at the back of my neck."

Thad grunted. "Good enough for me. Those instincts of yours kept ye alive on the field of battle. I'm not about to dismiss them. I'll search with ye."

Nathaniel sighed, obviously not liking to be left behind. "I'll keep watch over the girls. They'll probably regroup in Penelope's room anyway to study that idiotic book. Well, Beast. What do you think? Are Olivia's spells working on you?"

"What are you, an old hen? Come on, Thad."

"Bloody hell, you didn't deny it." Nathaniel threw his head back and laughed. "That's rich. The war hero brought to his knees by Little Goose. And you even bought her the damn book."

THE MEN HAD been particularly serious all day, Goose realized. Did it have something to do with her? Of course it did. She saw it in the fiercely protective way Beast looked at her.

He'd sat next to her at church.

And stood beside her while she chatted with Wellesford's new vicar, Adam Carstairs, who had received the living about six months ago and seemed to be fitting in quite nicely. She thought she'd detected a note of jealousy in Beast, for the vicar was a young man and reasonably good looking. He had dark hair and striking blue-gray eyes that every woman noticed.

But any resentment Beast might have felt slipped away the moment the talk turned to war. "You served on the Peninsula? At Salamanca?" Beast asked him, responding to the vicar's mention of one of the bloodier battles.

"I did, Your Grace. I was there to lend solace to the soldiers, but there were times when the enemy got too close and I had to fight beside our men… on the side of right, of course, and always for our Lord."

Beast shook the vicar's hand and gave a grudging nod of approval. "Welcome to Wellesford," he said, at the same time taking her arm and locking it in his so that she had to go with him as they moved on.

Surprisingly, he remained by her side as she bid farewell to Lord and Lady Plimpton, and the many locals who came forward to bid her good travels, for everyone knew she was returning to London and no one liked Lord Gosling. The fact that they'd never met her guardian was no obstacle to their disliking him. "Any man who cannot appreciate the beauty of these surroundings is a scurvy knave and not to be trusted, if you ask me," Mr. Baldridge, the local magistrate said with a harrumph.

Of course, no one had asked him. But he was the authority there and quite proud of his status in the community. "Good thing Lord Welles has been caring for your house. Quite a shame it has been left empty these past two years."

Olivia turned to Beast as they walked on. "I'll have to thank Nathaniel properly. He never said anything to me. Wouldn't even acknowledge it when I thanked him this morning. Of course, he had to be the one watching over Gosling Hall or it would have been ruined by now."

"You have many friends here, Goose. You are like family to many, especially the Sherbournes. Even Pip adores you. You've been very kind to him."

She shook her head and laughed lightly. "So have you. You've taken the time to read to him, making him feel as though he matters. Not that he doesn't love Nathaniel or Penelope or Lavinia. He obviously does, but you are England's hero. And you took the time to notice him. Did you see the way he walked to church? He strode like you. He crossed his arms over his chest and stood like you. I think when I see him next, he'll be wearing an eyepatch just like yours."

Beast laughed. "Lord, I hope not."

While Lavinia and Matilda returned to Sherbourne Manor in Nathaniel's carriage, the rest of them chose to walk back. It was a beautiful day and Olivia had the sense that none of them wished to leave and were already feeling nostalgic of their time spent together. But the men had duties that required their attention in London, and the ladies were to return to the whirlwind balls and other entertainments designed to have them married by the end of the Season.

The day had passed quietly, but Beast, Thad, and Nathaniel continued to pay her particular attention, casting protective looks and watching her every movement to the point of exasperating her.

They watched over Poppy and Penelope as well, but she was their main objective and they were quite oppressive at times. If she sneezed, they jumped to their feet. If she sighed, they were immediately beside her, asking what was wrong.

She could not wait until they finished supper for a reprieve, for the men customarily remained at the table to share a glass of port and talk business while the ladies retired to the drawing room. She eagerly rose along with the ladies and sauntered into the drawing room for tea and coffee. "At last, a moment alone."

But the men immediately joined them.

Olivia frowned at the three of them. "Stop following me everywhere I go. I can't even clear my throat without the three of you jumping to my side in alarm. You're being quite ridiculous."

Matilda frowned. "Indeed, you boys are behaving as though a battle is imminent. Is there something more we should know? Did you find out who was lurking about Gosling Hall?"

Olivia rolled her eyes. "I'm sure no one was lurking there. I think I would have sensed it had there been someone."

"Perhaps." Beast crossed his arms over his chest and stared at her. "But this is our last night here and this would be the perfect time for Lord Gosling to attempt something if–"

"Assuming he means to do anything," Olivia retorted, digging into the sugar cone set out with their tea and scraping off more than she intended. She scooped it into her tea anyway.

Beast arched an eyebrow and grinned, apparently amused she was taking out her frustration on the innocent sugar cone. "There's no harm in being cautious."

"Besides, Beast is never wrong," Thad said.

Lavinia cast him a worried look. "Oh, dear. Then you believe it, too, Thad? Our Olivia is in danger?"

Nathaniel added to the conversation. "Someone was there last night. Perhaps it was an innocent traveler seeking shelter for the night."

Beast nodded. "Nothing appeared to be stolen, but one of the bedchambers had been disturbed. I still want Goose to be careful. No sleeping with your balcony doors open this evening."

"The room will be stifling. I always sleep with them open." But her protest was mild, for she understood the danger. "Betsy can spend the night with me."

Beast leaned forward and frowned at her. "Your maid can't protect you. Those doors stay closed. Promise me, Goose."

She sighed. "Very well. I promise. But don't be surprised if you find nothing but a puddle of melted ginger in a pool on my bed in the morning."

"I have a better idea. I think you should sleep in my bed," Penelope said. "You too, Poppy. It will be our last night together. We can snuggle as we used to do when we were younger."

Lavinia cast them an indulgent look. "I think it's a wonderful idea. Don't you think so, Nathaniel? The girls will be easier to watch if they're together."

"And maybe we can keep my windows open since all three of us will be together and would hear any intruder," Penelope added hopefully. "You'd only need to post a watch outside my bedchamber."

Poppy clasped Olivia's hand. "It will be fun. Please don't fret,

Olivia. I'm glad the truth is finally coming out. Beast, Nathaniel, and Thad will keep you safe. Of course, Penelope and I will do our best as well, but it isn't quite the same as being protected by experienced soldiers."

Olivia nodded, but her stomach was still in knots. Why would Lord Gosling send someone to harm her now? Why at all? Unless Lord Plimpton had been right about her father providing for her. It would mean Lord Gosling had been stealing from her all the while. If he'd found out Bow Street runners were starting to ask questions, that would account for his panic.

"What happens when we return to London tomorrow?" Poppy asked, nibbling her lip. "Olivia obviously can't return to Lord Gosling."

Everyone responded at once.

"She'll stay with us," Nathaniel said, sparing a glance at his sister who was nodding emphatically.

At the same time Matilda intoned, "She'll stay with me."

Beast responded similarly. "She'll stay with Matilda."

Poppy grinned. "Olivia, you have all the choices before you. Add mine, too. You can stay with me."

Beast folded his arms across his chest. "No choices. It's settled. She will remain with Matilda while we investigate her guardian."

Olivia frowned. "But your aunt lives with you. I can't reside under the same roof as you."

He turned to her, his expression as determined as she'd ever seen him. "I'll stay at one of my clubs. Once we return to London, you are not to go near the Gosling townhouse on your own. Understood?"

She nodded. "I'll need to retrieve my clothes. And Beast, don't you dare suggest I don't need them because you'll buy me a new wardrobe. I will not accept it."

Beast was prowling back and forth in front of her now. "Then I'll send the Bow Street runners to collect your gowns. You won't go near that place."

She rose to stand in front of him. "This is turning into precisely the mess I wished to avoid."

He stopped and assumed his usual crossed-arm-over-chest stance. "No mess. You are not going back to him. Ever. Are we clear?"

"I am not one of your soldiers to order around." She folded her arms to mimic him, but that only drew his gaze to her chest and he grinned in appreciation. She sighed and dropped her arms to her sides. "We're clear. But you are still overbearing."

"Are you packed?"

"Yes. Just about done. A few last items to stow away in the morning and then my trunk can be loaded onto one of the carriages."

"My carriage," Beast corrected. "I'll be escorting you and my aunt to our townhouse."

She glanced at Penelope. "Then I had better take my book and pack it away now. I don't want to forget it in your bedchamber."

Penelope drew back her chair. "I'll get it. Where did you leave it?"

Olivia waved her down. "On your bureau, I think. I'll run up and take care of it now." She did not wait for a response, for she needed to be away from everyone's prying eyes. She was on edge because of a lurking stranger who quite possibly did not exist, but everyone believed he did because of Beast's intuition.

Now she was moving in with Matilda.

It felt awkward.

It all felt sudden and ill-conceived.

She turned on her heels and scurried upstairs, deciding to put the book under her reticule and take it in the carriage with her to read during tomorrow's ride. Was there a section in it dedicated to stubborn men? Or how one got over a stubborn man who did not love her but insisted on keeping her under his roof?

Well, she'd be residing there as a guest of Matilda's, but her home was Beast's since he was now duke and had inherited all the wealth and entailed properties. As dowager, Matilda would have received a comfortable settlement and could have maintained her own residence, but Beast doted on his aunt and was not going to move her out of the lavish ducal home she had lived in for decades.

But if she was to move in there for weeks, perhaps for months, what would Beast do? He could not take up residence at one of his clubs indefinitely. She shook her head and sighed. They would figure it out once back in London and his Bow Street runners discovered more about her situation.

Shaking off her distraction, Olivia entered Penelope's chamber and easily found the book. "You'd better have answers for me," she muttered, giving it a pat before tucking it under her arm and walking next door to her room.

Penelope's chamber had been sealed up and stifling, but there was a light breeze blowing through hers. "Betsy?" The room was dark, and since she was merely dropping the book on the chair where she'd left her reticule, she did not bother to light a candle.

But she paused by the door to glance around first and then frowned. The girl must have run off on an errand and would certainly be back shortly to finish up. Her trunk was still open and a few clothes remained strewn on her bed.

But she did not like that her balcony doors had been left open. After Beast's stern lecture to everyone, Betsy should not have been so scatterbrained as to ignore the warning.

She hesitated another moment.

Then, worried the girl might get in trouble, she set down her book and crossed the room to shut them. She was about to do so when a large figure suddenly loomed in front of her. She tried to scream, but the villain reached out and covered her mouth with his filthy hand. He drew her hard up against him. "Lud! Ye're not—"

She stomped on his foot and when he loosened his grip and howled, she poked her finger in his eye and then slammed her elbow into his belly. "Beast! Beast! Help!"

The man released her and raced off, leaping down from her balcony and heading into the darkness.

She was scared witless and her heart felt as though it might burst, but she had to think clearly. She heard the thunder of footsteps coming up the stairs and knew Beast would be there within moments, so she hurried back toward the balcony to peer out of it, hoping to get a sense of the intruder's direction as he ran off.

Her legs began to give way as soon as she reached it. She tried to lean on a nearby side table, but lost her balance and fell against it instead, spilling its contents, a vase, clock, and a charming ceramic dish, onto the floor.

The table made a soft thud as it toppled, and the delicate vase and dish merely dropped onto the carpet and fortunately did not shatter. The clock began to chime and would not stop.

As she bent to pick it up, her door slammed open so hard it flew off its hinges. Beast burst in. Thad and Nathaniel were right behind him. "Goose, what happened?"

"There was a man in here, but he ran off in the direction of Wellesford." She pointed into the distance.

"We'll get him," Nathaniel said, and in the next moment, he and Thad leaped off her balcony to chase after the man.

"Did he hurt you?" Beast remained behind, hastily running his hands down her arms and taking a moment to study her to make certain she hadn't been harmed. Then he searched her bedchamber to make certain no one else was lurking about.

"I'm all right." But the violent shaking of her hands told otherwise.

"Let's get you out of here." He lifted her into his arms and carried her to Penelope's room, setting her on the bed and then kneeling beside her. "You're trembling. Can you tell me what happened?"

It took her a moment to gather her thoughts and find her voice, but she nodded. "He was on my balcony and must have pried open the doors." She was afraid to mention that Betsy might have neglected to properly close them. "I thought I might have forgotten… when I went to close them, he clamped his hand over my mouth to quiet me. I managed to step on his foot and then I poked him in the eye."

Between shattered breaths and an occasional sob, she continued to relate what had happened. While she spoke, Beast once again ran his hands over her body to make certain she hadn't been injured. His touch felt warm and soothing. "When he let go of me, I hit him in the stomach."

Beast groaned. "Goose, I almost lost you. Thank the Graces you were able to fight him off." He caressed her cheek. "You protected yourself. I'm so proud of you."

She smiled at him even though she was still scared. "You may be proud, but I'm amazed. Stunned. Astonished. I've never had to do anything like this before."

He shook his head and groaned again. "Hopefully, you never will again. Lord, you were out of our sight for hardly a minute. There was someone, after all."

She was still seated on the bed, and he was kneeling beside her. Then suddenly, they were both standing and she was in his arms, clinging to him as he gave her a long, lingering kiss that stirred the deepest recesses of her heart.

"Goose, I–"

Whatever he was going to say was lost as Poppy and Penelope ran into the bedchamber and immediately came to a halt when they saw her wrapped in Beast's arms. She blushed and attempted to step away, but he refused to let her out of his embrace, and by his expression, she did not think he meant to release her any time soon. If he could have tied her to him, she sensed he would have.

"Did Thad and Nathaniel catch the intruder?" he asked Penelope.

"I don't know. They're not back yet." She turned to Olivia. "Are you hurt?"

"No, just shaken." No doubt Beast was shaken as well, for she could feel his turmoil in the protective way he held her and the muscled tension in his arms. He was obviously frustrated that someone had managed to slip into the house without his notice.

"Penelope," he said with a quiet calm that none of them felt, "send one of the footmen for the doctor. Poppy, run downstairs and fetch me a bottle of whiskey."

"I don't need a doctor," Olivia insisted, but Penelope was already scampering down the stairs to do Beast's bidding. Poppy followed on her heels.

Olivia looked down at her still shaking hands. "I don't need a doctor," she repeated, this time more insistently. All she'd suffered was a good scare. "Nor do I need whiskey to settle my nerves."

His laughter sounded pained. "The whiskey is for me. I need it to settle *my* nerves."

She sat back down on Penelope's bed, now having to tip her head upward to gaze at Beast since he'd remained standing. His arms were folded across his chest and he looked like a fierce warrior. She loved that look.

She loved the way his expression softened whenever he regarded her. She sighed. "I don't think I'll sleep at all tonight."

He knelt once more beside her and ran his knuckles gently across her cheek. "Nor will I."

Smiling with a tenderness he rarely showed to anyone, he uncurled his hand to brush back a few stray locks of her hair. Some of the pins must have fallen out during her struggle, but she'd been too distracted to notice. "Oh, my hair. It's–"

"Marry me."

She blinked. And gaped at him. "What?"

He leaned closer and gave her a soft kiss on the lips. "Marry me, Goose."

CHAPTER FIFTEEN

"SOAMES HAS SENT one of the footmen for the doctor," Penelope said, returning to the bedchamber in a breathless rush.

"And here's the whiskey," Poppy said, hurrying in behind her. "I brought up some glasses, too. What's wrong with Olivia? She looks dazed. Why is she blinking like that?"

Beast rose to take the glasses from Poppy's hands and set them on the night table beside the bed. "I've just asked her to marry me."

The bottle slipped from Poppy's grasp and thudded to the carpet.

Penelope froze. "Do you mean *The Book of Love* actually worked?"

Olivia shook to her senses. "You are the most infuriating man I've ever met. Was that a proposal or a command? I don't want you sacrificing yourself out of pity." She tried to say more, but her heart was pounding fiercely once again and she felt tears well in her eyes. She didn't know whether they should be tears of joy or of despair.

She tore out of Penelope's bedchamber and rushed downstairs, then stopped in the center of the hall, realizing she had nowhere to go. She'd just had the scare of her life and the intruder had not yet been captured. She was overset, but she wasn't so foolish as to simply run off blindly.

Beast caught up to her, but made no attempt to touch her. "Goose, I thought you loved me."

She nodded. "I do, but I'm not the problem. Do you love me? If so, then why can't you simply say it to me? I don't want you to lie to me. Merely tell me how you feel. But how can you offer for me if you don't love me? I'd never force you into a marriage you don't really want. Do you want to marry me?"

The questions went unanswered, for the front door suddenly burst open as Thad and Nathaniel returned with the now subdued culprit in their grasp. The stranger had obviously been on the losing end of their struggle. His lip was swollen and one eye was badly bruised. The damage appeared to be more from a fist than from her merely poking him in the eye.

Nathaniel cast her a nod of assurance that all was once more under control. "I'll send one of the footmen to fetch the magistrate."

The man's eyes widened in obvious terror. "It's all been a misunderstanding, m'lord. My Betsy will clear this up. I came to see 'er. She's lady's maid to one of yer guests, Lady Olivia Gosling. Please, ye must believe me. I never meant anyone no harm."

Matilda and Lavinia, who had been seated in the drawing room tensely awaiting Nathaniel and Thad's return, entered the hall. Penelope and Poppy had also hurried down the stairs and were staring at the culprit from the steps, obviously afraid to edge closer.

Olivia reached for Beast's hand, relieved he was standing beside her. He cast her a questioning glance and then tucked his arm lightly around her waist in a typically protective gesture. Her tension seemed to melt away, for Beast always made her feel safe. His tension eased as well, knowing she was not angry with him for proposing when he did not mean it.

The culprit fell to his knees, pleading and protesting his innocence. "It was dark. I thought she was my Betsy. Then she tried to scream and I knew I was in trouble. Where's my Betsy? She'll tell ye. I'd never harm no one."

Nathaniel had Olivia's maid summoned.

The girl hurried in, took one look at the man before her and paled. "Oh, sweet Lord! William Jennings, what have ye done? What are ye doing here? Were ye the one his lordship was chasing?"

William nodded. "I'm so sorry, Betsy. I know I shouldn't have come 'ere, but I was afraid they'd take ye back to London and I couldn't let ye leave without ye knowing how I feel."

Betsy stared at him. "What are you sayin'?"

"That I love ye. With all my heart. I came 'ere to ask ye to marry me."

Olivia gasped.

William turned to her and motioned to his pocket. "It's the truth, m'lady. I bought Betsy a locket. It's in the shape of a heart because she has my heart and always will." The little apple bobbing in his throat moved up and down as he swallowed hard and turned teary-eyed toward Betsy. "If his lordship don't hang me, will ye marry me?"

"Bollocks," Thad muttered, his grip still on the man as he stared at his own hand that looked swollen and bruised. "To think, I broke my hand over a damn marriage proposal."

Nathaniel sighed. "Seems we don't have a murderer in our midst after all."

"Murder!" William's eyes rounded in horror and the blood drained from his face. "Who said I'd ever kill anyone? M'lord, ye cannot believe I'd do such a thing. Betsy, tell 'im. I'll be hanged for sure."

Nathaniel turned to Olivia's maid. "Well? Is this true?"

Betsy nodded and turned in pleading to Olivia. "I know he did a very foolish thing, m'lady. But he's my sweetheart. I've known him all my life. He comes to see me sometimes. I know he meant no harm. Did ye mean it, William? Ye wish to marry me?"

He nodded. "I have the locket for ye right here in my breast pocket. I swear it."

Thad reached into the man's pocket and withdrew it. "Here it is."

"I love ye, Betsy. No matter what happens. Ye're the only girl I've ever loved and the only girl I'll take as m'wife. I want ye to know that before I'm hanged."

Nathaniel groaned and turned to Beast. "What do you think?"

Beast sighed. "William, if you live in town, then what were you doing at Gosling Hall last night?"

"I live on a farm just outside of Wellesford. I'm one of Magistrate Baldridge's tenant farmers." William frowned. "I wasn't at Gosling Hall, Yer Grace. But I might have seen the man that was."

"You did?" Olivia clasped Beast's hand. "Then who was he?"

"A stranger, m'lady. I know everyone around these parts and he wasn't from around 'ere. An unpleasant lookin' fellow."

"Describe him," Beast said.

"Big man, Yer Grace. Ugly fellow, as one might come across in a dockside tavern. The sort who wouldn't think nothin' of stickin' a knife in ye to steal yer purse."

"What do you think, Beast? Do we search for him?" Thad asked.

"The commotion probably scared him off. I doubt he'll make an attempt this evening. If he's Gosling's man, he must know we leave for London in the morning. Very likely he's on his way back to town to report on his failed mission." He turned to Thad. "Let William go."

"Thank ye, Yer Grace," both he and Betsy said at the same time.

"But William is to wait for the magistrate and lead him and his men to the spot where he last saw this ruffian," Beast continued. "Nathaniel, we should also have the magistrate search Gosling Hall and the surrounding area on the chance he's still lurking."

"Yes, I agree we must," Nathaniel said.

Beast frowned and rubbed his hand across the nape of his

neck. "Although I'm almost certain it will be a wasted effort. Still, we can't take anything for granted. But my bet is on London. Whatever he means to do, he'll now attempt it once we're back in town."

"Is that why you proposed to Olivia?" Penelope asked from her perch on the steps. "Two proposals in one evening. That's cause for celebration."

Nathaniel turned to his sister. "Don't jest at a time like this."

Poppy rose to her defense. "She isn't. I heard it, too."

"What?" His mouth opened as he turned to Beast in disbelief. "You proposed to Olivia?"

Penelope gave a huff. "Yes, he proposed. Why do you find the notion so shocking? Beast wants to marry her. Isn't that what I just told you?"

"Olivia, my dear," Lavinia said, coming to her side and giving her a heartfelt hug. "Is this true? How wonderful. Matilda and I have been watching you together. We hoped something would come of it."

Olivia squeezed her eyes shut as Lavinia gave her an exquisitely affectionate and motherly hug. This is what she'd missed so much since her parents had died. She wanted a family to turn to and to love. She wanted a husband who loved her. "He doesn't really want to marry me. He thinks it is the only way to protect me."

"Ah, I see." Lavinia took her hand. "Come sit beside me, child. Let me have a closer look at you. Are you hurt? Is this why Penelope sent for the doctor?"

"I'm all right. Just a little overset."

Matilda came forward and patted her arm. "With good reason." She turned to scowl at William. "Imagine finding a stranger in one's private quarters. You're fortunate Lady Olivia is so forgiving."

William looked stricken as he turned to Olivia. "I am forever in yer debt, m'lady."

Matilda then turned her scowl on Beast. "What's this about

you not really wanting to marry the girl? Is this what you've led Olivia to believe? I've never heard such utter rubbish in all my years. Nephew, you must swallow your pride and tell the girl the truth. How can a brilliant tactician such as yourself botch this proposal so badly?"

"Men are that way," Lavinia intoned. "They'd rather face death than surrender their hearts." She frowned at Beast. "Love is not a battle. The woman you love is not an enemy to be conquered. Even this farmer has more sense than you."

Beast seemed to be struggling to contain his mounting irritation, obviously not used to having his actions questioned or dissected in front of everyone. "Are you both quite through insulting me?"

"We aren't insulting you. We are supporting Olivia. She deserves better," Matilda insisted, and then apparently not done berating the men, she turned to Thad. "Why are you still holding Betsy's young man? Release him."

Thad did not look too happy. "He broke my hand."

"By getting his face in the way of your fist?" Penelope retorted, rolling her eyes at him. "Come here, you big Scottish oaf. Let me have a look at your hand."

He did so warily.

"Stop looking so scared. I won't hurt you." Penelope inspected it quite gently. In truth, Olivia was surprised. Her friend was often prickly around Thad, but she appeared genuinely concerned and took great care with his injury.

"William Jennings," Nathaniel said, sounding quite serious and commanding, very much as a powerful earl ought to sound. "I will not press charges this time. Don't ever break into my home again or I will see you hanged." He turned to Betsy. "Take five minutes to see him off, then return to your duties. And Betsy…"

"Yes, m'lord?" The girl's eyes were still wide with fear.

Nathaniel shook his head and sighed. "Congratulations. I wish you every happiness."

No one said anything until the pair went off. Then suddenly, all eyes were upon Olivia. Nathaniel stepped forward once more. "Are congratulations truly in order for the two of you? You don't look certain, Olivia."

She turned in alarm to Beast. Even her maid had gotten an 'I love you' from her somewhat dimwitted beau. Was she asking too much of Beast? And what of herself? He was the answer to all her problems.

More important, she loved him with all her heart. "Beast?"

He understood what she was asking. "I meant it, Goose. I'm not taking it back."

She released the breath she was holding. "Yes, congratulations are in order."

Poppy and Penelope cheered.

Thad and Nathaniel looked on in bemusement.

"Well I'll be damned," Thad muttered.

Nathaniel shook his head. "I need a drink."

Lavinia rang for champagne.

Matilda gave Olivia a hug. "Welcome to the family, my dear. Well, I'm glad that's settled. You'll never have to return to Lord Gosling now."

Olivia felt more numb than euphoric. Had Beast expressed his love for her, she might have felt gleeful. But he hadn't, and she was still concerned he'd assured every one of his seriousness merely to placate them. "But I'll still need my guardian's consent to marry."

Beast stepped to her side once more. "He'll give it if he knows what's good for him. Goose, don't worry about him. The man is inconsequential. He won't dare cross me."

The next hour was spent taking care of loose ends and toasting their betrothal. The local doctor, Angus Carmichael, took her aside and asked her a series of questions to determine whether she was suffering any ill effects from the evening's incident. "I can give you something to help you sleep, but otherwise, I see nothing wrong with you. You're healthy."

She declined to take any drugs. Her head was already in a fog and she needed clarity when dealing with Beast.

The magistrate congratulated her when he heard the news of their betrothal.

"We'd like to keep it quiet for now," Olivia said, noting that Beast looked awfully grim for a supposedly happy bridegroom. While the doctor was not one to spread gossip, the magistrate had no such qualms. Olivia expected the entire town of Wellesford would hear of Beast's proposal before the first carriage rolled out of Sherbourne Manor in the morning.

It was well after midnight by the time they were all finally ready to retire. The two dowagers went up first. Then Penelope and Poppy returned to Penelope's bedchamber. Olivia meant to follow them, but Beast held her back a moment.

Thad and Nathaniel bid them goodnight, but they weren't going to sleep. They had decided to stand guard outside Penelope's chamber on the chance there was another incident. Beast would join them in patrolling the grounds and house, but first he asked to speak to her.

Was he already regretting his proposal?

"You don't look happy, Goose."

"And you look like you just buried your best friend. How can I be happy when I've obviously forced you into offering for me?"

He drew her into his arms and kissed her with a surprising hunger. "You didn't push me into doing anything I did not wish to do."

"*The Book of Love–*"

"Forget that damn book. I know what it says." He sighed and cast her a wry smile. "I promise you I will not spill my seed into you and then leave you and my offspring behind to be eaten by wolves."

She wanted to be angry with him, but perhaps Matilda was right. *The Book of Love* had spoken of this as well. It was in a man's nature to spill his seed far and wide. To make that leap into connecting with one mate and protecting her for a lifetime was no easy feat. Also, Beast was used to being in command. Having to surrender something as precious as his heart would take time.

However, he'd given her the lovely bracelet. It had to mean something.

She reached up and kissed him back. "I love you, Beast."

She turned on her heels and hurried upstairs, preferring not to wait around for the silence that would surely linger between them when Beast said nothing back.

But not all hope was lost. Once they were married, they would have the sexual privileges afforded to a husband and wife. She'd need to read a different sort of book to learn about those, and it wouldn't be so hard to obtain one. Miss Billings carried such books in her Wellesford bookshop. She'd leave word for her to ship one of them to London for her. Hopefully one with vivid illustrations that explained the various positions.

She stopped suddenly and hurried back down the stairs. "Beast, I have an important question to ask you."

He nodded. "Ask it."

"Will we be sharing a bed once we're married?"

The question surprised him, but he seemed pleased by it. He arched an eyebrow and grinned. "Do you wish to?"

She nodded.

"Then, yes. We'll be sharing a bed." He chuckled lightly. "Dare I ask why you posed the question?"

"No, you may not." She was about to skitter back up the stairs when he laughingly groaned and started toward her with a smoldering look. Lord, he looked so handsome.

She loved this man.

He placed his hand lightly on her arm. "Is this about another book?"

"Goodnight, Beast."

"One of those lewd books?" he persisted, still holding on to her arm.

"It isn't lewd if one reads it when one is married, as I shall be to you."

"Bollocks, you're a little goose," he said with an aching groan. "But I think that's why I love you."

Had she just heard him correctly? Or was she asleep and this had all been a dream? "You love me?"

He nodded and took a step up to gather her in his arms. "I do."

"Truly?"

He nodded again and kissed her, this time with exquisite tenderness. His mouth felt warm and reassuring upon hers. "Truly."

"Promise."

His arms came around her, and they also felt solid and wonderful. "I promise, Goose. I'll love you till the day I die."

A sudden dreadful thought overwhelmed her.

If her guardian was stealing from her, then Beast now posed the greater threat to him. As her husband, he would take control of her inheritance as soon as they were married, assuming she had any inheritance to contribute to their marriage. Her guardian would be desperate to stop that from happening.

Would he dare murder a duke?

BEAST KNEW HE ought to have climbed in the carriage with Goose and behaved like a proper husband-to-be, but he did not like that everyone was now regarding him as a curiosity. He preferred his privacy and mildly resented the way his best friends and even his own aunt continued to gawk at him. Goose appeared to be relieved that he rode alongside the carriage instead of sitting in it beside her.

As it turned out, Lavinia and Matilda decided to ride together in his ducal carriage. Goose and her friends rode in Nathaniel's along with *The Book of Love* which had now taken on mythical proportions since Goose had conquered her duke… him.

"Having any regrets?" Nathaniel asked, riding up beside him as they neared Oxford.

Thad joined them. "Do ye think there's any truth to *The Book of Love?*"

"No regrets. And the book is just a book. Whatever spell has been cast on me is of Goose's own doing."

Thad grinned. "Will ye ever call her Olivia? It's her name, ye know. She might prefer it to Goose."

Beast shook his head and chuckled. "We'll see. She hasn't complained about it to me." But he regarded his companions thoughtfully. "Has she said anything to either of you?"

"No," Nathaniel said. "In truth, I've never known her to complain about anything. Not even about her odious guardian. I'm glad she'll soon be under your protection. We'll all rest easier knowing she's in safe hands. But you must pay some attention to her now, or Matilda will box your ears. We're almost at the Black Swan Inn. I'll order food and refreshments for all of us once we get there, but do start behaving like a man in love, or I'll be the one to catch hell for it from my own aunt and my opinionated sister."

Beast grumbled, but assured his friend. "Everyone's meddling isn't helping matters."

Thad laughed. "Ye have only yerself to blame for returning to England as a war hero. Ye're the catch of the Season. But now that ye're taken, perhaps Nathaniel and I will have more luck with the ladies."

"I've got my eye on one lady at the moment," Nathaniel admitted. "The Duke of Winthrow's daughter, Lady Charlotte. Her first Season and she's already considered an Incomparable."

Beast had seen her on his second day back in London. She was beautiful, but there was something icy in her character. Nothing like Goose. Ridiculously, he missed not having her beside him these past few hours. That she was in the carriage and he could have climbed in to join her at any point on their journey was not the same thing, not while surrounded by a host of prying eyes.

He liked having Goose close, liked the light lavender scent of her skin, the brightness of her eyes, and fullness of her smile. He also liked the idea of having her body pressed close to his.

He dismounted and strode to Goose's carriage.

Thad assisted the elderly ladies down from the first carriage while Nathaniel strode into the inn to make arrangements for their luncheon.

Poppy and Penelope walked ahead to join the others. Beast was left alone for the moment with Goose. "How are you holding up?"

She smiled. "Well, thank you. It feels strange knowing I'm not to return to Lord Gosling's townhouse. But I'm glad. Truly, it lightens my heart. I look forward to staying with Matilda."

"Even that won't be for long. I'll obtain the special license tomorrow."

Her eyes widened in obvious surprise and she began to nibble her lip, a sign she was fretting. "Assuming you gain Lord Gosling's cooperation."

He gave her cheek a light caress. "Goose, all will be well."

"I hope so. I can't seem to stop worrying. What if he attempts to harm you? If he truly has something to hide, then you pose the bigger threat to him. He might be making plans to stop our marriage as we speak." She sighed and shook her head. "Oh, Beast. Doesn't it feel odd? We were mere friends only a few days ago. Old friends who hadn't seen each other in years. And soon we'll be bound to each other for the rest of our lives."

"Have you heard me complain?"

She shook her head. "No."

"I'm not afraid of your guardian, nor am I regretting my offer. Just so we're clear, it wasn't made out of pity. I know what I want, Goose. Remember that day at the pond when the three of you caught us without our clothes? Instead of running off with mine, you neatly folded them. It was such a Goose thing to do. Kind and silly and sweet. It touched my heart. *You* touched my heart, and I never forgot you throughout the years."

He tucked her arm in his when he heard Nathaniel calling to him. "Let's join them. I don't want to delay our journey."

She nodded. "I never forgot you either, Beast. How could I? You saved me from drowning. That was our first meeting. I was a scared six-year-old, soaking wet and sputtering, probably bleeding from my forehead. You were all of fourteen. You carried me home in your arms and introduced yourself to my parents. 'Good afternoon,' you said to them. 'I'm Alexander Beastling, Duke of Hartford. I've found this little goose in my friend's pond. I believe she belongs to you.'"

He laughed. "Man of your dreams?"

"You still are. You'll always be."

"The dukes of Hartford are faithful by nature. They love once and always. You're the one for me, Goose. I'm telling you this now because London Society will be in an uproar when we return and they hear the news of our betrothal. The Prince Regent won't be happy. Many of the rich and powerful who hoped to put me forward for high political office will be disappointed, and some will be angry. Don't listen to any of the gossip. I need you to believe in me and trust me."

"I do."

"And most of all, I need you to marry me. You'll hear lots of reasons why you shouldn't. For the good of the country. For my own good. Malicious reasons. I want you to know I've given it serious thought. I'd already decided to offer for you before William Jennings frightened the wits out of you and all of us. That incident only spurred me into proposing to you sooner. It was never a question of *if* but *when*."

She listened in apparent earnestness and seemed to take his words to heart. They weren't flowery or particularly romantic, but such was not his nature. He was a military man. Decisive. Direct. Forthright. He hadn't even courted her. He'd bought her an inexpensive bracelet, that's all.

Should he say something more? Do something more?

He was never one for dramatic gestures.

Goose said nothing, just cast him a perfectly beautiful smile. He realized then no more words were needed. She understood his heart as no one else ever would. They'd have a good marriage if ever he got her to the altar.

Society and her toad-of-a-guardian were not going to make it easy for them.

He understood men like Gosling and could outwit his plans.

But Prinny was the bigger problem. What would he do to interfere?

CHAPTER SIXTEEN

OLIVIA HUGGED HER friends after they finished their repast at the Black Swan Inn and made plans to meet them at Lord Forster's ball tomorrow evening. This is where they parted ways, she and Matilda now to ride in Beast's carriage for the last leg of their journey. "Wait Poppy. Let me fetch *The Book of Love* for you." She grinned at her friend who suddenly appeared a little paler. "You're next. You know that's the plan."

"Oh, dear. I'm not in a rush. I'll pick it up later this week. Besides, Nathaniel will be riding in the carriage with us now." Poppy paused to peer beyond Penelope and Lavinia, settling her gaze on Penelope's brother who was just finishing a pint of ale with Beast and Thad. "I'd rather not have him mocking me the entire journey."

Penelope nodded. "He and Thad believe it was just coincidence that Beast fell in love with you. Perhaps you and Beast were fated to do so, but I know that book made it happen now."

Poppy agreed. "The men have no understanding of how powerful it is. In truth, it puts me a little on edge just holding onto it. What if I choose the wrong man to pursue? What if he falls in love with me and then I decide I don't really love him? That would be awful."

"It is potent," Penelope agreed, "but that's why you're going to practice on my brother. He's safe enough. Besides, the dolt has set his sights on Lady Charlotte, the Duke of Winthrow's daughter, and I don't like her." She rolled her eyes. "Why are men so dense? She's obviously completely wrong for him."

Poppy sighed. "She is beautiful."

"So are you," Olivia said. "Far prettier than she is because you have an inner glow while she's just a frosty exterior."

After another round of hugs, she and Matilda climbed into Beast's carriage while Penelope, Poppy, and Lavinia clambered into Nathaniel's carriage. Olivia smothered a grin when she noticed that Nathaniel had taken the seat beside Poppy. No doubt, he meant to tease her about the book, for he knew she was next to receive it, but Goose suspected there was a little fear in him as well.

The mighty Beast had fallen.

He and Thad had to know no man was safe now.

Olivia's heart felt a little heavier now that she was no longer with her friends, but this time alone with Beast's aunt also gave her the opportunity to get to know her better. She was quite surprised Matilda had accepted her so readily. Was it merely a ruse she maintained while among friends?

"I am quite the dragon, I'm told," Matilda said, seeming to read her thoughts. In the next moment, she laughed and shook her head. "Olivia, my dear. You needn't fear I am about to bite your head off."

Olivia's eyes rounded in horror. "Never, Your Grace."

"But that is exactly what you're thinking." The dowager gave an impatient wave of her hand. "That is my reputation and I've encouraged it. When one is in my position, one must strike a little fear in the hearts of all the toadies and fortune hunters who circle around me like vultures or else they'd never hesitate to approach. But you are nothing like those birds of prey. You need not fear me." She leaned forward and patted Olivia's hand. "You are the sweet bird my nephew adores. You must call me Matilda. Or Aunt Matilda, if you wish. We shall soon be family."

Olivia smiled at her. "Thank you, I'd love that, Aunt Matilda. I've missed having a loving family. I've wanted it so badly these past two years. But this *sweet bird*, as you call me, is merely a goose. A penniless goose, if my guardian is to be believed. So how can I not be worried about how you perceive me? You hardly know me, so why wouldn't you think me a fortune hunter? I bring nothing into the marriage."

"My dear, you bring the only thing that matters. True love. Nothing less will do for my nephew. Nor will I accept anything less from him. If I believed for a moment you were after his wealth and title, I would turn into the very dragon everyone fears." She took out her handkerchief and dabbed at the tears suddenly forming in her eyes. "Oh, I promised myself I would not turn into a watering pot. After all, dragons don't cry, do they?"

Olivia's smile softened.

"Beast is the dearest thing to my heart. His injuries in battle were so severe, some even worse than his damaged eye. And he'd hardly taken a step off his ship when it docked in London before everyone began to clamor for his attention."

Olivia nodded thoughtfully. "The Prince Regent most of all."

Matilda rolled her eyes. "The Austrian princess fiasco. Yes, Prinny was not thinking clearly. But everyone is demanding his attention. From the highest born to the lowest, they accost him. However, when he is with you, he is at peace. You make no demands on him."

Olivia shook her head. "Quite the opposite. I make the greatest demand. I want his heart. Nothing less will do for me."

"You soothe his heart," Matilda said with insistence.

"As he does mine." Olivia blushed. "I've always cared for him."

"I know, my dear. I had only to glance at you to know the truth. You are not very good at hiding your feelings."

She groaned. "That's what Beast says."

"My nephew is right. He is always right. Makes him insufferable at times, but this is why everyone trusts his instincts."

Olivia nibbled her lip as she began to fret. "I don't know that he's right about my guardian. He believes I am the one in danger, but what if I've put Beast in danger?"

"Are you suggesting your guardian would be insane enough to assault a duke? Possibly attempt murder?" Matilda shook her head. "I hadn't considered that. He would have to be completely mad to even harbor the thought."

"The problem is, I don't know the man at all. He's a distant cousin of my father's. My family had very little contact with him. I'd never met him until my parents passed away. Yet, he was put in charge of me because he was next in line to the title." She began to wring her hands. "I've mentioned my concerns to Beast, but he remains so calm about it. I want to shake him by the lapels and shout at him to be careful."

"He will be. He always is. He has Bow Street runners investigating your guardian as we speak."

Olivia allowed Matilda to shift the conversation to more pleasant topics. "You'll need a gown for Lord Forster's ball."

She hadn't given it a thought, but knew the dowager was right. She sighed. "I'll borrow one from Penelope or Poppy. We're all about the same size. The alterations, if any are needed, won't be drastic."

"A borrowed gown? Oh, no, my dear. We shall have none of that." Matilda gave a dismissive shake of her head. "The gossips will have a feast with that news. No, Beast will never allow it. You'll have a new gown for tomorrow's ball. We'll attend to your wardrobe the moment we reach London. We aren't far. It won't be long now."

Olivia did not like involving Beast or Matilda in her problems, but neither did she ever wish to return to her guardian. So, she said nothing when they reached London and settled into the townhouse residence of the dukes of Hartford located in fashionable Belgravia. This section of town was where the scions of old wealth and power had settled over the generations.

Matilda retired upstairs to change out of her dusty travel clothes while Beast gave her an abbreviated tour of the house. He'd ordered a guest bedchamber to be prepared for her, so they had time to casually stroll through the majestic rooms while her accommodations were prepared.

The entry hall alone was magnificent. The floor was of the finest quality marble and the matching oversized vases standing at either end of a medieval-looking table were made of exquisite Delft porcelain. The ducal portraits lining the walls of the visitor's salon were painted by renowned artists of their time. The furniture and draperies in the drawing room were of the finest Italian silks and velvets.

Everywhere Olivia looked, she was dazzled. The ornate silver was polished to a blinding shine and every detail, every piece of furniture and decorative art, spoke of the prominence of the dukes of Hartford from the time of the Norman conquest to the present.

Olivia had lived finely as the daughter of a viscount, but she felt like a pauper among this old-world opulence. It made her head spin to think this residence would be her home once she and Beast were married.

Matilda joined them in the drawing room. "Beast, will you stay for tea and light refreshments? I've told Hopkins to bring up a tray for us."

He nodded. "One cup and then I'll take my leave. I'll have Collingsworth send a few of my things over to my club."

"Oh, dear." Olivia frowned, not liking she was booting Beast out of his own home.

"I don't mind staying at my club until we're married, Goose. I'll be coming and going at all hours these next few days. It'll be easier for all. Of course, my Bow Street runners will be watching over you whenever I'm not around."

She nodded and settled on the emerald silk settee beside Matilda, not knowing what else to say. It all felt so rushed to her, not for herself. Being with Beast felt very right. But he was the one being pushed toward marriage, and she did not want him to regret his decision once it was too late to do anything about it.

If only they had more time.

But that was the one thing they lacked.

Beast took a matching chair opposite hers, not looking at all put upon or concerned. "You'll get used to this place, Goose. And don't think you're kicking me out of my own home. I often stay over at my club. This is nothing unusual."

"All that will change once you are married, of course," Matilda said with a casual wave of her hand. "I'll retire to the country—"

"Only if you wish to," Olivia hurried to assure her. "I would love to have you with us. That is…" She should not have spoken without consulting Beast. This was his home to do with as he pleased. She cleared her throat. "What I mean is, if my opinion is sought, then I'd like to be clear that Matilda is most welcome to stay."

"I hope I am as enthusiastically received," Beast teased.

Olivia shook her head and laughed softly. "I'll think about it."

"You do that." He took her hand in his and tossed her a private look that was quite wicked and full of promise. "In the meanwhile, I'll attend to the business of securing the special license and paying a call on your guardian. I'll see you later this evening."

Her momentary merriment fled. "Oh, Beast. Do be careful."

He caressed her cheek. "Don't wait up for me. I may run late. If so, I'll go straight to my club and come around to see you in the morning."

"I'll wait up for you. Stop by whenever you've finished." She wanted to see him, needed to be certain no harm had come to him. She did not trust her guardian.

He drank the last of his tea and then rose to bid them both farewell. "Don't see me to the door, Goose. And don't fret if I fail to stop by this evening. I have plenty to do. I promise to come around first thing in the morning."

Matilda turned to her once Beast had gone. "Honestly, the man must stop calling you Goose. It will slip out in public one day and we'll never hear the end of it."

Olivia managed a chuckle, but she could not hide her worry now or later when Beast did not return by suppertime. He'd warned her his duties would delay him.

Still, she'd hoped.

Supper was a quiet affair, she and Matilda dining in the summer parlor that overlooked a neatly maintained garden. The roses were in full splendor at this time of year and Olivia was enchanted.

She also enjoyed getting to know Matilda better and could see why Beast doted on her. She was fiercely protective and affectionate toward those she loved. Olivia wasn't quite certain what she had done to gain Matilda's favor, but was glad they got along well. The dowager would have been a formidable adversary had she taken a dislike to Beast's intended bride.

When the grandfather clock in the drawing room chimed ten o'clock, Matilda could no longer hold off her exhaustion and excused herself. "Olivia, you ought to retire as well. Beast is not likely to stop by tonight. He'll report any news to us in the morning."

Olivia nodded, but was too much on edge to sleep. However, she took pity on the maid assigned to assist her. She accompanied Matilda upstairs, but only for the purpose of dismissing the girl for the evening.

Having changed out of her travel gown after tea earlier in the day and donned one of her simpler, formal gowns, a delicate ecru silk that had few buttons or laces, she had no need of assistance. Although she had not thought of it at the time, it would also offer little impediment should Beast return tonight and wish to... she dared not finish the thought.

Matilda cast her a knowing grin. "Sweet dreams, Olivia."

Drat, she really ought to learn to hide her feelings. "Thank you for everything, Matilda."

She hurried downstairs to the library to bury her nose in a book. If Beast did not return by midnight, she would go to bed.

But she hoped he would come before then.

As the midnight hour approached, Olivia gave up hope. She shut the book she had been reading, if one could call falling asleep in one's chair before finishing the first page, reading. It hardly counted as that. Setting it aside, she muffled a yawn along with her disappointment.

She was about to rise when the library door opened and Beast strode in. "Collingsworth said I'd find you in here," he said, referring to his valet. Olivia had met the man earlier this evening when introduced to the staff.

Beast came to her side and cast her an appealing grin. "I'm glad you waited up for me. Although you look as though I just woke you from a dead sleep."

She laughed and rose to meet his outstretched arms. "These elegant leather chairs are quite comfortable. It took me less than a paragraph to fall into oblivion. But I hoped you'd stop by. I missed you, Beast. It's silly, isn't it? We were together all week and only apart for an evening."

"Not silly. I felt the same. My news could have waited until tomorrow. But I was eager to look upon your lovely face. *The Book of Love* exerting its force on me again, I suppose."

"Ah, the higher brain function at work. Do you recall the words? You don't have to be beautiful, just beautiful to the one you love."

"You are beautiful by any measure. But you grow even lovelier every time I see you." He lowered his mouth to hers and gave her a long, lingering kiss that turned her legs to pudding. "I'll never grow tired of this," she said in a breathless whisper.

"Nor will I." He eased back and patted his breast pocket. "I have the special license."

Her eyes widened. "Oh, my goodness. Now this feels very real."

He frowned. "And it didn't before? Did you think I'd beg off?"

"No, but can you blame me for having to pinch myself? Look at you, England's most sought-after bachelor." She waved her hand. "And this place. It's magnificent and elegant and perfect.

Within the span of a week, I've gone from a living nightmare into this dream."

She sighed and continued. "What did Lord Gosling say to you? Did you have the chance to speak to him?"

"No, he wasn't at home."

"Oh." She did not bother to hide her disappointment since Beast always knew what she was thinking anyway. "Did the bounder slip out the back way to avoid you? I wouldn't be surprised."

"No, he was already out of the house. I've had my Bow Street runners watching him." He nudged her back into her chair and took the one beside her as they continued their discussion. "They weren't there either, so they must have followed him when he stepped out."

"I wonder where he went."

"Nowhere sinister, I expect. Gentlemen usually stop by their clubs in the evening." He ran a hand through his thick mane. "I won't have time to see him tomorrow before Lord Forster's ball. Prinny has summoned me."

"Again?"

Beast nodded. "He'll keep summoning me until I apologize for refusing to marry the Austrian princess, no matter that he now realizes it was a mistake and no one ever thought it was a good idea in the first place. Still, he wants me to kiss his royal arse. I'm not going to do it. So, I expect I'll be stuck at St. James's all day."

"Like an errant schoolboy forced to stay after class."

He shrugged and stretched his long legs before him. "I'll pay your guardian a call the day after tomorrow. It will also give me time to speak to Homer Barrow, my Bow Street man. He'll give me a full report. I'll also arrange to meet your father's solicitor. Might as well gather as much information as I can if I'm to wait a few more days before confronting Lord Gosling."

"Do be careful, Beast. He's a wicked and desperate man."

He grinned. "So am I. While I may appear calm on the outside, I am a volcano about to erupt. I'm aching to have my way with you, Goose. You look delicious."

She shook her head and laughed. "You must be hungry, indeed. Have you eaten since we stopped at the Black Swan at midday?"

He nodded. "I dined with Prinny. He served a succulent breast of goose. Made me think of you. I savored every bite."

She laughed again. "I hope you were not as obvious as Pip was that night at Sherbourne Manor. He slobbered over his bite of goose."

"I was much worse. I licked every bit of it off my fork. Made overt love to my fork."

Olivia emitted a snorting chuckle, but after a moment, she turned serious. "Beast, I appreciate everything you're doing. But I feel so useless. What can I do to help?"

"Nothing yet. Just stay safe. Remain here with Matilda. Don't go out. I'll come by tomorrow evening to escort you both to the ball."

She nibbled her lip, fretting again. "What if the prince keeps you too late?"

Beast tucked his finger under her chin and drew her gaze to his. "You are going to chew a hole in that very pretty lip of yours if you don't stop worrying. If I'm late, I'll send word to Thad to escort you. He plans to meet me here anyway."

"I suppose I'll be occupied with the modiste most of the day. She's coming around noontime with cloth samples and an entourage of workers. I'm told nothing less than the best will do for a new duchess."

"You don't seem pleased."

"It feels odd, that's all. Matilda wants me to wear one of your family heirloom necklaces, her way of announcing to the world I'm about to marry you. I'm not the Duchess of Hartford yet. It feels presumptuous. And what if the Prince Regent refuses to give his permission? My guardian isn't the only one we have to worry about."

"We'll compromise. I'll buy you a new necklace to wear to the ball."

She did not know whether to laugh or groan. "Oh, excellent. Then they'll believe I'm your mistress."

"Nothing of the sort. You'll walk in with Matilda even if I'm not there to escort you. She'll lend respectability to your status." He drew her onto his lap and wrapped his arms around her. "Goose…"

She melted into his embrace. "Don't worry about me. I'll be fine, no matter what happens."

"What will happen is you will become my wife. No one is going to stop me."

"I could stop you." Although his arms were as solid as iron bands, he held her gently. "You know I won't allow you to be ruined over me."

"Women are ruined. Men are always forgiven their vices." He bent his head to hers and kissed her with ravenous longing, his lips warm and crushing against hers.

She returned his kiss with equal ardor, for there was no other way she would ever respond to him.

He had her heart.

Always and forever.

To her surprise, he ended the kiss with a whispered groan. "You are too much temptation. I had better go."

"Must you? So soon?"

"Yes." He still held her in his embrace, but eased his hold on her. "I will not have you outside of marriage. When I claim you, it shall be in our marriage bed and you shall be my wife."

She smothered her disappointment. "Is it because you're worried our marriage might never take place?"

He kissed her again, cupping her cheek and gently running his thumb along it. "Not worried. It will happen. Even if we have to make a run for it and elope to Gretna Green. Are you up for the mad dash north?"

She smiled and rested her head against his shoulder, loving

his strength and the masculine heat of him. "A Scottish wedding. I hear they're the best."

BEAST WAS A member of many clubs, but his favorite was Whitcomb's in St. Giles, not far from Holborn and Chancery Lane. It was an elegant club and well maintained, but there were only a few guest chambers available for members who wished to stay overnight. Those accommodations usually remained empty in the summer, for most members were in residence with their families during the Season, and those who had no daughters of age to make their come-out usually spent their summers in the country.

So, it came as no surprise to Beast that he was the only one staying overnight.

He enjoyed the privacy, especially since he'd arranged to meet Homer Barrow there this morning to hear his report. Depending on what the man told him, he would either meet next with Goose's family attorney or head straight to the Gosling's townhouse to confront her guardian.

"Mr. Barrow, do come in," he said, motioning for the runner to enter the private meeting room he had reserved for them. "Would you care for a cup of coffee?"

"Thank you, Your Grace. That would be quite welcome." The man took the offered seat across the table from Beast and accepted the cup handed to him by one of the club's stewards.

Beast waited for the steward to leave and then turned to his investigator. "What have you found out, Mr. Barrow?"

"There's dodgy business going on for certain, Your Grace. I'm not certain yet whether the solicitor, Sir Winston Aubrey, is involved or if he's another victim. He failed to show up at his office yesterday. His clerks are concerned. He had appointments that he missed and they say it isn't like him to forget. I sent my associate, Mick, around to his home to question his family. They're gone as well."

The man paused to sip his coffee. "I doubt they were all abducted. There would be some trace. But they might have gone into hiding. The question is, are they hiding from you or from Lord Gosling?"

"What do you think, Mr. Barrow?"

"Haven't quite made up my mind yet, Your Grace. Right now, I'm inclined to believe he is hiding from Lord Gosling, afraid the viscount means to kill him in order to silence him. His clerks mentioned his office had been broken into several days ago, but they don't think the culprits found what they were after."

Beast arched an eyebrow. "The old Viscount Gosling's testament? Or perhaps certain trust documents or financial records?"

His companion nodded. "They were forthcoming when I mentioned your name and were eager to assist in clearing up this mystery. They like their employer. They don't believe he was involved in anything underhanded. But I've been around too long to accept their word for it. Some men can appear pious as saints, but they're up to their elbows in dirt."

Beast nodded.

"They gave me the name of the bank where Lady Olivia's trust account is established and the banker in charge."

Beast quirked an eyebrow. "She has a trust account?"

"With the Royal Bank of London. That's what Sir Winston's clerks say. What's more, they claim the income from her investments is deposited monthly into that trust account. It is managed by the solicitor, not Lord Gosling. However, as her guardian, Lord Gosling has access to the funds and frequently dips into it. More so this year, but they all believed the income was spent on Lady Olivia's entrance into Society."

Beast grunted. "It wasn't."

"I'll be speaking with the bank manager this morning to confirm all this. However, if you were to join me, I'm certain the gentleman would be far more forthcoming with the details."

"I'll make the time for it." Beast checked his pocket watch. "The bank should open within the hour. We'll stop by my townhouse and pick up Lady Olivia, then ride straight there. I think she'll be interested in speaking with the manager."

"Very well, Your Grace."

Mr. Barrow did not appear at all concerned about bringing Goose along, nor did Beast feel apprehensive about it. She'd felt frustrated about being unable to help him, and this was a perfect way to expedite the investigation and safely bring her in on their progress. He wanted her to know what had been going on with her assets. In truth, he'd never been the sort to shield anyone, male or female, from the truth.

Information was power, and he wanted Goose to have all the power necessary to protect herself against her guardian. Of course, he intended to be at her side to protect her. But nothing in life was ever certain. "She has an appointment with her modiste at midday, so we'll drop her back home and then I'd like us to stop by Sir Winston's office to review the trust documents. A cursory review. I'll have my own solicitors look over her father's affairs in greater depth. His testament, his investments, the assets comprising his estate, those entailed and those he was free to give to Lady Olivia. Now tell me, what have you learned about Lord Gosling himself?"

Mr. Barrow shook his head sadly. "The man ran up significant debts from a string of bad investments, but he's been paying them off suddenly. However, they're massive, and Lord Marston holds the bulk of the debt vouchers."

"Marston?"

"Yes, Your Grace."

"That's why he's been visiting the Gosling townhouse recently."

"Lord Marston's been talking at the gaming tables, as well. I had one of my men follow him yesterday." Mr. Barrow ran a hand across the nape of his neck. "He's a recently widowed gentleman, and…"

Beast leaned forward, scowling. "And he wants Olivia."

"Aye, he'll forgive Lord Gosling's debts if he gives her over to him."

"Bastard. And Gosling will do it, too. We can't give him the opportunity." He'd take her to Gretna Green, if necessary. He hoped it wouldn't be. The special license was burning a hole in his pocket. All he needed was Prinny's consent and that would override any objections Gosling might express.

He swallowed hard, knowing what he needed to do. Apologize to Prinny. Get down on his damn knees and beg for this favor.

Kiss his pasty, royal arse.

"Let's go, Mr. Barrow. We have much to accomplish this morning."

CHAPTER SEVENTEEN

OLIVIA'S HEART FLUTTERED when she heard Beast's voice in the entry hall. She was seated alone in the summer salon, Matilda's intimate reception room, having a cup of hot chocolate and enjoying a quiet moment before diving into the day's activities. The ball was this evening. Madame de Bressard, London's most sought after modiste, was coming to see her at noon.

It was early yet, so she had intended to write notes to Penelope and Poppy to let them know she had comfortably settled in with the dowager duchess. She was also hoping Beast would stop by before Matilda awoke, for she wanted him all to herself for what she expected would be a brief visit before he rushed off again.

She rose and hurried out to meet him, surprised he'd brought someone along with him. She stopped herself from addressing him with the familiarity to which they'd grown accustomed. *Beast.* "Er, Your Grace. I'm so glad you found the time to stop in."

He grinned and bowed courteously over her outstretched hand, but his gaze revealed his thoughts were not at all courteous. "I'm glad you're up and dressed. Do you have time for me this morning?"

She nodded. "Always."

"Good." He introduced her to Homer Barrow, one of the runners he'd spoken about to her. "We are going to pay a call on your banker."

She tipped her head in confusion. "I have a banker?"

He nodded. "And a trust fund, it seems."

Her eyes rounded in surprise. "I'll fetch my reticule and be right back."

Beast and Mr. Barrow filled Goose in on as much as they knew while the carriage slowly made its way toward Bond Street where the bank was located. "Wait for us here, Hawkins," Beast said to his driver, wanting the bank manager to notice the elegant, polished black conveyance and his ducal crest embossed on the door as soon as the bank opened for business.

He did not expect any of the bank's directors to be there at this hour of the morning. Those gentlemen were of the Upper Crust and not likely to stir until noon. But the manager was someone who could be persuaded into revealing all he knew about Goose's trust fund.

Beast expected that a mere scowl from him would be enough to have the manager cowering. "Mr. Barrow, wait here for us," he said, motioning to a row of chairs. "Do let me know if you see Lord Marston or Lord Gosling come in. For that matter, keep your eye out for anyone suspicious who might be following us."

He then turned to Goose. "Let me do the talking."

She nodded. "Yes, of course. I'm not certain I would know what to ask. Finances are not in a young lady's curriculum. Playing a musical instrument or pouring tea gracefully is what's deemed important for us to know. Utterly useless, of course. I'd like our daughters to be prepared to–"

She stopped suddenly and her eyes widened in horror. "Oh, Beast. I didn't mean to presume… oh, dear. We aren't even married yet and I'm thinking of our children."

He grinned. "The female brain at work? Just as men are driven to spread our seed, women are driven to nest?"

She eased and smiled back at him. "It must be true. It's written in *The Book of Love*."

Her hand had been resting on his arm as they'd walked into

the bank. He placed his hand over hers where it still rested on his arm. "It is no small thing, Goose. Women are the givers of life. And although men are given the credit as protectors, it is no less true that a woman will fight fiercely to protect her children. But that discussion is for another time. Right now, we need to find out about your trust fund and if your guardian had assistance at this bank to hide his theft."

"Your Grace, how may I be of help?" The manager, Mr. Pershing, a small, thin man and quite obsequious, introduced himself as he rushed forward.

"Let's speak in your office, Mr. Pershing."

"Yes. Yes, of course. Do come this way, Your Grace." He bowed repeatedly as he spoke, reminding Beast of a bird pecking at seeds that had fallen on the ground.

Beast escorted Goose in and they sat beside each other in the two guest chairs placed in front of the manager's desk. "Lady Olivia Gosling," he said, nodding toward her, "and I are soon to be married. She has a trust account established by her father with your bank. As her husband, I will be taking over management of it shortly. I'd like to know what has been coming in and going out over these past two years."

The manager's face reddened. "It will take me a few days to–"

"Now, Mr. Pershing. I do not give a fig what instructions Lord Gosling or Lord Marston may have given you. I am now overriding them. Show me her account ledgers."

"But, Your Grace–"

It troubled Beast the man did not appear at all surprised or confused by the mention of Lord Marston's name. He'd brought it up on a mere hunch. But it was now obvious Lord Gosling did not always come alone when making his withdrawals. "Do you wish to continue this pretense, Mr. Pershing? I am good friends with the Duke of Lotheil, your bank's chairman of the board. Neither he nor the other board members will be happy when I notify them of the theft that has systematically been occurring in this account."

Beast leaned forward, his expression severe. "I suspect we will find matching deposits into the account of Lord Marston as well as that of Lord Gosling. The only question is, do you wish to cooperate? Or will I bring you down along with them?"

The man shot out of the seat he'd settled in only a moment ago. "I shall retrieve the ledgers for you. Rest assured, Your Grace. If those gentlemen stole from Lady Olivia, I shall cooperate in every way possible."

"Excellent. Mr. Barrow will accompany you." He walked out with the manager and motioned to his Bow Street runner to join the man. He did not want a warning sent to Lord Gosling or Lord Marston before he was ready to confront them.

Goose smiled at him when he returned to her side. "You were brilliant."

He shook his head. "It's the eyepatch. Scares everyone."

"And your fierce scowl. I would not like to be on the receiving end of it." She glanced toward the door and sighed. "I'm glad you are doing this for me, but I wish I had thought to do it for myself."

"Your guardian purposely kept you in the dark. Had you known of this account, I'm sure he and Lord Marston would have lied to you about its value and made certain you were never told the truth."

"They didn't have to try very hard to convince me. I never questioned what I was told."

He took her hand in his. "Goose, they fed you the lies while you were grieving and vulnerable. Both Gosling and Marston knew exactly what they were doing. Perhaps Marston wasn't involved from the beginning, but I have no doubt he's in it up to his neck now."

"Why would he do this? Surely, he doesn't care what happens to Lord Gosling."

"He probably loathes the man, but he advanced him funds and now he wants his loan repaid. I think he wants more than that. He wants you, too."

Goose shivered. "The man makes me uncomfortable. He looks at me in an unsettling way."

"So do I. You have a way of rousing a man's desire."

She shook her head vehemently. "No, he doesn't regard me in the noble way you do."

"You are a beautiful girl, Goose. Even a venal, old goat such as Marston could fall in love with you. He's a widower now. He may wish to marry you."

She snorted in disdain. "I would have sensed it if he were. The man is driven by greed. And now it is obvious Lord Gosling is driven to save his own hide. I would not be surprised if they'd hatched a plan to have Lord Marston marry me so he can then get his hands on my inheritance. Of course, my guardian would only give his consent if he were released from all his debts."

"I was thinking the same." He cast her a grim nod. "I should have thought to ask Sir Winston's clerks if Lord Marston ever stopped by their chambers."

"We can stop there next, if we have time."

"You have an appointment with your modiste. I shall catch hell from Matilda if I don't have you back in time."

"It's early yet. We'll have time to visit my father's solicitor before my meeting with the modiste or yours with Prinny. It will be easy enough for us to find out if Lord Marston was involved in feeding Sir Winston false information about the funds drawn out."

"Very well." Since he still held Goose's hand, he gave it another light squeeze. "I'm glad we're just figuring this out now. Had you grown suspicious sooner, they might have been forced to act quickly. Who knows what harm they might have done you."

"Beast, I'm glad you wish to marry me." She gave a light, laughing groan. "Gretna Green is looking better and better. I wish we were on our way there already."

He rubbed his thumb across the back of her hand. "Hopefully, we'll save ourselves the trip. The special license is right here in my breast pocket. A consent from Prinny is all we need. I shall obtain it today. It is my priority."

"You're awfully confident all of a sudden. What makes you think he will agree?" Her eyes widened and she gasped. "You're going to give up something important to accomplish it. Oh, Beast. Don't do this because of me. What do you have in mind to give him? What will he demand of you?"

"It doesn't matter." He cast her a wistful smile. "I don't care. You're more important to me than any piece of property."

She leaned forward and kissed him lightly on the lips. "It galls me to think our Prince Regent would hold up England's finest war hero. He ought to be bestowing gifts on you, not taking them from you. If our running off to Gretna Green will avoid a royal extortion, then I'm ready to go this instant."

He laughed. "Duly noted."

"More important," she said, now serious and quite distressed, "if our running off to Gretna Green will put you in greater trouble with the royal family, then let's end the betrothal now. The last person I'd ever wish to see hurt is you."

There was no opportunity for further conversation as Mr. Pershing scurried back into his office with several ledgers in hand. "This one is Lady Olivia's account record. These are Lord Gosling's and Lord Marston's." He glanced nervously toward the door. "Please do hurry, Your Grace. I'd rather not have anyone know I've taken them."

It did not take Beast long to sift through them. Gosling and Marston were sloppy and arrogant, neither one taking pains to hide what they were doing, especially with the recent withdrawals and deposits. It gave him a sense of unease. These were not stupid men, but they obviously appeared no longer concerned about hiding their tracks. That indicated to him they'd struck their devil's bargain and would act fast now that Goose was back in town.

Thank goodness he'd insisted on her staying with Matilda.

He struggled to suppress his seething rage. They would have

put their nefarious plan into action the moment she walked through the door of the Gosling townhouse.

It was clear Lord Marston wanted Goose.

It was also clear Lord Gosling wanted his debts forgiven.

Her marriage to Lord Marston would solve both men's problems. As her husband, odious or not, Lord Marston would have full access and right to her inheritance. No man, not even a powerful duke such as he, could have interceded.

"The deposits match exactly," Goose muttered, tossing him a questioning glance. "Whatever was taken out on a particular day showed up the same day in my guardian's account or Lord Marston's. Why be so obvious in their theft? What does it all mean?"

He rose and took her hand to assist her to her feet, not wishing to explain it all in front of Mr. Pershing. Goose had figured out most of it already. He'd respond to her question once she was back in his carriage.

Beast turned to the manager whose face was ashen and who was wringing his hands. "Not a word of this visit to Lord Marston or Lady Olivia's guardian. Do you understand me, Mr. Pershing?"

He nodded. "But others will have noticed your carriage out front, Your Grace. And my staff has seen you in my office."

Beast dropped a hundred-pound note on the manager's desk. "Open up an account in the name of Lady Olivia Gosling, the soon-to-be Duchess of Hartford. If anyone asks, that is what we came here to do."

He strode out with Olivia at his side.

She looked up at him as they walked out of the bank. "Will anyone believe it, Beast?"

He shrugged. "They might. They might not. It doesn't matter. Marston and your guardian are bound to find out soon enough. I want them to know I'm breathing down their necks. No one is going to marry you but me."

She cast him an apprehensive glance. "They'll try to hurt you."

"No, they won't. I'm a duke."

She sighed. "They won't care."

"They won't *dare*. It's over, Goose." He lifted her into the carriage and motioned for Mr. Barrow to ride up front with the driver. He then climbed in and settled beside her, needing to have her by his side and liking that she would soon be the one always beside him. "If they have any sense, they'll steal whatever else is left to steal and leave England this very afternoon. And if they are idiots and don't understand I will kill them slowly and painfully if they so much as set a finger on you, I have four Bow Street runners guarding you with orders to shoot them on sight."

She cast him an impatient glance. "They need me alive. They need you dead before you can marry me."

"We'll speak more on the matter this evening." He withdrew his watch fob and glanced at the time. "Let's make a quick stop at Sir Winston's office and then I'll drop you off at home."

She tucked her arm in the crook of his. "Beast, that sounds wonderful. *At home.* You said it so naturally, as though it is ours to share."

"It is. Or soon will be."

"Assuming the Prince Regent does not have you arrested and shipped off to the farthest reaches of the British Empire."

He cast her a wry smile. "He won't."

She leaned her head against his shoulder. "I wish *The Book of Love* had the power to bend monarchs to its will as well as eligible bachelors."

"That book ought to be kept under lock and key."

Goose nodded. "It is a prize indeed. Every young woman in England will be itching to get their hands on it. But Poppy has it next."

"Heaven help the unsuspecting bachelor. Does the poor bloke stand a chance?"

She grinned. "Did you?"

"No, I suppose I was done from the moment I entered Gresham's bookshop. I'm not complaining, mind you." He took advantage of her closeness and their privacy to steal a kiss. Her mouth felt warm and soft on his, her body sweet and willing as he drew her closer and deepened the kiss.

He drew away as the carriage came to a halt. The ride from the bank to Sir Winston's chambers was not nearly long enough. "Ready?"

She nodded as she fussed with her gown that might have gotten a bit rumpled during their exchange of kisses. "Give me a moment to right myself. You are a fiend, surely you know that." She gave a mirthful chuckle. "You've left me quite foggy-brained."

"You seem to rattle my senses, too. Every one of them." He helped her down from the carriage and escorted her up the stairs to Sir Winston's office.

The solicitor's clerks rushed forward to greet him. By their expressions, Beast realized they had not heard from their employer and were now beyond merely concerned but frantic with worry. "I have put my Bow Street runners on the matter of his disappearance," he said, introducing the senior clerk, an earnest young man by the name of Mr. Poole, to Goose and Mr. Barrow. "Have faith that Mr. Barrow and his men shall find Sir Winston and his family. He's here to ask you questions. Be as helpful as you can. Does he have a home outside of his London residence? What about his wife's family? But first, show me and Lady Olivia the documents you've gathered for us."

"Right away, Your Grace." The young man led them to Sir Winston's desk and drew up a chair for each of them before bowing his way out and leaving them alone to peruse the gathered material.

After a moment, Goose looked up at him in confusion. "Can this be right? My father left me a generous inheritance. Gosling Hall in Wellesford is mine, just as Lord Plimpton suggested. So is the family's London townhouse. And a trust fund, managed by Sir Winston. Thank goodness my father left him in charge of it, for it is obvious from our review of the bank accounts this morning that Sir Winston was diligent in his duties. Income was deposited into my account, but diverted by Lord Gosling."

She shook her head and began to seethe. "How dare that toad do this to me. My father left him well provided for. The entailed properties and the funds to manage them were more than ample. He could have had a substantial income with little effort had he used the slightest care."

Beast placed his hand over hers. "It will all be made right."

She sank back in her chair and put her hands to her now aching temples. "I hope so. I won't rest until I know Sir Winston and his family have been found unharmed. Look at these letters, Beast. He obviously had no idea what Lord Gosling was doing at first, but had begun to grow suspicious. Oh, dear. I shall never forgive myself if he or his family has been hurt."

"Mr. Barrow is the best. He'll find them." He understood Goose's frustration. Had her father realized how corrupt his cousin was, he would never have given the bounder guardianship of his precious daughter. The solicitor had no choice but to adhere to the terms of the testament and allow Lord Gosling to oversee her affairs until she came of age or sooner married.

What a mess her father unwittingly created.

Mr. Barrow knocked on the door to Sir Winston's office that had been left open. But he was not about to step in without Beast's permission. "Your Grace, it seems Sir Winston has a house in Ipswich. I think I ought to send a man to search there. With your approval, of course."

"You have it, Mr. Barrow." He turned to Goose. "They'll be found there. Safe."

She nodded. "Your instincts?"

"Yes." He cast her an affectionate grin. "I am never wrong. It irks my aunt to no end."

After making arrangements with Mr. Poole for his own solicitors to take possession of the Gosling documents, Beast returned Goose to his townhouse. It was almost noon and her modiste would soon arrive.

He had no wish to remain and be dragged into ogling the fabrics or forced to gush over them as though he actually cared what Goose wore. She would look lovely no matter what she had on.

He cleared his throat.

In truth, she would look best with nothing on, but that was just his depraved male brain weighing in since he'd vowed not to touch her until their marriage, and perversely, could think of nothing else since.

The morning had gone better than expected. He hoped Prinny would not turn the afternoon hellish with his unreasonable demands.

However, since Beast was still with Goose at the moment, the girl with heaven in her smile, he wasn't going to worry about his upcoming meeting. She gazed at him with her dazzling blue eyes and he felt the power of her love shine through. "Beast, thank you for letting me join you this morning. It meant a lot to me."

He tucked a finger under her chin and bent to kiss her lightly on the lips. "Enjoy your afternoon. I'll see you this evening."

Poppy and Penelope arrived as he was leaving. The modiste and her entourage swept in immediately after them. Beast hurried off before he was dragged back inside.

His carriage felt empty without Goose beside him.

She was a little thing, but had a large, soothing presence.

It did not take him long to reach St. James's Palace.

Prinny was already riled and pacing in his private salon, no doubt expecting more defiance from him. "You're late."

Beast grinned. "No, I'm not. You are impatient and itching for a fight which I have no intention of giving you."

"Is that any way to speak to your betters?" But Prinny waved his hand and motioned for him to take one of the two red silk chairs set beside the massive, decorative alabaster hearth. There was no fire lit because of the warmth of the day, but it was a comfortable space where they could speak to each other without his staff overhearing.

"That is the way I speak to a friend, as I hope you and I still are."

"Bah, I hate it when you are reasonable." They waited while his steward poured each of them a glass of port from a crystal decanter. Then the man quietly backed out of the room, shutting the gilt-trimmed doors behind him.

Beast settled in the chair beside Prinny. He sighed and ran his hand across the back of his neck. "I meant it when I said I have no wish to fight with you. What do you want from me in exchange for your consent? It is urgent that I marry Lady Olivia."

"Ah, dipping your wick in—"

"Nothing of the sort. What do you want from me? You've won. I want Olivia and will give you whatever you ask in return."

Prinny arched an eyebrow as he turned to him in surprise. "What? A humbled hero? Am I to have no further argument from you? No condescension or insufferable superiority? Are you ill?" He laughed at his own jest. "I don't think I've ever seen a more submissive Beast."

Beast held his frustration in check knowing Prinny was purposely goading him. "Lady Olivia is in danger. Marriage to me is the only way I can protect her. We've run out of time. Her guardian is desperate and ready to do something drastic. I don't wish to argue with you. What do you want in exchange for your consent to our marriage?"

Prinny set down his glass of port with a *thunk* against the demi-lune side table. "Even when submissive you have an irritating air of superiority." He sighed and steepled his fingers under his chin in contemplation. "I can have him removed as her guardian with the stroke of my pen."

"It isn't enough."

"Only marriage will do? That is utter nonsense."

"I haven't time to put up with your petulance. She is in danger unless I marry her. Nothing less will do. And just to be clear. I will not have anyone but Olivia as my wife."

"You are a most irritating man. Love is overrated, you know. It fades over time. Ah, but you are a Duke of Hartford, and everyone knows the Hartford men are loyal hounds. Too bad. We could have had such fun, you and I. A different woman every night." He arched an eyebrow again, this time adding a wicked grin. "More than one woman a night. Young, beautiful ladies of the court experienced in the sexual arts."

"Not interested." He'd outgrown that sort of pleasure, and although he and his friends had made noise about doing exactly that, now they'd returned home from war, the truth was, he wanted to settle down and build a life with the woman he loved.

Prinny leaned forward and pinned him with an icy stare. "Here's the bargain, my friend. Join me after Lord Forster's ball for a night of debauchery. I know women who will give you pleasure beyond your wildest imaginings. If you still wish to marry Lady Olivia afterward, then I shall give my consent." He slapped his hands on his thighs, feeling quite gleeful over his proposition. "You don't look pleased."

"I'm not."

"Be grateful I haven't asked for any of your fine properties. Spending a night on the town with me is little to ask of you. I think my proposal is quite generous. Where's the harm? You'll have your consent tomorrow. Besides, my lady friends are eager to meet you. They've been hounding me for an introduction. Perhaps we'll share one or two of them."

Nothing sounded less appealing.

Prinny slapped his hands on his thighs again and rose. "Come, I have a meeting with the prime minister. He's going to drone on and on about the economic disaster that will strike once our soldiers return to England and we have no jobs for them."

Beast frowned. "It is a grave problem."

"I know, but all he does is talk in circles as do both houses of Parliament. You're experienced in commanding armies. Perhaps you can add a fresh perspective to this problem."

Sitting with politicians was as appealing as having a sore tooth pulled, but he knew it was an important issue that would affect the very men who'd served under him. Many had lost their lives. Some of the survivors had lost limbs. He could not abandon them to politicians.

So, he remained in conference for the rest of the afternoon with Prinny, the prime minister, and representatives of both houses of Parliament.

Since Prinny and those in the House of Lords had been invited to Lord Forster's ball, the meeting broke up by late afternoon. However, he was not given permission to leave. Prinny drew him aside. "Stay, Hartford. Have a light supper with me before the ball. I want your thoughts on the meeting. Do you think we accomplished anything?"

"Do you want the polite response or the honest one?"

"The honest one. Lud, you are so infuriatingly superior."

But Prinny was in genuinely better spirits than when Beast had first arrived. Beast hoped he would remain in good humor through Lord Forster's ball and relent on the requirement to join him afterward.

They walked to the prince's private dining room, another opulent chamber decorated in gilt trim, blue silk drapery, and chairs padded in blue velvet. Their place settings were already set out, everything polished and gleaming, from the silverware, to the crystal glasses, to the gold-rimmed royal plates.

Servants lit the candles in the ornate silver candlesticks, poured wine for them, served them an assortment of cold meats, and then stepped back to blend into the walls.

"Well, Hartford? What are your thoughts?"

He twirled the wine glass in his hands, concentrating on the blood red liquid sparkling in the exquisite crystal. "The war has changed things. There will be no going back to the old ways. Those in the House of Lords will have to accept this."

Prinny laughed. "They never will."

"I know. That's why we're going to be in for some tough years ahead. We've demanded our soldiers risk their lives and they've done their duty. Now they're coming back and these lords believe we owe them nothing for their sacrifice. We must put them to work. We must offer them jobs. We must support those who are injured and can no longer work."

"All well and good, but how? Our royal coffers are drained." He rubbed his hand tiredly across his face. "War is the obvious solution to keep these men occupied, but the world is tired of it. Bah! Enough of this discussion. We have a ball to attend."

Hours had passed since the last mention of the courtesans he was to meet afterward, Beast hoped that Prinny had forgotten about that demand. It wasn't something he could ever explain to Goose. Not that he intended to do anything with Prinny's elegant whores.

He glanced up and noticed Prinny eyeing him speculatively. "You don't wish to join me after the ball, do you?"

"No."

He cast Beast a petulant smile. "But you will."

Beast nodded. "Do I have a choice?"

"No. I command it. And will you participate?"

"No." Beast stiffened in his chair.

Prinny snorted. "What's the expression? You can lead a horse to water but you can't make him drink. Hartford, think about it. We'll have fun this evening. And my lady friends will be most put out if you sit aside with a beastly scowl on your face. What's wrong with having a little sport? You aren't married yet." He paused a moment, and then sighed when met with Beast's stony silence. "Fine. I won't force you. But you still must come along because I've promised them that you will."

Beast strode out of St. James's Palace uncertain how to explain this to Goose if she asked questions. He wasn't going to lie to her, but neither was he going to bring up the topic. Prinny seemed to be mellowing. Hopefully, he would only need to put in a brief appearance, bow over a few hands, and then take his leave. Hopefully. Anything could set Prinny off and then there would be more demands foisted on him.

Most men would be honored to spend an evening with the prince and his beautiful courtesans. But he wasn't most men.

Goose would be hurt.

He shook his head and sighed.

Did *The Book of Love* have any advice on how to get out of this coil?

CHAPTER EIGHTEEN

OLIVIA HADN'T SEEN or heard from Beast since they'd left Sir Winston's office and was now concerned matters had gone poorly with the prince. It was a warm evening with just a hint of moisture in the air. She and Matilda were in queue on Lord Forster's receiving line waiting to be announced. Thad stood beside them, looking quite elegant in his formal attire, and doing his best to reassure her. But not even he sounded convinced.

"Och, Goose. Beast will get his way. It may take a few days, but Prinny is beholden to him. He's not going to risk the ire of every soldier in England by denying him the right to marry you."

She wasn't convinced, but did not have the chance to respond before Penelope and Poppy hurried over to greet her and Matilda.

"Good evening, Loopy," Thad said, casting her friend an arrogant grin.

Olivia and Poppy glanced at each other with slight smirks as Penelope tipped her nose up, prepared as usual to shoot Thad a waspish retort. To their surprise, she merely reached out to straighten his tie and then she smiled at him. "You clean up quite nicely for a Scottish oaf."

He covered his heart with his hand. "Am I hearing right? A compliment from the incomparable Lady Loopy Sherbourne?"

She sighed. "Stop calling me that. My name is Penelope." She turned away before he could respond. "Oh, Olivia. You look beautiful. I can't believe Madame de Bressard managed to finish your gown in less than a day. The ivory silk suits you to perfection. How did she work all those pearls into the lace bodice and hem in a matter of a few hours? She must have had an army of seamstresses working on it."

"It was a little rushed," Olivia admitted. "I'm afraid to breathe for fear the gown will fall apart if I do."

"My maid fashioned her hair," Matilda said, giving a nod of approval. "The braided twist is simple yet elegant. Suits Olivia to perfection. Beast won't be able to take his eyes off you, my dear." She glanced around, obviously hoping to find her nephew. "Oh, dear. I hope Prinny hasn't delayed him."

Olivia hoped it did not bode ill for their chances of marrying. Was Prinny resisting? Of course, he was. She'd been a fool to hope love could conquer all.

"He'll be along soon," Thad assured.

Nathaniel joined them. "Goose, you look smashing. All you ladies do." He slowly raked his gaze over each of them, seeming to take a little longer over Poppy, which caused her to blush. But then his gaze shifted to a young woman by the door. "Excuse me, ladies."

Olivia glanced worriedly at Poppy. She'd gone from blushing to crestfallen as Nathaniel strode away to greet Lady Charlotte Winthrow. Thad, to her delight, held out his arm to Poppy. "I believe they've just opened the ball. Care for the first dance?"

Poppy was obviously too overset to speak, so she simply nodded.

Olivia watched them walk into the ballroom.

Penelope sighed. "The Scottish oaf can be quite wonderful when he tries. I never thought I'd say this, but Thad has more sense than my idiot brother."

Olivia laughed.

She, Matilda, and Penelope greeted Lord and Lady Forster and then entered the ballroom. Lavinia was already seated along the wall beside the terrace doors chatting with friends. They joined her and were engaged in quite a pleasant conversation when the first set ended and Thad returned Poppy to their side. He then offered to dance with Penelope.

Penelope's nose tipped up again. "Will you step on my toes?"

Thad grinned. "Repeatedly."

Penelope shook her head and laughed. "Very well, let's see how bad a dancer you are."

She and Poppy grinned as the two of them walked off. "They are a pair," Poppy said. "I'm not sure whether they'll fall in love or kill each other. My bet is on kill each other."

Olivia nodded. "You're probably right. Ah, here comes Nathaniel."

Poppy frowned. "Where? Is he alone or with Lady Charlotte?"

"Alone."

Poppy's frown deepened. "I'm going to refuse him if he offers to dance with me."

Olivia gave her a little hug. "Don't you dare. How else will he realize he's made a mistake? Grab every chance to show yourself off. You are far superior to Lady Charlotte in every way."

"She's a nobleman's daughter. I'm the daughter of a merchant."

"But you will have *The Book of Love* and she won't."

"Oh, that." She cast Olivia a sheepish grin. "I want to believe the book is magical, but Beast insists it isn't. And I'm not certain I fit in an Upper Crust world. You and Penelope are wonderful, of course. But you are the only ones who have befriended me. I do like Nathaniel very much. But I don't know that he will suit as a husband for me."

Their discussion ended as Nathaniel reached them. "Poppy, may I have this dance?"

It was a waltz.

Poppy's eyes rounded in surprise.

Olivia nudged her. "She'd love to, Nathaniel."

He laughed. "Next dance is yours, Goose. I'm not sure what's delaying Beast, but Thad and I promised to look after you until he arrives. Unfortunately, the Bow Street runners are not permitted inside. They've been forced to stand watch on the street, which won't help if there's to be trouble at this party."

"Do you think there will be?" She rose on tiptoes to look around. "I don't see Lord Gosling or Lord Marston."

"Neither do I, but that signifies nothing. Don't walk away. Stay near Matilda."

"I won't budge," she assured him.

She watched her friends on the dance floor and chatted with acquaintances who stopped by to pay their respects to Matilda and Lavinia as well as to her. But as the waltz neared its conclusion, the elderly Lord Walton accidentally stomped on the hem of her gown with his walking cane, and Olivia felt it rip. A few pearls fell off the lace and rolled onto the polished floor.

Oh, perfect.

She had wanted to impress Beast, not greet him with a torn dress. She excused herself, intending to dash upstairs to the ladies retiring room. But the stairs were on the opposite side of the crowded ballroom. What if more of her hem unraveled as she made her way through the crush of guests?

The terrace was right behind her, no more than a few steps away. She decided to slip out there. It would only take her a moment to apply a strategic pin or two to the hem. She had tucked a few into her silk waistband as a precaution. "I'll be just outside," she whispered to Matilda, motioning to her hem.

"Lord Walton, that doddering, old goat," Matilda muttered with a roll of her eyes. "I was afraid he'd topple onto me. Do hurry, Olivia."

"I will." She stepped onto the terrace, nodding to a few acquaintances who were now walking inside, for the Prince Regent had just been announced with great fanfare, and everyone who had been outside did not want to miss his entrance.

Although Olivia did not like suddenly finding herself alone outdoors, she only needed a moment to pin the hem and then join everyone back inside. But as she dug into her waistband to remove one of the pins, someone grabbed her from behind, muffling her mouth as he attempted to drag her toward the terrace steps and into the darkened garden.

"Thought you could outwit me, you insolent girl."

She shuddered, recognizing Lord Gosling's triumphant, snarling voice, and then shuddered again as she felt the press of a cold blade against her throat. "We have you now and you won't slip away from us this time."

"Stop gloating and get her out of here before anyone notices she's missing." The deeper voice belonged to Lord Marston.

She saw the outline of two other men, but could not make out their identities in the darkness. If they'd been invited to attend Lord Forster's ball, she expected they were dissolute younger sons of noblemen who were in need of funds to subsidize their wastrel ways.

Panic overwhelmed her, but she forced herself to remain calm. Even though her guardian held a knife to her throat, he dared not use it. Did he? She was of no use to him dead. And she had a weapon of a sort at her fingertips, the pin she meant to use for her hem. She plunged it into Lord Gosling's fleshy hand, the one that had been covering her mouth.

"Bitch!" he cried, dropping his knife and releasing her to pull out the pin she'd jammed deep into his skin.

She screamed at the top of her lungs and tried to run, but Lord Marston grabbed her. She fought against him, not realizing he had picked up the knife her guardian had dropped. It sliced into her skin just above her breast.

"Fool!" Lord Gosling hissed. "You've wounded her."

Pain shot through Olivia and she fell to her knees, for Lord Marston realized too late what he'd done and released her with a muffled curse.

Wounded me?

She did feel a burning pain. As she looked down, she noticed blood beginning to spew from her chest and cover the ivory-silk bodice of her gown. "Oh, God."

"No one said she'd be hurt," one of Lord Gosling's cohorts cried. "We never agreed to this."

All four of them abandoned her and ran away.

She felt the vibration of their footsteps along the ground, for she'd now collapsed and was lying on the cold stone of the terrace floor.

She heard shouts. Felt a breeze against her hair as men began to rush out of the ballroom to chase her attackers.

Through the blur of her tears, she saw Beast leap over the balustrade like a wild animal hunting its prey, and then heard grunts and panicked cries as he took down those fleeing men. Thad and Nathaniel followed on his heels, and several other gentlemen who were not quite as spry also gave chase.

Her head was spinning.

She tried to rise but staggered and fell back to her knees.

Penelope and Poppy were now beside her, both calling for Beast. "Olivia, don't try to get up. It will be all right." But they were both crying, for blood was still spewing from her wound and crimson now stained the entire bodice of her gown. Her hand was soaked in blood as well, for she'd put it over the cut in an attempt to stop the bleeding.

She saw the liquid crimson everywhere, even in a little pool on the ground. Her chest hurt like blazes.

"Oh, God! Olivia!" Beast was now at her side. He lifted her into his arms. "Hold on, my love," he said in a raw and raspy whisper as he carried her through the ballroom, toward Lord Forster's library.

"Not there, Beast," she said with a sob, "I want to go home."

"Soon, my love. I need to stop the bleeding first. Fetch a doctor," he called out to Lord Forster as he made his way through the stunned and now hushed crowd.

Poppy and Penelope were trailing behind Beast. "I'll fetch my uncle," Poppy said. "He's the most highly regarded physician in London. He doesn't live far."

"Of course, George Farthingale." Beast sounded relieved. "Is he at home now, Poppy?"

"Yes, I'll run all the way."

Olivia heard more murmurs of "doctor" and "Farthingale" and then heard Nathaniel's voice as he caught up to them. "I'll go with you, Poppy. We'll take my carriage. It's being brought around now. Beast, shall we bring him here or to your home?"

"Here. I dare not move Olivia yet. But have my carriage brought around as well. Where's Thad?"

"With the other men. They're holding her guardian and his cohorts. Lord Forster has allowed your Bow Street runners in. They'll guard them and see they're properly put under arrest."

Beast muttered a curse in frustration. "They should have been in here tonight. I ought to have insisted. I knew what they were up to."

"They were determined to abduct Olivia no matter what precautions were put in place," Nathaniel insisted. "You did all you could."

Olivia tried to nod her assurance, but every little movement hurt. Besides, she knew it would do little to change Beast's mind. He blamed himself, no matter that he hadn't held the knife to her throat or stabbed her or attempted to abduct her.

They reached the library, and Beast set her down gently on the leather sofa. "Hold on, love. I'm going to try to stop the bleeding." His voice was still raspy and barely above a whisper. "Hold on to me as I am holding on to you. I won't let go of you. I won't ever let go of you."

He knelt beside her and kissed her lightly on the forehead.

"Beast, it wasn't supposed to be like this," she said in a sob.

"I know." He removed a handkerchief from the breast pocket of his evening jacket and ever so carefully used it to dab around the edges of her wound. "My love, I have to tear away the fabric. It doesn't appear to be a deep cut, thank The Graces. He didn't stab you."

"No, I struggled not realizing Lord Marston held a knife against me."

"You'll need a few stitches. Poppy's uncle will take care of that."

"Hartford," said someone with an authoritative voice. The man was standing over Beast's shoulder. "I'm sorry. I never realized. You have my consent. Freely given. I'll deal with the culprits." The man then turned and walked away.

She tried to sit up but Beast gently held her down. "Lie still, my love."

"Who was that?"

Beast caressed her cheek. "Prinny."

She closed her eyes and gave a little nod. "Then we won't need to dash to Gretna Green?"

"No, love."

"Good, I'm not up to travel at the moment."

CHAPTER NINETEEN

BEAST HAD BEEN late to arrive at Lord Forster's ball and wasn't happy about it. The ballroom was crowded and he did not doubt that all of London Society had been invited, including Lord Gosling and Lord Marston. For this reason alone, he'd wanted to return home in time to escort Goose and remain close to her side throughout the evening.

But Prinny was suddenly his best friend and not letting go of him, so he had to send for his valet to bring his evening clothes to the prince's residence. He'd been given one of the guest chambers in which to wash and dress and then been invited to ride in the royal carriage to Lord Forster's home.

Since all the royals were political animals, perhaps a necessity for their survival, he knew Prinny's wanting to make his grand entrance alongside him had little do with Goose and all to do with currying favor with the Parliament elite. Since he and Wellington were England's favorites at the moment, Prinny was going to keep them close.

A chill ran up his spine the moment he surveyed the ballroom. He was standing at the top of the imposing staircase, he and Prinny side by side, giving the revelers time to adore and worship them. He scanned the crowd, not certain why his attention was suddenly drawn to the terrace, but he'd noticed a flash of white silk and then it was gone.

Lavinia and Matilda were seated beside the terrace doors.

No sign of Goose.

Then he knew.

He just knew.

He leaped down the stairs and shoved his way through the crowd, ignoring the gasps and grumbles of those he'd pushed aside. He heard Goose scream as he neared the terrace. She'd fallen to her knees, but he saw the men who were now running away and recognized her odious guardian and Lord Marston. He couldn't make out the identity of the other two, but it mattered little at the moment.

He jumped over the terrace balustrade and brought two of them down as he landed. He did not know if they were reaching for weapons, but he punched each one in the jaw, knocking both out. He'd sort out the details later.

"I've got them," Nathaniel said, reaching his side. "Thad's chasing the others."

Beast took off to assist his friend.

Perhaps it was a good thing that Thad had reached Lord Gosling first and subdued him. Beast was blind with rage and would have killed the man if Thad hadn't held him back. He went after Marston and hauled him back, dropping him at Thad's feet.

"We've got them all, Beast. Lord Forster's footmen will help me bring them back inside," Thad said. "Olivia fell down. Go see how she's doing."

Beast pushed his way through the small crowd gathered around Olivia. Penelope and Poppy were in tears beside her. She was still on the ground. He knelt beside her and his heart suddenly exploded.

She was covered in blood.

"Goose, no." His voice was a strangled whisper. He wrapped her in his arms and felt her body trembling as he carried her toward Lord Forster's library. He resolved to kill her guardian and Marston with his bare hands if... no, she had to live.

She had to.

He'd carried her like this before, the little girl he'd pulled out of the pond, her forehead bleeding and her tiny body soaking wet. She was his Little Goose.

She was sunshine and smiles and all things good.

Prinny stepped forward.

The lethal glower he cast Prinny turned him ashen. "Hartford… I…"

"Not now. She needs a doctor." He dared say no more, for his thoughts were murderous and filled with rage toward everyone who had let this happen, even himself.

He settled Goose on the sofa in the library, holding on to her with all the strength in his heart and soul. She needed him to remain calm and tend to her, so he entwined his fingers in hers and stroked her hair while he called for Lord Forster's staff to bring him water, clean cloths, and a bottle of whiskey with which to cleanse her wound.

Goose's blood had soaked through his own handkerchief as he ever so gently pressed it to the cut. Within moments, a footman returned with all he'd asked. He took the whiskey and linens from his hands, and motioned for him to place the water ewer on a nearby side table. "Wait outside the door. Stay close enough to hear if I call for you."

"Yes, Your Grace."

Penelope was standing quietly behind him. "What can I do?"

"Stand next to her. Stroke her hair. Help me clean off her hands." He opened the whiskey bottle and poured some of the amber liquid onto the cloth. "Goose, I have to peel away the fabric around the area of the wound. I'm going to use the whiskey to cleanse it."

"Breast of goose," she murmured, casting him a wan smile. "Will it hurt?"

"Yes, love. Quite a bit. But your injury isn't as bad as I'd first feared. What you have is a nasty cut, not a stab wound. Try to hold as still as possible, Olivia."

"You called me Olivia," she said, as he was about to rub the cloth over the top of her breast.

This is what she took from his words? He shook his head and groaned. "What can I say? What happened this evening shook me to the core."

"Me too, Beast."

"I know, love. You gave me quite a scare. My heart is still in my throat and my entire body is shaking. But now that the blood is cleared away, I can see the blade made a superficial slice across the swell of your breast."

She cast him another small smile. "Just like *The Book of Love* says. It always comes down to breasts. Oh, Beast! Now mine will always be scarred."

He placed a gentle kiss on her forehead. "I didn't fall in love with one breast. I fell in love with you. All of you. The scar will fade in time, but my love for you never will."

Her eyes widened in obvious surprise. "What a lovely thing to say. I never realized you were a romantic."

He glanced over at Penelope who was still beside her and now smirking at him. He winced. "Don't you start on me, Loopy. You're not going to repeat this to Nathaniel or Thad, are you?"

Penelope's expression softened. "I can be bribed to keep quiet. Do you want me to leave? I didn't mean to intrude. The two of you must have much to say to each other."

"No, stay. I need you to put your hands on her shoulders to hold her down. I'm about to cleanse the wound, and as I said, it will hurt. Goose, I think you're going to hate me now. Just remember, I'm doing this to save your life." He lowered the cloth to her breast. "Hold your breath."

"The devil!" she blurted as he pressed the whiskey-soaked cloth to her skin and obviously felt the intense burn along the length of her wound.

Tears streamed down her cheeks. "You're right. I hate you."

"I know. It can't be helped. An infection of the blood will hurt a thousand times more."

She groaned. "I don't really hate you, Beast."

He ran his thumb along her cheek. "I know."

He took another cloth and gently pressed it against the now cleansed wound. "The bleeding has slowed down. Lie still, Goose. All we have to do now is wait for Dr. Farthingale."

"I liked it when you called me Olivia. But now that I'm back to being Goose, I think it is a good sign. It means you think I'm going to survive." She smiled at him, a fragile smile that sparkled like sunlight on a crystal-blue lake.

Penelope cleared her throat. "Do you need me any longer? I really feel as though I'm intruding here."

"You're not," he and Goose said at the same time.

She laughed. "Oh, yes. Indeed I am. I think Lavinia and Matilda must be frantic with worry. They'll want to know Olivia's condition." She frowned suddenly and cast Beast an uncertain look. "Can I tell them she will recover?"

He nodded. "She will recover fully. Tell them I said so and that I am never wrong."

Goose turned to him as soon as Penelope left. "Is it true, Beast? Will I survive or did you just tell her that so she wouldn't fall apart in front of me?"

"It's true. I've seen plenty of war wounds and treated too many to count. We all become healers of a sort on the field of battle. I'm sorry I had to pour whiskey on your cut. I know it burned like blazes. But it was necessary."

"You did what you had to. I trust you." She glanced down at her gown and her face paled. "Oh, dear. What a horrible sight. And it was such a lovely design. Madame de Bressard and her seamstresses worked tirelessly to finish it in time."

"I'll buy you a hundred others. Madame de Bressard and her seamstresses will be very happy. How do you feel, love?"

He was still changing out the cloths on her breast, putting slight pressure on the wound in order to stop the bleeding. Although he did not want to think of when he touched her breast the first time, he couldn't help himself. He was touching her because she was injured, but the fullness and softness of her felt so right and perfect.

She licked her lips. "I'm thirsty. A little hungry, too."

"I dare not give you food or drink just yet. I'll dab some water on your lips. Dr. Farthingale will be here shortly. I'm not sure what medicine he'll give you to help numb the area around the wound. You'll need four or five stitches to close it properly, perhaps more."

She closed her eyes. "I'm glad you're beside me, Beast."

He leaned forward and kissed her on the lips. "Nowhere else I'd rather be, my love."

"I've read so many romantic stories where the heroine dies tragically in the arms of the man she loves. I–"

"You're not going to die," he said with a growl. "I won't let you. Besides, death is not romantic."

"No, I don't suppose it is. Oh, Beast, don't frown. I have no intention of doing so. Those heroines died gracefully. I would fight and curse to the very end. Besides, if I did die, then what is the point of *The Book of Love* falling on my head? Twice."

"No point at all."

He said no more as Dr. Farthingale arrived. He'd never met the man, but had heard his name mentioned often enough to know he was one of the most highly regarded doctors in London. He'd intended to pay a call on him to seek treatment for his injured eye. That would have to wait until after he and Goose were married. Protecting her was first among the items on his list of priorities.

Poppy had spoken often of her relatives, so Beast wasn't surprised that George Farthingale had blue eyes and dark hair just like Poppy. Seemed the dark hair and blue eyes was a fairly common trait among the Farthingales.

"Your Grace, would you mind stepping aside while I examine Lady Olivia?" But it took him only a moment to notice that her wound had already been tended to. "Did you do this?"

"I cleansed it with whiskey," Beast muttered, realizing he should have done more to clean Goose up, for blood was still all over her gown and much of her body, although he and Penelope had wiped most of it off her hands.

"Well done." He then turned to Olivia and began to explain what he needed to do. "You'll need stitches. Five or six at most."

Beast took an instant liking to the man, for he had an aura of competence and quiet authority without being full of himself. He looked on as Dr. Farthingale dug through his medicine bag and brought out his sutures and needle.

The doctor cast Goose a wry smile. "I think you're going to detest me as much as you must have detested His Grace when he poured the whiskey onto your wound. I have to stitch it, and it will hurt. I'm going to give you some laudanum first to help ease the pain as I work on you, but it will make you quite lightheaded. Hopefully, it will put you out for a few hours but not leave you nauseated. You'll be in pain when you wake up. I'll leave you enough laudanum to get you through the next few days. However, I recommend you use it sparingly."

She nodded.

The doctor waited until the drug began to take effect.

"Olivia, I love you," Beast said, kissing her on the forehead and taking hold of her hand when the doctor doused more whiskey on the wound and began to apply the sutures.

OLIVIA AWOKE TO find herself in a large, comfortable bed. The last thing she remembered was Beast wrapping his arms around her as Dr. Farthingale began to stitch along the area of the cut. She tried to get up, but immediately fell back against the pillows that had been propped behind her. Pain tore through her chest. "Where am I?" she muttered, believing herself alone and merely talking to herself.

She was surprised to hear a deep, rumbling voice give answer. "You're home, love."

"Beast?" She gave a shaky laugh, now realizing she was in her guest bedchamber at Beast's townhouse. He must have brought her here after Poppy's relative had finished tending to her, but she had no memory of it. "Have you been with me all this time?"

"Yes, I'll never leave your side again."

"That's quite an ardent statement. Romantic, really. Are you hiding a secretly poetic soul?" She smiled at him, wanting to tell him how wonderful he looked.

He had changed out of his evening clothes. She knew he'd gotten her blood all over them, and now had on buff breeches and a white shirt of softest lawn that clung to his muscled arms and broad chest. He must have recently washed and shaved, for she caught the scent of lather on his jaw as he drew closer and his hair was damp and curling at the nape of his neck.

"Romantic?" He chuckled. "Perhaps. My heart is still lodged in my throat. I wish I could have taken your pain. I hated to see you suffer."

"Was I a hideous, whining infant? Did I shout and scream and cry? I wanted to be brave, like one of your soldiers on the battlefield, but I must have failed miserably." She could not hide her disappointment. "I've gained infinite respect for you and all those who were injured during the war. I had the finest doctor. I had you by my side to hold and comfort me. I'm sorry I wasn't brave."

"Goose, you were as stoic as a Spartan warrior." He sat beside her on the bed and leaned forward to kiss her lightly on the lips. When he drew away, he had a wry smile on his own lips. "I was the one who cried and whined, if you must know."

Her eyes widened in surprise, and then she laughed when she realized he was teasing her. "Oh, Beast. Don't make me laugh. My chest feels so tight, like someone is stepping on it."

"Are you in a lot of pain? Do you want some laudanum?"

"No, I'll let you know when it becomes unbearable. I don't think it will, not while you're beside me." She looked down at herself, afraid she'd find more blood on her nightgown and bed sheets, but there was none. Still, the color of dark crimson flashed before her eyes. "My ballgown…"

"Matilda and I brought you back here last night after Dr. Farthingale finished tending to you. Poppy and Penelope helped our maids get you out of your gown and prepare you for bed." He groaned in anguish. "They carefully washed off the blood. There was so much of it, Goose. It terrified me when I first saw you. I believed the bastard had stabbed you and I could do nothing to save you."

"Where are Lord Gosling and Lord Marston now?"

"Prinny has them in custody. Lord Marston will be heavily fined as well as confined to his estate for the remainder of his life. If he steps foot off it, he'll serve out the rest of his punishment rotting in a debtor's prison. Lord Gosling has agreed to forfeit his title in exchange for living out his life in the country home he resided in before inheriting. But he has also been forbidden to step foot off the property unless he wishes to rot in prison to the end of his days."

"What will happen to my father's title?"

"I spoke to Prinny briefly about it. He stopped by earlier this morning. The title won't perish. It will be given to our second son. I thought it only fair since our first son will inherit the Hartford dukedom."

"And nothing for our daughters?"

He groaned again. "We will provide for them generously, of course. I can't take on another battle right now, Goose. Just let me marry you before Prinny has a change of heart. We'll fight to overturn the laws of primogeniture afterward."

"Very well, no crusades for now." She'd had enough excitement to last her for a good long while. In any event, she'd be able to accomplish much more as the wife of a powerful duke. "But I'm curious, who were Lord Gosling's accomplices?"

"Scoundrels. Wastrel sons of aristocrats. Their punishment has been left up to me. I can have them imprisoned. However, their fathers have offered to purchase them commissions in the navy and have them shipped out of England as quickly as possible."

"Which will you choose?"

He arched an eyebrow as he cast her a wry smile. "Which do you want me to choose?"

She hadn't expected the question and regarded him in surprise. But she liked that he was confiding in her. They were alone, speaking quietly together and he cared about her opinion. "I know what they did was vile and reprehensible. But they refused to cooperate with Lord Gosling when they realized I might be physically harmed."

"Refused to cooperate? Those bastards ran off and left you defenseless."

"Yes, well. I don't mean to excuse their actions, but I think a commission might serve them better than years of confinement."

He did not look pleased, but after a moment, he nodded. "So be it. They'll be sent to the navy. Their fathers will be eternally grateful to you. Hopefully, those scoundrels will appreciate your generosity. I'd like to run both of them through with my saber."

"But you won't." She reached out and placed her hand against his cheek. "Because you know how I feel. You care about how I feel. That's why you gave me the choice."

He kissed her palm and placed soft kisses along her wrist, grinning when he felt the tingle run up her arm. His smile turned wicked. "Nathaniel suggested we return to Sherbourne Manor. He thinks we ought to hold our wedding in Wellesford. Vicar Carstairs is willing to officiate the ceremony. Penelope and Poppy thought it a good idea. They said you'd want to invite the villagers. Lavinia and Matilda will return to Sherbourne with us, of course. Those dowagers would risk Hannibal's trek across the Alps to attend our wedding."

"I adore them," she said with a genuinely mirthful laugh.

He nodded. "Or we could marry here today. Simple and quick."

"Will Prinny allow you to have a quiet wedding here? Won't all of London Society be up in arms if we marry in town and they aren't invited?" She gazed at him and laughed again. "But you don't care what anyone thinks. You want to do what makes me happy."

"Are you surprised?"

"I shouldn't be. It seems my war hero does have an utterly romantic soul. Or perhaps it is just *The Book of Love* working its magic on you. And don't say it was me who worked the magic. I didn't. I was just the little nuisance who used to visit Penelope over the summers."

"Perhaps the book merely helped me to understand the treasure before my very eyes. Even if I only have one functioning eye."

"I think your vision is perfect. You see me as no one else ever could, for you look at me with your heart." Nor would she ever tire of looking at him, this proud, beast-of-a-man with his eyepatch and formidable frown. "I love you, Beast. Are you giving me the choice of where and when we marry?"

He nodded again. "I don't care about the details, but you've had an opinion on this ever since you were a little girl. Sentiment means everything to you."

She shook her head in denial. "You mean everything to me."

"I know. But this will be your wedding day. What's your preference?"

CHAPTER TWENTY

O LIVIA'S PREFERENCE WAS to marry Beast quietly at his townhouse that very day even though she had yet to recover from her injury. But the wedding she'd dreamed of ever since she was a little girl had to be held in the town of Wellesford. "I suppose it would be a mistake to be married in my nightgown, barely able to stand on my own two feet while under the influence of laudanum. That would be a juicy courtroom confession if ever the legitimacy of our marriage was challenged."

"Who would dare challenge it?" But he gave no argument despite his obvious frustration which matched her own. "Then Sherbourne Manor it is. I'll let Penelope and Nathaniel know."

"Waiting another week is the right decision." She needed to convince herself as much as Beast, but her stitches were still tugging on her chest and her wound still felt raw and painful.

No bride wished for that memory on her wedding day.

The days passed in a blur of activity, not that she had much to do other than make herself available to Madame de Bressard who came by every day to fit her for new clothes. There were also decisions to be made about restoring Gosling Hall now that it was properly put in her hands by her father's solicitor, Sir Winston Aubrey. "I'm so glad you and your family are safe," she said, sincerely relieved he looked none the worse for wear.

"I thought it best for the safety of my family to settle them in Ipswich while I returned to London to take on your guardian in the courts. But His Grace's Bow Street runner found me first. I must say, I was vastly relieved to know you had a powerful friend fighting on your side."

She invited him and his family to their wedding. "We're to be married in Wellesford at the end of the week."

Now she and Beast stood in front of the altar at Saint Mary's Church in Wellesford. The pews were already filled to overflowing with villagers who'd come for the ceremony. Matilda and all four Sherbournes were seated in the front row.

Pip cast her an impish grin.

"Bollocks," Beast muttered, suddenly frowning at the boy. "He has that look."

"What look?" Olivia asked.

"He's planning to launch a spider at you during the ceremony." He turned once more to Pip. "You'd better not be hiding any eight-legged creatures in your pocket."

"I'll search him," Nathaniel said, casting a sideways glance at his young cousin.

Goose laughed. "Don't be silly. He'd never... would you, Pip? Not at my wedding."

Thad and Poppy were seated in the pew behind them along with Sir Winston. Thad clamped a hand on the boy's shoulder. "Open your fist, lad. Hand it over."

Pip sighed. "I wasn't going to release it *during* the ceremony."

Goose's eyes rounded in horror, but in the next moment, she was laughing again. She took Beast's hand as Vicar Carstairs cleared his throat to signal the ceremony was about to begin. "All is perfect," she whispered. "All is just as it should be... even Pip and his spider."

"Indeed, perfect. But without the spider." Beast recited his vows, unable to take his gaze off Goose as she recited hers.

Nor could she take her gaze off him.

"You look as radiant as an angel," he whispered.

She supposed her happiness showed. Indeed, she was probably glowing with it.

Since beasts did not smile or glow, Beast stood there in all his ducal severity. But she knew that warmth flooded his heart. When the ceremony ended, he leaned forward to kiss her cheek. "Little Goose, you are now mine and I will love you forever."

When the wedding breakfast finally ended late into the night and the villagers had all returned to their homes, Beast took her hand as they made their way across the meadow to Gosling Hall. He'd hired half the village to work on the house to prepare it for them in time for their wedding day.

He'd surprised her by hiring most of the old staff, much to her delight.

"Beast, this is perfect. I'm going to turn into a watering pot." Every beautiful memory rushed forward as they strolled past the deer and rabbits quietly grazing upon the low-lying shrubs. "These were my happiest days, tearing across this meadow every morning and skipping back home to my parents in the early evening. And now you and I will make our own memories here. Beautiful ones."

"Starting tonight. We have a second son to create who will inherit this house."

She laughed and put her arms around his neck as he lifted her into his arms to carry her over the threshold. "You don't waste time, do you?"

Her old butler, Milford, opened the door to them before he could respond.

If the poor man was surprised to find her in Beast's arms, he did not betray it. "Good evening, Lady Olivia. Or should I say, Your Grace?"

She cast him a sincere smile. "Good evening, Milford. It's good to have you back with us."

"It's good to be back."

Her smile broadened. "This is my husband, the Duke of Hartford. Have you met him yet? Isn't he the handsomest man in all the realm?"

Her butler could not contain his chuckle. "I have met him,

Your Grace. It shall be my greatest pleasure to serve you both."

"Milford, my wife and I are not to be disturbed this evening."

"I'll advise your maid and valet." He began to close up the house as Beast carried her upstairs to the old viscount's quarters that had been freshened and upgraded with a new bed and damask silk drapes to replace the moth-eaten ones that had been hanging in disrepair for the past few years.

Her heart beat a little faster as he shut the door behind them before setting her down in the center of the room. A lone lamp cast a golden glow about their chamber and caught the brilliant warmth of his smile.

He looked big and powerful, and she could not believe he was now hers to love forever.

"How do you feel, my love?" They were alone now, the world around them shut out for the night. The only sounds to be heard were the soft rustle of the wind outside their open window and their own breaths, his calm and even while hers were short and erratic with excitement.

"Happy, Beast."

They may as well have been the only two people left in England, for nothing and no one else mattered to her at the moment.

"How is your injury?" He reached out to caress her shoulder, no doubt afraid to move his hand lower for fear he'd hurt her. Madame de Bressard had fashioned her wedding gown so the scoop of her neckline fell just a little above her breasts to hide her stitches which had not yet been removed and would not be until next week.

Her smile faded a little. "It was a long day for me, but I'm not in pain."

"We can wait—"

"No… that is, unless you'd rather wait."

He gave a pained laugh. "Me? Are you jesting? I've waited all week to finally get you into my bed."

"I'm eager, too. But I'm not certain what I'm supposed to do."

He caressed her cheek, his smile appealingly wicked. "Obviously, you have not read the book you acquired from Miss Billings yesterday, the one you thought I did not see."

Her eyes rounded in surprise. "You know about that book? How?"

"Goose, you have the most expressive face. It hides nothing of your feelings. Besides, I saw you come out of her bookshop with a package under your arm that you were doing your best to hide. I knew at once what it was." His smile became an affectionate smirk. "You won't need it. Not tonight."

"I won't?"

He shook his head. "Love is not about body positions."

She breathed a sigh of relief. "My eyes crossed when I glanced at the illustrations on the pages. I don't think my body can contort the way…" She sighed again. "You're about to burst out laughing."

"I'd never laugh at you." But his lips twitched and then slowly curled up in a delicious grin that was sinfully wicked and tender all in one. "Forget that book. Love is about the senses."

"Described in *The Book of Love*?" She wished she had listened more closely to Penelope's aunt, Lavinia, when the kindly dowager had tried to talk to her about the wedding night. But the talk had come too soon, Lavinia sitting her down while back in London, and she had been too foggy from the laudanum she'd taken to ease her pain.

She hadn't taken any laudanum for the past few days, and perhaps she ought to have asked Lavinia to talk to her again instead of sneaking out to buy the naughty book. Hopefully, something would be salvaged from it. She hated to waste good coin on something useless.

"Yes, the senses described in *The Book of Love*," he said in a velvet rumble, running his thumb along the line of her jaw and then lightly across her lower lip. "It's about the way I touch you."

She closed her eyes to better absorb the excitement of his fingers upon her skin. His hands were those of a warrior, calloused from the rigors of battle.

"And the way I taste you." He bent his head and kissed her on the lips, wrapping his arms around her and drawing her close as he dipped his tongue into her mouth to probe and tease it.

"You taste of wine and honey cake," she said in a breathless whisper when he ended the kiss but kept her pressed up against his body. "I like the feel of your lips on mine."

She also loved the hardness of his body as he still held her in his embrace. Surprisingly, they seemed to fit perfectly, like a glove to a hand or like two halves of a broken locket that fell into place seamlessly when slid together.

"And the scent of your body. The hint of lavender on your warm, silken skin."

"Your scent is sandalwood." It was an arousing scent when mixed with his male heat. She felt herself responding to it like a wild creature desperate to mate. This hungry need for him came from a place deep within her soul and the power of this feeling frightened her a little.

But she trusted Beast and knew she was safe with him.

She closed her eyes and moaned softly when he began to undress her, his fingers deftly unfastening her laces and buttons. "Done," he whispered as the tea rose silk slid down her body, leaving her clad only in her thin camisole and wedding slippers.

Still holding her, he bent and gently trailed his hand down her right leg to remove her slipper. He did the same with her left leg, the soft caress of his fingers leaving her in fiery torment by the time he removed that slipper.

He set aside the gown that was a pool of silk around her feet.

His arm had remained around her waist all the while, but when he'd bent to attend to her slippers and gown, his lips were at the level of the junction between her thighs. She felt his warm breath against her most intimate spot and it did shocking things to her body.

Her legs had turned to butter and would not have held her up were it not for his support. Her blood was thick and molten.

Was he going to touch her there?

Mother in heaven. Was he going to touch her with his mouth?

He slowly rose to his full height with a knowing smile and a gleam in his eye that held promise of what was to come.

He said nothing, just placed his hands on either side of her hips and slowly lifted the camisole off her body so she was standing before him naked. Wordlessly, he unpinned her hair so it fell in waves down her back. "You look beautiful, Olivia."

Her cheeks heated, surprised he'd called her by her given name. "My sutures–"

"Everything about you is perfect." She believed he meant it, for he was looking at her with such wonder and an aching need that revealed she wasn't the only one in fiery torment.

She wrapped her arms around his neck as he carried her to the bed and set her down on the mattress. He quickly undressed, removing his trousers last. He settled his big body over her, his chest lightly pressing against hers, although he took care to avoid touching her wound. "I love you," he whispered and claimed her mouth in a scorching kiss that left no doubt of his desire.

The Book of Love spoke of connections between a man and a woman. Beast spent the night showing her how intimacy was built in so many ways. In the gentleness of his touch. In the coiled tension of his release when he entered her and claimed her for his own. In the affectionate way he held her in his glorious arms as they lay hot and spent.

In the way he touched her.

In the way he tasted her.

In the morning, she awoke to find herself still cradled in the circle of his arms. She turned to look at the beautiful beast-of-a-man as he slept, unable to resist the urge to run her hand lightly over the spray of gold hair along his chest.

Her curves were soft, but his big body was lean and hard, and the strength of him was exciting.

She caressed his muscled arms. She traced her finger along his jaw and felt the rough stubble of his morning beard.

He'd taken off his eyepatch, and her heart tightened at the sight of the scar that ran across his eye.

"How long do you mean to inspect me?" he asked in a sexy rumble, turning onto his back and stretching like a magnificent lion basking in the sun. He grinned and opened his good eye to stare back at her.

"As long as you'll allow me. I love you, Beast. I never thought such happiness was possible. I look at you and my heart bursts with joy." She liked that he felt comfortable enough with her not to reach for his eyepatch. But she felt similarly about her stitched wound that was still healing. He'd been so careful around that still tender spot even as they'd both lost themselves in shattering release.

Three times last night.

By the look of him, he looked ready to couple again, and she had no intention of denying him. He'd held back last night, refusing to claim her a fourth time. But it was now morning and the sun was shining through the window. A gentle breeze rustled through the sea-blue curtains so that they looked like ripples upon the water.

"You have starlight in your eyes, Little Goose."

"It's the sunlight. It's glistening in my eyes."

"No, it's starlight." He took her in his arms and rolled atop her. "I like that you have that starry look just for me."

"I always will, you know." She loved the weight of him atop her, even as he rested most of it on his elbows.

He nodded again. "I hope so, for that look feeds my famished soul."

She melted as he kissed her hungrily on the lips.

"It's the look of love," he said. "It's the same as I have for you." He repeated words similar to what he'd said at their wedding. "I'll love you forever, Little Goose." He gave a devastatingly sexy growl before claiming her willing body along with her heart that he'd captured long ago.

Also by Meara Platt

FARTHINGALE SERIES
My Fair Lily
The Duke I'm Going To Marry
Rules For Reforming A Rake
A Midsummer's Kiss
The Viscount's Rose
Earl Of Hearts
The Viscount and the Vicar's Daughter
A Duke For Adela
If You Wished For Me
Never Dare A Duke
Capturing The Heart Of A Cameron

BOOK OF LOVE SERIES
The Look of Love
The Touch of Love
The Taste of Love
The Song of Love
The Scent of Love
The Kiss of Love
The Chance of Love
The Gift of Love
The Heart of Love
The Hope of Love (novella)
The Promise of Love
The Wonder of Love
The Journey of Love
The Treasure of Love
The Dance of Love
The Miracle of Love
The Dream of Love (novella)
The Remembrance of Love (novella)
All I Want For Christmas (novella)

MOONSTONE LANDING
Moonstone Landing (novella)
Moonstone Angel (novella)
The Moonstone Duke
The Moonstone Marquess
The Moonstone Major

DARK GARDENS SERIES
Garden of Shadows
Garden of Light
Garden of Dragons
Garden of Destiny
Garden of Angels

LYON'S DEN
The Lyon's Surprise
Kiss of the Lyon
Lyon in the Rough

THE BRAYDENS
A Match Made In Duty
Earl of Westcliff
Fortune's Dragon
Earl of Kinross
Earl of Alnwick
Aislin
Gennalyn
Pearls of Fire
A Rescued Heart
Tempting Taffy

DeWOLFE PACK ANGELS SERIES
Nobody's Angel
Kiss An Angel
Bhrodi's Angel

About the Author

Meara Platt is a *USA Today* bestselling author and an award winning, Amazon UK All-star. Her favorite place in all the world is England's Lake District, which may not come as a surprise, since many of her stories are set in that idyllic landscape, including her award-winning fantasy-romance Dark Gardens series. If you'd like to learn more about the ancient Fae prophecy that is about to unfold in the Dark Gardens series, as well as Meara's lighthearted, international bestselling Regency romances in the Farthingale series and Book of Love series, or her more emotional Braydens series, please visit her website at www.meara platt.com.

9 781960 184955